Feelings were important to Billy Ray. He had strong feelings about everything, but especially about killing. And he'd killed a lot of stray animals—cats, dogs, even a stupid cow once. He even remembered his first kill, when he was only four or five years old. It was only a cat, not a human, but he still remembered the thrill of drowning it in a bird cage, dipping the cage into the old cistern and raising it to watch the cat going crazy with fear, and each time holding it under a little longer, until finally the terrorized, squalling, clawing cat was reduced to a lump of soggy, silent fur in the bottom of the cage, lifeless.

The pleasure of its dying had been like waves of limpid warmth washing over him. And now, when the feelings got too strong, when his control slipped away and he killed a kid, the sheer joy of the experience was indescribable. And he trembled with the knowledge it would soon happen again—this time deliberately.

KINDERKILL

RICHARD HARPER

LYNX BOOKS
New York

KINDERKILL

ISBN: 1-55802-225-2

First Printing/March 1989

This is a work of fiction. Names, characters, places, and incidents are either the product of the author's imagination or are used fictitiously. Any resemblance to actual events, locales, or persons, living or dead, is entirely coincidental.

Copyright © 1989 by Richard Harper
All rights reserved. No part of this book may be reproduced or transmitted in any form or by any means electronic or mechanical, including by photocopying, by recording, or by any information storage and retrieval system, without the express written permission of the Publisher, except where permitted by law. For information, contact Lynx Communications, Inc.

This book is published by Lynx Books, a division of Lynx Communications, Inc., 41 Madison Avenue, New York, New York, 10010. The name "Lynx" and the logo consisting of a stylized head of a lynx are trademarks of Lynx Communications, Inc.

Printed in the United States of America

0 9 8 7 6 5 4 3 2 1

*For the Family,
God bless 'em all.*

KINDERKILL

PROLOGUE

Inside the old, abandoned stable the darkness was terrifying. But not as terrifying as what was outside. The boy's rapid breathing slowed as he paused in the shadows by a broken window, cobwebbed over, listening for his pursuer and sensing the overwhelming presence of imminent death. But even this close, death was still unreal.

After all, he was just a kid. He whispered it aloud in the blackness, as if that would somehow explain things, solve things. "I'm just a kid." But the words broke in a sob, and he knew they wouldn't save him anyway; hadn't saved him yet from the crushing burden of his guilt. And he knew now they wouldn't, couldn't save him from his death.

At the sudden scraping sound he froze, pressing against the raw adobe wall of the empty stable. He saw the shadowy face peer briefly through the dingy, broken pane of glass, and heard him moving around to the broken stable door. His heart pounded in his ears. His mouth was dry, his hands sweating. He cringed against the wall. "No," he whispered hoarsely, "I'll be good. I'm just a kid. I'll be good—"

Aware of the mound of loose, dry straw at his feet, he plunged into it, only to find it old and brittle and pungently strong. It filled his nostrils as he burrowed deeper, trying desperately not to sneeze while the sagging stable door, pushed wider to admit his pursuer, creaked on one rusty hinge.

And then he did sneeze—and burst from the straw, and was caught; whining and begging uselessly under the sudden onslaught of brutal, painful blows; his fear of death almost all-consuming now, except for that tiny, tragic part of him that welcomed its release. And his killer was obligingly merciless, making his dying small and mean and senseless; an act of craven stupidity, of mindless terror and violence and pain.

Minutes later his limp and lifeless body was hoisted easily across the shoulder of his killer, and carried from the place of death.

PART I
The Investigation

ONE

Leaning back in the creaking old captain's chair at the Mimbres County sheriff's substation in Pontatoc, Detective-Sergeant Tom Ragnon laced his fingers behind his head, crossed his dusty boots on the desktop, and stared at the blank crime report rolled into the old manual typewriter.

Then his gaze shifted to the wall calender, where he had already x'ed out the date—September 25th. One more month left in his exile, his three-month disciplinary transfer down here to the boonies; a dozen dusty miles from the Mexican border and a hundred miles from nowhere. He was sick of working burglaries and car thefts and family disputes. Incredibly, he missed his speciality—homicide. And there hadn't been a homicide in Pontatoc, Arizona, since Billy the Kid had strayed this way from over in New Mexico.

The crime report he was not writing was another burglary—another hit-and-run, the perpetrators backtracked to the border with their loot, including a late-model pickup. The report would be filed on the Mexican side and probably forgotten. Sometimes they actually got a stolen vehicle back. More often it turned up with some Mexican police chief driving it for his personal transportation.

A sudden gust of wind rattled the casement window beside him, and he looked outside. The late September sky was yellow, the clouds reflecting the coppery, almost liquid glow of the dying sun. The very air seemed yellow, an eerie phenomenon that signaled a late summer monsoon moving steadily across the valley. A dust devil swirled violently along the street, a tumbleweed following in its wake to lodge under the rear bumper of the Jeep parked at the curb. Another storm, Ragnon thought, pushing the heat and humidity and dust before it, until finally loosing the thundering wind and lightning and rain, breaking the oppressive heat, at least for a little while.

"Should be the last storm of summer, right, Rags?" The duty deputy walked in from the back room carrying a fresh mug of coffee just as the big fat drops of rain began to slap the pavement outside, and a clap of thunder seemed to lift the roof as the yellow air dissolved into an ominous gray-black afternoon.

"Let's hope so, kid." Ragnon looked over at Ruben Montoya, who was twenty-three years old and had been with the sheriff's department for two years.

"Sure you don't want another cup, man?" the deputy offered. "It's fresh."

"No, thanks. My brain's turning to caffeine now." He sat there, watching the violence of the storm, always glad for the last of them because it signaled the coming of fall and a break in the relentless summer. Next month would be his favorite—October, with warm days and cool desert nights. The best month of the year in southern Arizona, Ragnon thought. That and April, before the brutal heat descended once again upon the land.

The old Seth Thomas on the wall behind the reception

desk bonged softly—four o'clock. A relic of the past, as if time stood still in Pontatoc. The whole town was a relic of the past: a couple of bars and a gas station, a mercantile store, a bank and post office, a restaurant and hotel. And this place—an old railway station refurbished and converted into a sheriff's substation and jail.

Freshly painted a traditional yellow with brown trim, it squatted in the center of the town's main street, dividing it into two thoroughfares. An old iron-wheeled baggage wagon was also freshly painted and parked beside the heavy double doors, but the tracks themselves and the trains were long gone. Mexican produce moved north in trucks now, and Ragnon, reflecting on the steady beat of the old swamp cooler and the ticking pendulum of the Seth Thomas on the wall, wondered if progress was really all that great. After all, what was lacking in Pontatoc besides sex, drugs, and break-dancing?

When the phone jangled suddenly, he heard Ruben answer it: "Pontatoc substation. Deputy Montoya. Yes, Lieutenant. Ragnon?" He glanced over at the detective, who quickly shook his head. "No, sir," he said into the receiver. "He checked in a while ago but he's not here now. Right, I'll tell him." He hung up. "Your *jefe* wants you to call him as soon as—says if you don't check in within the next hour for me to send somebody to run you down. Says it's important."

"Which means it's important to him, not me," Ragnon said. "And I don't want to report the lack of progress on another damned burglary." He sat there while another full forty-five seconds of his life ticked away on the old Seth Thomas before ripping the blank report out of the typewriter and picking up the phone. "Shit, might as well face it." Even talking to the chief was better than trying to fill in the blanks of a nothing case.

Not that he hadn't had nothing cases before, he thought, dialing the number at county headquarters in the city. But since his disciplinary transfer down here to the Gulag, he was batting nothing but zeros. He caught everything in the southern part of the county now and worked it alone. Usually there wasn't that much—they figured he'd die of boredom or quit, with nothing to think about except his problems—and Lord knows he had them. His personal life was withering on the vine with his wife filing for a divorce this time, not just a separation, and his father dying in a vet hospital in Prescott while he tried to cut through the red tape of transferring him to Tucson, where he'd be closer. "Chief?" He'd finally gotten through on the switchboard. "Just heard you called—what's up?"

"Oh, nothing much, Ragnon." The gruff voice was dripping sarcasm. "I just wanted to pass the time of day. Where in hell you been? I expected a crime report on my desk this morning. You owe me three now."

"The wheels of the gods, Chief. They grind a lot slower down here. But I'm working on them, really."

"Sure you are. Well, I've got a real one for your plate now, hotshot. A kid. Sex male, age estimated eight or nine, naked body found at a county dump on Tres Lomas Road ten miles south of here. 'Abusive trauma inflicted prior to death by asphyxiation' is the preliminary report. Dead about twelve to eighteen hours."

"Sweet Jesus," Ragnon breathed. "But you've already got a prelim? When did they find him?"

"Day before yesterday—just after dawn—an old guy was scavenging the trash."

"Day before—and you're just now telling me? What the fuck, Chief—"

"Don't get your balls in an uproar, Rags. I tried to call you earlier, remember?"

KINDERKILL

"Yeah, ten minutes ago!"

"The world doesn't turn on your every whim and desire, Ragnon," the chief said patiently. "We had to establish jurisdiction. That particular dump belongs to the county, but the city limits runs right through it. Anyway, it's ours. But you don't want this one, Rags, it's not a case that's gonna move. It's not gonna get you a gold star, it's just a messy no-win deal, and frankly I fought it. I even tried to assign it to someone else, but everybody's tied up. Murder's becoming an epidemic in Mimbres County this year. They must of heard you were off the line. Besides, there's political heat on this one—parents of missing kids, child-abuse nuts—you know the type, it's all the rage now."

"Yeah, people that are hurting . . ."

"Now, don't pull your bleeding-heart act on me, Rags. Just get your bad ass back here and get on it."

Tom Ragnon had pulled out his pouch of Red Man tobacco and was tucking a pinch in his cheek. "I'd take anything right now to get off this shit detail early, Chief, but you'll have to go through the higher brass. They're the ones who put me down here."

"I know. It's already been cleared. And maybe now you'll learn to kiss their ass once in a while like the rest of us."

"And what about Antone, is he on it yet?"

"He's on vacation—hunting somewhere on that goddamn reservation of his. I've got their Law and Order people looking for him."

"Shit."

"My comment exactly, but he's *your* partner. So fold your tent like a good little Arab and come in from the cold. And by the way, Rags, what do you know about horses?"

"Horses? Only that they leave those greenish-brown lumps behind them after a parade, Chief. Why?"

"Forensics found straw in the victim's hair. That's known as a clue, Rags, in case you've been away too long. It's about the only one. So you can look for a stable."

"Terrific." Ragnon sent a squirt of tobacco juice twanging into the metal wastebasket. "Or maybe a scarecrow or a hayride."

"So how's the weather down there? There's a flash-flood watch up here."

"Lousy. Storm's headed your way, and it's nothing to go out in chasing a cold trail."

"Shit, Rags, I just heard the snow's ass high to a tall Indian up in Denver this afternoon, an early blizzard, so count your blessings and get humping."

"I've got my trailer to move and—"

"Just so you get those crime reports in, then have your butt back here by eight in the morning. Maybe I'll have found Antone by then and you can cry in each other's beer. But at least you're back in Homicide, where you belong."

Tom Ragnon hung up the phone and stared out the window again, not quite so sure now he wanted back in Homicide. A kid savaged. He hadn't hunted down a childkiller since the Valdez raid when he'd lost his Mexican partner, and he still had bad dreams about that one. He looked mournfully over at Ruben Montoya. "You get any of that?"

"Enough. Sounds like you're off the hook again, Rags."

"Yeah." He spat. "But at what price? Somehow I feel like I just passed Go and forgot to collect two hundred dollars."

"Why do I get the feeling your chief's not one of your favorite people?"

"Lieutenant Sidney Clayton Poole," Ragnon mused, shifting his tobacco to his other cheek. "Next to Moammar Qaddafi I like him best. Count my blessings, the man says." He thought again of his father and his soon-to-be ex-wife, and moving that goddamned trailer again—and a child-killer. "I've got so many blessings I can't count that high," he said, and spat again.

Deputy Montoya had taken a call on the radio and missed the last remark. "What'd you say, Rags?" he asked as the old Seth Thomas bonged softly again. Four-thirty.

"I said I'll have to get these crime reports finished before the old walrus has apoplexy or breaks out in hives. Then I'll need to fill my thermos from your coffeepot, because it looks like I'm back in business, Rube, and I've caught a nasty one."

TWO

"How did the old walrus find you?" Tom Ragnon asked, tossing his crumpled, sweat-stained Stetson on his desk and filling his coffee mug at the big aluminum urn mounted at one end of the detective squad bay at headquarters in the city.

"Not by sending up smoke signals." Detective John Antone smiled at some secret recollection. "No, *I* found *him*, Sergeant. I checked in with Law and Order from Hickiwan and they told me he was after my red Injun ass."

"That's the first thing you learn in Homicide, John." Ragnon sipped at the freshly brewed coffee, but it was still too hot. "Never check in."

Ragnon had never quite figured out if Antone was a cop first and an Indian second or vice versa. Short and solid and barrel-chested with eyes like dark flint set in the brown planes of a smooth, hairless face, he wore his long hair tied in a ponytail and would admit only to being part Papago, part Apache, and part coyote. He took life as it came and still greeted each dawn with gratitude and grace. But he was a good cop. He had helped Ragnon on cases

KINDERKILL 13

before, as a deputy sheriff, and when he had passed the exam for detective, Ragnon had not only recommended him, but asked for him as a partner.

So far the partnership had amounted to zilch, with Antone working off and on with other detectives while Ragnon served out his disciplinary exile alone, having wised-off to the top brass once too often. This would be their first official case together, and the senior detective wanted it to work. The twenty-eight-year-old Indian, eleven years his junior, had been a good deputy, and Ragnon knew he'd make a good detective, too, if burnout and disillusionment didn't get to him first.

"You working anything now?" Ragnon asked, glancing up at the clock that hung above the large wall map of Mimbres County. It was 6:20 A.M.

Antone shook his head and drew his own mug of coffee. "Just cleared a family killing before I went hunting. Guy sat down beside his wife's body, the gun still in his hand."

"That was how I was hoping to ease back into homicide—with a nice, neat smoking-gun case. Instead, we've drawn some kind of sex freak." He picked up the report. "A kid. 'Extreme trauma to the anal area.' Jesus, John, we didn't really need this." And sinking down heavily on a chair at the conference table, he brushed his fingers through his thinning, gray-flecked hair and stared at the autopsy report, and then at the grisly color photos of the young victim, shutting out the images of his own two kids, age seven and five.

"But we've got it, Sergeant," Antone said softly. "It's ours. The kid got it, and we've got it."

They had agreed to meet here, on the third floor of the County Sheriff's Department, at 6:00 A.M., and hopefully be out on the case before Chief Poole came in at 7:30. Antone had brought the coroner's report and pictures, and

Ragnon had already gone through it once. It didn't read any better the second time: "Ante-mortem contusions and lacerations and broken bones." He looked up at the Indian. "Someone beat hell out of him, John, and then suffocated him."

"Strangled?"

"No." Tom Ragnon shook his head. "No ligature or finger marks. Probably used a plastic bag." Now he didn't feel like any breakfast, and even the coffee was making him a little queasy.

"There's not much to go on, is there, Sergeant?" Antone had sat down on the opposite side of the table and was studying Ragnon's expression for some clue to his real thoughts.

"There never is on the nasty ones, John." Outside the squad bay window, the day had dawned clear and clean and bright, but once again Tom Ragnon was faced with trouble in paradise. The easy ones were no challenge, but the toughies drove him crazy.

Half an hour later they had gone over the entire report again, and Ragnon still wasn't satisfied. Something wasn't right. It didn't click. He pushed the paper across the table to his partner. "Read that part again about where they found the body."

"—face down in the garbage," Antone quoted, and looked up.

"I thought it said *on* the garbage."

"No." The Indian looked again. "*In* the garbage."

"Then look at the lab analysis. Where does it say anything about the garbage that must have been on top of him?"

Antone studied it a few moments more and looked up. "You're right. Doesn't say anything about that, does it? Maybe it's just a matter of semantics—in or on."

"And maybe it isn't. When you're working a homicide, John, you find out. You look at everything, list everything, then you sort out what's important." Tom Ragnon leaned back in the chair and thought a moment. "Who found the body—a transient?"

"No, a local guy. He was garbage-picking at the dump."

"His record clean?"

"Yeah. One of the uniforms already checked." He pulled a notebook from his pocket and consulted it. "Delbert Gardner, seventy-two years old and lives alone. But he was playing shuffleboard at the park with two other old guys all day the estimated time of death."

"Let's go talk to him anyway," Ragnon said.

"You think it will do any good?"

"No." The senior detective was tucking a pinch of Red Man comfortably in his cheek as he watched the Indian put away the report and pictures. "But even the nasty ones have to start somewhere, partner."

They found Delbert Gardner already at the shuffleboard court in the park, even though it was only 7:40 A.M. They showed him their shields and invited him to breakfast at the corner café.

Settled in a red-padded booth over coffee and sweet rolls, Ragnon remarked, "A lady at your rooming house told us you'd be in the park. Kind of early for fun and games, isn't it, old-timer?"

Delbert Gardner met his gaze with fierce, rheumy eyes as he munched toothlessly on his roll after dunking it. "Still too hot to play in the afternoons, Sergeant. 'Sides, I'm always up come daybreak anyways. So." He eyed them both. "You're detectives, huh?"

"That's right." Ragnon took a bite of his own roll as

Antone sipped his coffee and silently watched the exchange.

"Never met any real detectives before. You don't look like the ones on the boob tube. Ever watch that Mike Hammer? Now, that's what I call a detective!"

"Never miss him," Ragnon said. "Now can we get down to this case?"

The old man smiled slyly. His fingers holding the roll were yellowed from too many cigarettes, the nails cracked and dirty. "Caper—that's what you call it, don't you? A caper?"

"A kid was killed, Mr. Gardner," Ragnon said patiently, "and not very gently."

"And you're gonna find who done him in?"

"We're gonna try." Ragnon glanced at Antone and back at the old man. "Are you gonna help us, Mr. Gardner?"

The old man snorted, dribbling crumbs down his chin and brushing them away. "What can I tell you? I was trashing that dump, picking up a few odds and ends to sell at the swap meet, while the guard was down at the other end, and there he was."

"There who was?"

"The boy. At least his legs—just the bare little legs sticking out—the feet bare too." The old man put down the remains of his roll and lit a cigarette. "Roll 'em myself," he said, taking the first deep drag and letting it out slowly. "Got me one o'them little rolling machines. It's lots cheaper than ready-mades."

They sure smelled cheaper, Ragnon thought.

"Then he was actually *under* the garbage, Mr. Gardner?" Antone asked. "Not on top of it?"

"Yeah, under it, some of it. I had to pull off a bag and

an old rug. It was the rug caught my eye. Thought maybe it was still good, but it wasn't."

"But the report doesn't mention any of this, Mr. Gardner," Ragnon said cautiously. "According to your statement, you told the officers the body was in the garbage, but you didn't mention moving anything to get a look at it."

"No? You got exactly what I said? They wrote all that stuff down?"

"They sure did. So which is it? It's important, Mr. Gardner. Was the child's body lying on top of the refuse, or did you have to uncover it?"

Delbert Gardner shrugged. "Practically on top, but like I said, I only saw the legs at first. I had to pull aside the trash before I could believe what I was seeing."

"The bag and the rug," Ragnon said. "Describe them."

"What can I say—a bulging clear plastic bag full of papers, and the rug. Gold color, but too old and ragged and stained to be any good."

"So the rug and the bag are still there?" Antone asked. "They never took them?"

"Not to my notice."

"Will you go back to the dump, Mr. Gardner?" Ragnon asked. "Show us the rug and the bag?"

The old man's bushy brows rose. "Go back—now?"

"You have something better to do, Mr. Gardner?" Antone asked.

"Naw. Hell, no. Say, you fellas wouldn't have a cigarette on you, would you? This is my last one."

"We don't smoke," Ragnon said, "but we'll stop and buy you a whole carton, Mr. Gardner, ready-mades. How's that?"

"Del. Call me Del." The old man's toothless grin was no improvement to his gaunt, grizzled cheeks and rheumy eyes, but his face had brightened with anticipation. "You wouldn't throw in a pint o' red-eye too, would you, Sergeant?" he asked slyly.

"Don't get carried away, Del," Tom Ragnon said.

THREE

At the dump, greasy black smoke curled against the blue morning sky, rising with the day's advancing heat, but it was coming from the far end, where the bulldozers were working, covering the refuse of a throwaway society.

In a lot of ways the whole country was becoming a garbage dump, Ragnon thought as he drove the unmarked county car along a temporary dirt road and the old man in the back seat directed them to the place where the "crime scene" signs and yellow streamers had already been removed.

"Another day and we'd have been too late," John Antone said. "The 'dozers will be working this end by tomorrow."

"Maybe you guys are just lucky." Del Gardner paused to cup a match to a fresh, unfiltered Camel as they pulled up at the site.

"I get the feeling we're going to have to make our own luck on this one," Tom Ragnon said. "Point out the spot, Del."

They all got out and the old man walked ahead of them

without hesitation. "There." He pointed. "That's the rug."

They stopped. The small throw rug had once been brown or yellow or maybe brownish-yellow, or even gold. Now it was ragged and stained. They stood there, staring down at it.

"And this rug was covering the body?" Ragnon asked.

"Yeah, the rug and that clear plastic bag of trash there." He pointed again. "They were both on top of the body, but I saw the legs."

"And you pulled the body out," John Antone said, testing him.

"Hell, no!" Del Gardner pulled back himself as if stung by the accusation. "I never touched it. I just dragged off the rug and the bag of trash to be sure I knew what I was lookin' at. It was a little kid's body—naked."

"And this is the bag of trash." Antone made the statement while walking over to the bulging clear plastic.

"You're sure that's the one?" Ragnon had his own notebook out now.

"You don't see no other clear plastic bag around, do you, Sergeant? Of course that's the one. And that's the gold rug."

"Funny," Ragnon said, "this wasn't in the report." He had jotted fresh notes and then turned back a few pages. "You didn't mention the body being covered by anything. You just said it was there, *in* the garbage." He looked at Del Gardner. "Sure you didn't touch it, maybe move it?"

"Goddammit, I told you no, I never touched it. I couldn't. I could see he was dead. There was even flies buzzing around him. It was awful."

"But you moved the rug and bag that covered him and didn't mention that to the other officers." Ragnon kept his tone carefully neutral, nonaccusatory.

"I just forgot, Sergeant. And nobody asked. Never thought it might be important. Is it?"

"Anything else you haven't told us, Del? Let us decide what's important." He spat a stream of tobacco juice onto the ground at his feet. "Was the body maybe wrapped in the rug, for instance?"

"No, Christ, it was just like I told you—face down, under the rug and bag, legs sticking out. That's it."

"Okay, Del." Ragnon looked around at the dump a moment, then he and Antone gathered up the rug and bag, unopened, tagged them for evidence, and put them in the trunk of the car. They let Gardner sit alone in the back seat while they poked around some more, not looking for anything special, just looking. The tire tracks on the road leading in were multiple and overlapping and useless. Maybe an analysis of the trash in the bag or the bag itself would tell them something. Or of the rug. And maybe it wouldn't.

"What do you think, John?" Ragnon asked, spitting. "He's a trash collector. Would he trash a kid?"

"He has an alibi, Sergeant. The other guys at the park. He even took two of them up to his room for soup at lunchtime. They were all questioned and checked out."

"Sure they were. And we'll go over it all again. Because it doesn't leave us much, does it? A rug and a trash bag."

John Antone smiled and unwrapped a stick of gum. "One step at a time, Sergeant, right? Maybe it will turn out to be a grab bag full of goodies. At least it's more than we had this morning, so we're on our way."

"I'll say one thing for you, John," Ragnon said, spitting as they walked back to the car. "I sure as hell do like your attitude."

* * *

In the basement of the sheriff's building they dumped out the contents of the bag on the cement floor and put on their plastic gloves, then canted a flood lamp and went through it all, listing everything. "Another small sign the gods might be smiling on us," Ragnon said. "There's no stinking mess to sift through, no rotting potatoes and squashed melons or used tampons—just dry trash. Looks like mostly paper—newspapers, and from three different cities: Pueblo, Colorado; Albuquerque, New Mexico; and Las Cruces, New Mexico."

"What are the dates?"

"They're current. Pueblo *Chieftain*, September seventeenth; Albuquerque *Journal*, September eighteenth and nineteenth; Las Cruces *Sun Times*, September twentieth—two days before the killing in Arizona."

"Travelers?" Antone wondered aloud. "Headed south out of Colorado and turned west into Arizona?"

"So where are they now, the twenty-sixth? California? Old Mexico?"

John Antone scratched his head. "Unless, of course, the killer did deposit the victim *on* the garbage, Sergeant, then simply grabbed someone else's nearby trash and piled it on top."

"Which would put us back to square one." He shook his head in frustration and began spreading more of the trash around—a bloody Band-Aid, some used facial tissue, a crumpled news article about an opera festival in Aspen, Colorado, with no date, and what looked like sheets of blank photographic paper along with some exposed negatives. He picked up one of the negatives with tweezers, held it to the light, and frowned. "I think we got the right trash, John. What do you make of this?"

Antone's eyes narrowed as he took the tweezers and held the negative to the light himself. "Looks like a kid,

Sergeant—two children—on a bed. But the picture's badly exposed."

"Same with this one—and this one." He handed two more spoiled negatives to the Indian, one at a time. "That's why there's no finished prints. Just bad negatives they threw away."

"I'll buy that," Ragnon said. "But what about the subject matter? What do you make of that?"

"The kids look naked. And they're posed—funny." He looked at Ragnon. "Pornography?"

"The worst kind. Kiddie porn. We'll have to get 'em printed and blown up."

"The negatives might also explain this, Sergeant." Antone had picked up an empty plastic jug and sniffed it. "That's photo-developer."

Tom Ragnon squatted down by the empty trash bag and tugged out his pouch of Red Man. Since his exile he'd grown a mustache and started jogging again, but he'd also picked up the bad habit of working on his days off. Now that he was back to the serious business of murder, he had sworn to get back on a regular schedule—keep his life simple, sensible, under control—but he knew he was lying. "Shit, John," he said now, "it's gonna be nastier than I thought."

By early afternoon they'd grabbed a quick sandwich in the basement cafeteria and were back upstairs in the detective squad bay, where Ragnon sat down at his desk and smoothed out another crumpled piece of paper—possibly the best piece of information they'd found in their "grab bag"—a handwritten receipt for three half gallons of strawberry ice cream at $3.19, total $9.57. No store name, no address, no date, but on the "name of purchaser" line was Rancho Malaguena. He looked up at his partner. "And nobody's ever heard of it?"

John Antone shook his head. "But at least it's something, Sergeant. We've got a name."

Everything had been checked for latent prints without a single positive result, and they'd sent the other stuff on to the lab for further analysis, and the negatives for development. This receipt would go to the lab, too, but Ragnon had kept it a little longer, trying to puzzle it out. It looked vaguely familiar, but he couldn't place it.

"I hate a mystery, John," he said, reaching for his pouch of Red Man. "And that's what we've got already— a mystery. Because you notice something that wasn't in the trash? Something that's in everybody's trash, but not in this guy's, aside from this?"

"Receipts?"

"Right." Ragnon tucked a pinch of tobacco in his cheek. "Receipts. Except for this one, nothing with a simple name or address on it. That's all we need, John. With the trash dumped on top of the victim, it would have to be the killer, right? Anyone else would have reported the body. Jesus, unless he *did* grab someone else's trash . . . But even then there'd be bills, receipts, torn envelopes, something we could have pieced together for a name and address. Instead, we've still got zip, zilch, *nada*."

"Unless the lab turns up something, Sergeant. Or the negatives. And we've still got the name of that ranch. And doesn't the lack of bills and addresses just support the evidence that they were traveling?"

"But not even a motel or a gas credit receipt?"

"Maybe they saved them," Antone suggested, "for taxes."

Ragnon spat into the wastebasket. "Tell you what, John.

Speaking of taxes, why don't you go check out the name—Rancho Malaguena—at the recorder's office, while I get this receipt over to the lab. Then I'll give the chief a tinkle to let him know how great we're doing."

"Why not just stop in his office before you leave?"

"That's another thing you've got to learn, John." Ragnon picked up his crumpled Stetson. "The chief is better kept at a distance when you've got only bad news. So meet me at the lab."

"Rancho Malaguena?" Chief Poole's voice on the phone line was skeptical. Ragnon could almost see his little walrus eyes squinch up over his half glasses. "What the fuck's a Rancho Malaguena? A new taco sauce?"

"I don't know yet, Chief. Antone's looking it up at the tax office. He's gonna meet me here at the lab. Just thought I'd break my own rule and check in, because we could use a little help on this one. Unless, of course, we got lucky. No sudden signed confession or a call from an eyewitness, I suppose?"

"You're gonna have to break your ass on this one, Rags. Not even an ID on the victim yet. We put a composite in the papers, and we've had fifty thousand calls from parents, but none gave us this victim's description."

"I thought people were printing their kids nowadays."

"Evidently not this one. Nothing's matched. But who knows how long he's been missing or run away or whatever. You got any idea how many kids disappear in this country every year, Rags?"

"I don't think I want to know. And I'm just concerned right now about this one. Hang on a minute, Antone's here with something already." He looked at the note the Indian had handed him and read it into the phone: "Rancho Malaguena, part of an old Spanish land grant, owned now by a multinational corporation. A working cattle ranch up to the early 1900s. Guest ranch off and on into the sixties, and used as a movie location by big companies—made a lot of Westerns. Caretaker lives on the place now, down near the border. But I don't believe this part, Chief. Nearest town is Pontatoc. I just hauled my trailer back from there!"

"Homicide is a small world, Rags. And I saw your negatives before they went over to the lab. Looks like some kind of porno racket, so we *are* going to get a little help from our friends the feds. They're loaning us a porn specialist."

"A porn specialist? But what are the feds—"

"Who knows about the feds. There's that new Child Protection Act, or maybe they just figure the kid's civil rights were violated. But help is help, right?"

"What I had in mind was another of our own teams—"

"Not a chance, Rags. Two more homicides popped last night in the northern part of the county. Be grateful you're getting this much. You may just have to turn your trailer around and take the Indian and the porn specialist with you."

"What makes you think the perp is still there?"

"Who knows? Southern Arizona gets nice this time of year, and you've got to start somewhere. And believe me, Rags, it's not going to be that bad, because I've saved the best news till last. Your porn specialist—I just met her over at the Federal Building, and she's a real fox!"

"She?" Ragnon almost swallowed his Red Man. "The porno specialist is a female?"

"Tits, ass, and everything, Rags, a well-packaged

pussy." He could hear the lecherous laughter in the chief's voice. "You're gonna love her!"

"Jesus H. Christ," Tom Ragnon said as he hung up the phone and looked at Antone. "We're getting ourselves a porno specialist." He still couldn't believe they'd do this to him. "A *female* porno specialist."

Four

"She's in there—with Old Iron Balls." The duty officer indicated the closed door with the bold letters CHIEF OF HOMICIDE stenciled in black on the frosted glass. "You maybe should of brought your elephant gun, bwana," he added, grinning. "She's all done out in some kind of African bush garb. Looks like she's going on safari."

"Wonderful," Ragnon grunted. He had delayed the meeting this morning as long as possible. Still reluctant, he knocked once and opened the door.

Lieutenant Sidney Clayton Poole sat behind his desk like a brooding walrus at bay. He actually looked grateful for the detective's intrusion. "Here he is now. Sergeant Tom Ragnon, meet Lucinda Ann Crown, your porno specialist." The chief had nipped the end off one of his fat greenish cigars and was lighting it with his bronze-horse desk lighter, puffing clouds of foul blue smoke to get it going while Lucinda Crown held out a slim, firm hand to Ragnon, who shook it carefully and returned her uncertain smile.

"Didn't I tell you she was gorgeous, Rags?" The chief

was beaming behind his cigar, a contented walrus now that he had someone to shuck her off on.

Crown offered Ragnon one of her own slim brown cigarillos, and when he shook his head, she lit one for herself with a slim pencil lighter. He judged her several years his junior, about five-feet-six, and a well-proportioned 126 pounds. And the duty officer was right. Her figure was contained by a neatly tailored tan bush jacket and slacks tucked into boots. A blue scarf encircled a slim throat, and a wide-brim bush hat rested on Poole's desk beside her. Her ash-blond hair was cropped boyishly short, yet it somehow made her seem even more feminine. She had thin, angular features, a firm chin, full lips, and eyes—he got hung up immediately on her smoky-gray eyes. Startlingly bold and carefully defined by mascara, they were calm and quiet and serious. It was her smile that was a little sharky.

"At least you don't look like a cop," he managed to say.

"I'll take that as a compliment, Sergeant." She glanced back at Poole, exhaling her own smoke, and their combined pollution would have delighted Jesse Helms and R. J. Reynolds both. "But let's clear up something first," she added unkindly. "I'm told you're something of a smartass, Sergeant, with a crude sense of humor. So please, no Dickless Tracy jokes. I've heard them all."

Tom Ragnon's smile grew a little wider as he tugged his pouch of Red Man from his pocket and tucked a pinch in his cheek, reluctantly adding his own small contribution to the tobacco industry's tidy profits and thinking, Dammit, the chief was right, she really is gorgeous. "Okay," he said agreeably. "So when can you start?"

"I've already started, Sergeant. I've read the autopsy report, and the field interviews with Gardner, the old man who found the body, and his cronies who alibied him. And I just finished the lab report that came in this morning."

"Then you know as much as we do." He glanced at the digital clock on the chief's desk. It was 10:25. "Shall we go meet my partner?"

"That would be John Antone? I pulled his jacket a few minutes ago. I noticed he only just made detective, but his record as a deputy seems excellent."

Tom Ragnon's smile faded as he spat hard into Poole's metal wastebasket and watched the chief wince. "He'll do to ride the river with," he said quietly.

"I pulled your jacket too, Sergeant." Her smoky-gray eyes sparkled as she watched him smolder.

"And you're suddenly grinning like a skunk eating grits. Did my record amuse you?" Damn, but he liked her sharky little smile almost better than her eyes.

"You've got as many suspensions as 'attaboys.' "

"I like to keep life on an even keel."

"I think you're going to be a real challenge to work with, Sergeant."

Ragnon spat again, violently, making the metal basket ring. "I'll try to keep it interesting, Lucy. Shall we go?"

"My name's Lucinda, Sergeant." She ground out her cigarillo in Poole's polished onyx ashtray.

"Of course . . . Lucinda. Mine's Thomas. Now, shall we go?"

"Yeah, go," Poole said, laughing, "both of you, before the blood starts to flow. And have fun," he added facetiously.

As Ragnon held the door for her, the chief added one more kindly gem of admonishment. "And, Lucinda, try to get this turkey to write me a progress report occasionally. He tends to neglect that sort of thing, and then I have to whack his balls."

* * *

On the elevator down to the basement, where Ragnon could check them out in an unmarked car, she was still smiling sharkily. "Does he do it often?"

"Does who do what often?" Ragnon grumbled.

"Poole. Whack your balls."

"More often than I like to admit, and it's not my favorite thing." He tried unsuccessfully to fix his eyes on the descending lighted numbers of the floors, then couldn't help smiling himself. He noticed her looking at him oddly.

"Now *you're* grinning like a skunk eating grits, Sergeant," she said. "What's so amusing?"

"Nothing. It's just that I never had a partner who wore perfume before. It's kind of nice."

"Don't let it go to your head, Sergeant," Lucinda Crown said.

He held the elevator door while she stepped out, and their boots echoed among the supporting pillars and stale exhaust fumes of the parking bays. At the garage office he got a log book and keys, and as they walked to the designated car he mentioned something as casually as he could. "You have me at a disadvantage."

"How's that?"

"Since I didn't get to peek at your personnel jacket, you might enlighten me as to your claim to fame." He opened the car door for her, feeling like a real gentleman.

When he got in on the driver's side and started the engine, she said, "We're dancing around it, aren't we, Sergeant?"

"Are we?" He headed up the ramp and out into the city traffic.

"What you really want to know is my personal situation—socially."

"Is that what I want to know, your social situation?"

"Believe me, it's nothing sensational."

"Maybe we can fix that."

She ignored him. "As to my 'claim to fame,' I started out in law school but ran out of money. I also became disillusioned quickly, the idealism replaced by cynicism. There seemed to be an overabundance of law but not much real justice in the American legal system. It's a game lawyers play—the best system in the world maybe—but still a game. Anyway, I got into enforcement instead, and the last couple of years I've been a special kind of cop. Pornography. Violence against women and children." She looked at him. "I'm even fairly good at it, Sergeant."

He glanced at her, beginning to suspect she was very good at it.

"And yes, I've been married," she continued with an audible sigh. "Once. No kids. And I'm presently going with a lieutenant in your vice department—Jack McKittrick."

Ragnon braked a little too hard at the light. "Not Jumping Jack McKittrick!" The light changed and he squealed the tires taking off.

"You sound like you don't approve, Sergeant. And what do you mean by 'jumping'?"

"Only that it's said he'll jump the bones of a corpse if it's wearing a skirt."

"Thanks a lot." She colored slightly.

"Nothing personal," he added weakly. "Other than that, I'm sure he's a wonderful human being." But the sarcasm hung as heavily as the sudden silence inside the car.

"You must see a different side of him than I do," she

said stiffly, trying again. "Can we change the subject? What about you? No Jumping Janes in your life?"

"My divorce is in the works, for the usual stupid reasons. And I do have kids, my wife's by a previous, aged five and seven. No current Jane, jumping or otherwise, I'm sad to say."

"So now I guess we're even—socially."

"Sort of, I guess." Why did he feel like a fish out of water with this woman?

"So what about your latest fiasco, a three-month disciplinary transfer? What did you do, goose the governor?"

"Almost. I wised-off to a county supervisor with mucho clout in the sheriff's department."

"About what?"

"He didn't think the detective division should have any additional appropriations under the newly tightened budget until we proved ourselves worthy with more cleared cases and less overtime. He made the crack in my hearing, and I responded a bit crudely as to where he could stick his appropriations. But I thought you read my jacket."

"That little tidbit hasn't been added yet. But now that we've cleared it up, let's get to work. And I assure you, I'm ready to hold up my end of this case, Sergeant. We can work together or separately. Separately will be harder on both of us, but take your pick."

"Oh, I'm with you, Crown," Ragnon assured her. "Help is help and I appreciate it—especially on a ballbuster like this one."

"So where are we meeting your partner?"

"You like Mexican food?"

He glanced at her while they waited for another light to change, and there was that sharky little smile again. "Does Michael Jackson wear a glove?"

"That's good, because Antone's meeting us at a Mexican joint in the barrio called the Tequila Mockingbird. It's away from the tourist traps, and the food's so authentic you'd better not drink the water. They've got a sign that says so."

Her laughter seemed light but genuine. "Then lunch is on me, but just this once."

"You'll be sorry. You haven't seen John Antone eat—or me."

As he turned the wheel, guiding the car across the railroad tracks and into the Mexican barrio, she lit another of her slim cigarillos. "What have you got on this case, Sergeant?" she asked seriously. "Really. Just the receipt for the ice cream from that ranch?"

"That's about it."

"Three half gallons, that would indicate several people, but it's a pretty thin lead."

"We work with what we've got in Homicide."

She seemed thoughtful as he pulled into the shade of a row of olive trees lining a low patio wall, parked, and looked at her. "You know we've got us a grungy one, don't you?"

She nodded. "I told you, I studied the pix, the autopsy report. I've seen it before."

"Oh? The pattern? The same MO?" he asked hopefully.

"No, but the abuse, the trauma, and then the death—of a child. Something inflicted often by parents or stepparents, and sometimes by strangers, but always by someone the child has turned to, depended on, and been betrayed by. Seven to eight hundred kids were reported missing in this city alone last year. Most were runaways, of course, or abducted by relatives, but it includes a small percentage seduced away by strangers."

"And we don't know yet what we've got here," Ragnon said as they got out and walked inside the restaurant, and on through to the patio out back. There they found a table with a checkered oilcloth under more olive trees. "The receipt's just a plain dime-store variety, torn from a pad," Ragnon told her. "Deputies are checking ice cream stores all over the city, but most use the regular printed cash-register receipts now like the supermarkets, or one with their own name on it—nothing old-fashioned and handwritten like this—and yet it seems familiar somehow."

"Where is this ranch?"

"About forty-five miles southeast of here, near Pontatoc."

"But since they appear to be traveling—and pornographers do move around a lot—they could be back in New Mexico by now, or old Mexico or even California."

"Or Texas, or Timbuktu."

"But you don't think so." The waitress brought them glasses of water and silverware and two menus, and Ragnon asked for a third setting, telling her someone else would be joining them.

"Like the chief says," he went on, turning back to Lucinda, "southern Arizona gets nice this time of year."

"I know. The place to be, come winter. And maybe our killers think the same way. Except what if they don't?"

"Then we've got a whole new ball game, lady," Tom Ragnon said.

"Hey." Lucinda Crown had put down her menu and nodded as the waitress brought the third setting. "They really do have a sign about the water!"

"Would I lie to a partner?"

She looked at him. "I hope not, Sergeant." She was suddenly serious again. "But even if you're right about the killers still being here somewhere, how do we go about finding them?"

Tom Ragnon smiled beguilingly. "I was kind of hoping maybe you could help us with that one, Crown." He sipped his water, tempting fate, and then nodded toward the doorway. "Here comes our other partner now. Maybe he's got something."

FIVE

Over a chili relleno, green chili burro, and a fat chimichanga, the three of them chewed on what they had and where to go from there. Ragnon and Crown washed theirs down with sweating cold bottles of golden "lite" beer, while Antone stuck to an icy "uncola." He had gotten drunk on hard liquor once when he was seventeen and nearly killed a man, and had never touched more than an occasional beer since.

"I stopped by the tax office again," the Indian was saying. "Rancho Malaguena's are paid through the multilayer corporation. No delinquency."

"A Mafia holding?" Lucinda Crown wondered.

Ragnon shrugged. "Why not? Those bastards are into every nasty business that turns a buck."

"Including pornography."

"But a child-killing doesn't make sense," Antone said.

"No, it doesn't compute," Ragnon agreed. "It attracts people like us."

"Unless they did a snuff film," Crown suggested. She looked at them both. "It happens, but there's been nothing on the street about one lately."

They paused while the waitress cleared away their empty plates and then brought two fresh beers and another uncola. Then Ragnon unfolded a state roadmap and spread it on the table. "Body is found, less than twenty-four hours old, at Tres Lomas dump south of the city." He marked an X with a black felt-tip pen. "But blood lividity indicated he was moved after he was killed, and Rancho Malaguena is about here"—he x'ed another spot—"forty-five miles southeast, less than an hour's drive from the dump." He looked up at both Antone and Crown. "A ranch where movies are made? Where maybe horses are kept? And straw?" Ragnon sat back and refolded the map on its creases. "I think it's worth a closer look, partners."

Lucinda Crown lit a cigarillo and inhaled thoughtfully. "If we could just ID the victim, we might have some even harder evidence, something to feed on. The autopsy showed some dental work, a couple of fillings in the right lower jaw."

"I'm having a check run on local dentists," Ragnon said, "especially children's dentists."

"But what if he's not a local kid?" Antone asked. "What if he's not even an Arizona kid?"

"I'm trying not to think about that, John," Tom Ragnon answered.

Crown let out a forceful jet of smoke. "The deputies are also checking on a computer list I compiled of known pedophiles in this area to see if any of them can be placed near the scene. But if the ones we want were traveling like the newspapers indicated . . ." She shrugged.

"And I went over the lab report again, Sergeant," Antone said, "but there's not much that really helps. Bloodstain on the Band-Aid wasn't enough to type. Stains on the rug *are* photo-developer, and there was dirt that may have come from a stable, but the spoiled negatives, even blown up, show only what appears to be a cheap motel room and no clear features on the kids."

"If the pessimism around here gets any deeper," Ragnon said, "we're gonna need hip boots. I think what we need is more from the victim himself. There's a black guy in the coroner's office named Parker. He's good. We'll see if he'll go over the body again. Meanwhile, I guess that's it for now." He signaled the waitress for their check.

"Not quite, Sergeant," Crown said, mashing out her cigarillo in the ashtray. "I've got something else going with the computer artist at headquarters on identifying the victim. It's called computer imaging."

"I know about computer imaging," Ragnon said. "Using a photo of a missing child and aging it, enhancing it to how they might look today, depending on how long they've been missing. Only we don't have a photo. We've got the child—dead—and no telling how long he's been missing. So what good is your imaging in our case?"

"It's just experimental, and a long shot, but I'm having the artist try to build enhancements based on the photos of various missing kids that would be about the victim's age now."

"But there must be hundreds—"

"Not when you sort out only the eight-to-nine-year-old Anglo males, then first take those missing up to a year, then two years, three, and so on, and computer-age them to what they might look like now and compare them to our victim."

Ragnon whistled. "That could still mean a lot of kids. And aging each one individually to compare with the victim—and how accurate could it be anyway, comparing them to a corpse?"

"I said it was a long shot; not like when the child is known to start with. Then they can even use a relative's features—eyes from the mother, mouth from the father, and so on—to blend a computer composite of what the child might look like today. But I think it's worth a try. They've already started sorting local Anglo males who would be about nine now for the artist to work on. Those missing from the city first, then Arizona. Then we'll try contiguous states."

Ragnon raised his brows. "You really did get started quick on this case, Crown." And he couldn't quite keep the admiration completely out of his tone as the waitress finally brought their check and Crown intercepted it. "My treat, remember?"

"I think I'm gonna love a partner like you," the senior detective said.

"Don't count on it, Sergeant. I don't mellow with age." But she smiled when she said it.

"Those cancer sticks will kill you, Crown," Ragnon observed softly as they all got up and she mashed out another cigarillo before heading for the cashier.

"What do you think that stuff is you spit into Poole's wastebasket, Sergeant? Vitamins?"

"The man makes me nervous." Ragnon rolled a toothpick from the dispenser at the counter. "I chew when I'm nervous, but I'm trying to kick that habit too." He looked around at Antone. "How come you got no bad habits, John? Don't you ever feel left out?"

John Antone smiled. "Me? A red man in a white man's world? Does an eagle soar?"

As they walked out toward the parking area, Ragnon said, "Why don't you stay with the computer-imaging thing, Crown, and maybe follow up on the dental checks while John and I look into this Malaguena Ranch. If we turn anything, I'll probably have to move my trailer back down to Pontatoc, the nearest town, and base out of there." Then he paused at the restaurant's patio gate, suddenly reluctant to leave the pleasant shade of the olive trees and the peace of flowering hibiscus and bougainvillea, reluctant to go back out into the real world of a child-killer. "Look," he said, "I've got to make a quick personal phone call, and then we'll go."

While they waited for Ragnon beside the patio wall, Lucinda Crown started to light another cigarillo, then changed her mind. "I hear he's quite a bulldog on a case," she said, "once he sets his teeth."

The Indian nodded. "That's his reputation. He seems to have a talent for it. Eight years in Homicide—he lives and breathes it. They say sometimes when it's slow he'll go to the office and review unsolved cases, use cross-indexes, feed old names and MOs into the computer, just fooling around, and zap, something clicks and a dead-end case is back in the active file."

"I know. Computers certainly help, but they still need the legwork of a good detective to feed them. Electronics can bring the whole complex mess together, but only if it's fed the right information and asked the right questions."

When Ragnon returned he handed Crown the keys to the county car. "You take this one back and stick with the ID on the victim. Like you say, once we know that, it ought to make the what, why, and who a hell of a lot easier."

But Lucinda Crown was staring at him oddly again, her expression laced with her sharky, mistrustful little grin. "You're not going to try to waltz me around on this, are you, Sergeant? I'm really after something with this computer imaging, and I'll share anything I get with you guys, but I'll expect the same. Don't put me out to pasture. This is *our* case—the three of us." And her gaze included the

Indian, who was standing very still, watching her. "A cooperative effort—partners—agreed?"

Tom Ragnon glanced at Antone, and then looked back at the lady. But it was the Indian who answered, smiling. "We wouldn't have it any other way, Lucinda." And he even reached over and shook hands with her on it.

Minutes later Antone was behind the wheel of the department 4×4 Jeep Cherokee, and with Ragnon beside him they headed onto the interstate and southeast out of the city. They drove in silence until the turnoff on a two-lane paved county road with the sign PONTATOC 45M.

"Lucinda," Tom Ragnon said at last.

Antone glanced at him. "What?"

"You called her Lucinda. Why not Lucy? When I first met her I called her Lucy and she corrected me."

"Because she said her name was Lucinda."

Tom Ragnon looked over at his partner. "That some kind of funny Indian logic, John?"

"No, Sergeant." Antone smiled. "It's called courtesy."

The narrow blacktop road began climbing through the high desert, the grama grass, and cacti-studded hills stretching endlessly under a vast blue sky to distant ragged mountains that ranged all around the horizon. Across the miles-wide valley a few puffed white clouds piled high, but they were far to the east and mostly over New Mexico. The radio had just forecast a high of only seventy-nine, with winds gusting to twenty miles an hour. Fall was in the air.

"I'm betting she's good, Sergeant," Antone said, breaking the silence between them again.

"Lucinda Crown?"

"Yes. She's got a way about her I like, a kind of gutsy, no-nonsense efficiency—besides being good-looking."

"She's good-looking, all right," Tom Ragnon admitted. "We'll have to see about the rest of it." But he'd gotten the same impression. In fact, he was beginning to think maybe having her help out on the case wasn't going to be the drag he was at first sure it would be. Though he wasn't about to admit it, even to Antone. Maybe especially to Antone. He dug out his pouch of Red Man and tucked a pinch in his cheek.

"That phone call I made back at the restaurant was to my dad up in Prescott."

"Oh? How's he doing?"

"Not so good. He knows now it's the big C—a tumor on his spine. I've got to get up there to see him. Doesn't look like that damn transfer to the hospital here is ever coming through."

"How old is your father?" the Indian asked.

"Not old. Sixty-three. Just retired last year and moved up to Flagstaff."

"My grandfather died last year at seventy-eight. Just passed to the other side in his sleep, lean and mean and raunchy as an old wolf."

"That's the way to go," Ragnon said. "I hope when my time comes I'll still have the strength to climb high up in those San Francisco peaks near Flag in the middle of winter and bare my bones to the icy winds. Don't your people say any day the sun shines and the wind blows free is a good day to die?"

John Antone smiled tolerantly. "Sometimes I think you talk more like an injun than me, Sergeant."

Twenty minutes later Antone slowed the Cherokee at another road sign that said PONTATOC 12M. But as he pulled off on the shoulder, he pointed across the highway toward an open gate with cow skulls mounted on the gateposts and an ancient, weathered sign arched above them. They could still make out the faded letters: RANCHO MALAGUENA. There was no mailbox, but just inside the open gate was another, newer sign posted: NO HUNTING, NO CAMPING, NO TRESPASSING—VIOLATORS WILL BE PROSECUTED TO THE FULL EXTENT OF THE LAW.

"Looks like the welcome mat is always out," Tom Ragnon said, spitting out the open window. "Wonder if they shoot first and ask questions later."

Antone, his arms crossed and resting on the steering wheel while the Cherokee's engine idled, was suddenly glad they had brought a marked vehicle, with its sheriff's star on the doors and bar lights on the roof. "So what now?" he asked. There were no ranch buildings in sight, just a narrow, weed-grown dirt trace leading up and over a grassy hill. An arroyo ran off to the right and was lined with mesquite trees. "That road's been used," he said, "but not much—no recent traffic—not in the last day or so."

"Well," Ragnon said, spitting again, "why don't we just meander on over there, John, and see where life takes us?"

SIX

With Antone guiding the 4×4, bumping across the grated rails of a cattle guard in the open gate, they followed the rutted, weed-grown trace while Ragnon kept one eye on the odometer. They topped the first rise and saw the road ahead disappear over another grassy hill as the arroyo continued to veer away on their right. On their left an old windmill stood silent, locked down tight, its blades motionless in the ten-to-twelve-knot wind that was gusting across the hills. The concrete water tank beneath it was dry.

"Evidently not running any cattle on the place," Antone commented, "or much of anything else."

Over the next hill the road angled farther left, and Ragnon clocked them at 2.8 miles into the property as they headed down into a shallow valley and spotted another windmill standing stark against the sky. On this one the blades were turning, and as the wind shifted they could hear its raucous clatter and the rhythmic squeak of gears crying for grease. Set into a leveled spot on the hill below it, shaded by an ancient oak, was a small, battered aluminum trailer.

Antone braked the 4×4 and let the engine idle while they both sat and studied the trailer and the working windmill. There was nothing else in sight. No ranch house, no stables, no other signs of habitation. Ragnon shifted his tobacco from one cheek to the other and spat. "That look to you like somebody sitting there in the shade by the trailer door?" he asked.

Antone had taken a pair of binoculars from their case and raised them. "It's a man, Sergeant. His chair's tilted back against the side of the trailer. He's not moving, doesn't even act like like he sees us. Maybe he's dead."

"Let's go find out."

With the wind and the sounds of the windmill still in their faces, Antone eased the Cherokee closer in. Still the figure in front of the trailer didn't move, didn't wave, didn't do anything. They could see now his hat was tilted down over his eyes, and his legs were dangling, his feet a couple of inches off the ground.

When they were within thirty yards, Ragnon told his partner to stop and shut off the engine. "Don't even see a dog or anything," the detective said as they sat there a moment longer, staring. "Well, let's go see if he *is* alive—and friendly."

They got out of the Cherokee, but when they were only twenty yards away Antone spotted the gun. "Hold it, Sergeant. He's armed."

They both stopped, and Ragnon could see the gun now—an old hog-leg revolver holstered on the man's right hip, butt forward and only inches away from his hands, which were crossed in his lap. He still hadn't moved. His chin was down, his hat still tilted over his eyes.

Signaling Antone away to the right, Ragnon drew his Cobra from the holster clipped to his belt at the small of his back, and saw the Indian pull his .41 Magnum Red-

KINDERKILL 47

hawk from the shoulder holster beneath his light nylon jacket.

When Antone had reached the end of the trailer, Ragnon moved forward, walking softly, and stopped a few feet away. Still the man had not moved, and there was no sound or movement from inside the trailer either. A carton of empty wine bottles sat on the opposite side of the trailer door, and he could see a partially empty bottle leaning against the trailer steps at the man's feet. Ragnon could even hear his light snoring now as he said casually, "Wake up, friend. You've got company."

The startled man crashed down in his chair, knocking over the wine bottle as his left hand went for his holstered gun.

"Freeze!" Ragnon shouted, crouching, his own gun hand extended and braced at the wrist by his left. "Police! Don't move!"

The man froze. "What the fuck—"

"Don't touch that hog-leg, Mister," Antone said from the end of the trailer. His Redhawk was leveled, too, and cocked. "Don't even breathe funny."

Ragnon could see the web of thin blue veins on the man's bulbous nose. The red-rimmed eyes were wary, fear-filled, and angry. Keeping his gun hand extended in the man's face, the detective tugged his shield and ID from his shirt pocket with his left and held it out. "Detectives—Mimbres County Sheriff's Department—just came by for a little chat, okay?"

"Where the hell'd you guys come from?" The man glanced anxiously from one cop to the other. "What the fuck are you doin' here?"

"First," Ragnon said, "reach down with just the thumb and forefinger of your right hand and ease that hog-leg out—now. That's it. Lay it down gently there on the steps where my partner can get it."

As Antone walked over and picked up the gun, Ragnon asked the man, "Who's inside?"

"Nobody. I live here alone." His voice was sullen now, recovered from his surprise. He looked like he needed a shave and a bath both. "I'm the watchman."

"Well, you weren't watching too close today, were you, friend?" He nodded to Antone. "Take a peek inside."

As the Indian stepped to the door, his own gun still in front of him, and looked inside, the man said, "This is private property. Didn't you see the signs? You got a warrant?"

Antone stepped inside the trailer a moment, then came back out, putting away his revolver and shaking his head. "He's alone. There's an old car parked out back."

"What's your name?" Ragnon asked him.

"Leo. Leo Kranzky. I asked if you got a warrant."

"Well, Leo"—Ragnon put away his own gun now—"it's like this. You aren't gonna make us go all the way back to the city for a warrant, are you? Just to look around this place? Just to ask a few questions? Because if we have to go to that kind of trouble, we'll come back and take everything we can find around here apart piece by piece—including your car and trailer. So what's it gonna be?"

"What do you guys want anyways? When do I get my gun back?"

Ah, Ragnon thought, he's going to be reasonable, he doesn't want a hassle. "When we leave, Leo. You got a permit for it?"

"Don't need a permit in this state. I carry it in the open, on my hip, not concealed."

"Okay, so just answer a few questions and you get your piece back."

"Like what?"

"Like what goes on around here? What are you supposed to be watching so careful like?"

Leo Kranzky wiped his nose with the back of his hand and then picked up the overturned wine bottle. Tilting it back, he drained what was left of it. "Nothing," he said, tossing it in the weeds by the steps. "This ain't a real ranch, not a working ranch. Not a dude ranch either."

"What is it, then, Leo? What needs to be guarded day and night by a man with a gun?"

"Gun's for my own protection." Kranzky wiped his nose again on his sleeve. "Nothing here worth stealin'. They just don't want nobody on the property, no tourists poking around, or hunters starting range fires."

"Who's 'they,' Leo?"

"My employer, Westering, Inc. Real estate outfit in Phoenix hired me. Check comes outta California."

"And what's here that's not worth stealing—besides your trailer and car?"

"Buildings. Over the ridge yonder. Phony buildings in a valley over there. Old movie sets. They don't film here anymore, but they don't want nobody carrying stuff off either, or destroying it." He cocked his head against the sunlight and lit a cigarette. "What's it to the cops anyways? I ain't done nothin'—ain't stole nothin'—ain't even growin' no marijuana."

"They keep horses around here, Leo?" Ragnon asked, turning and sitting down on the trailer steps while he tucked a fresh pinch of Red Man in his cheek.

"Horses? Ain't been any horses here in two, maybe three years. Why?"

Ragnon nodded to Antone, who handed Kranzky his gun. "Put it back in your holster and keep it there, Leo," the senior detective said. He pulled out the ice cream receipt and held it out to him. "How about ice cream, Leo? You like strawberry ice cream?"

Kranzky glanced at the paper, then looked quizzically at the detective, glancing from him to his partner as he shoved his revolver back in the holster. "What the fuck you talking about? Horses? Ice cream? You guys are nuts." But he finally took the receipt from Ragnon's hand, dug out a pair of wire-rim glasses, and studied it a moment. He handed it back, shaking his head. "Rancho Malaguena—that's this place, but I never saw that before—never bought no ice cream. Where'd you get it?"

"Where do you do your shopping?" Antone asked him. "Your groceries—where do you buy food?"

"In the city. It's less than an hour from here, and—"

"How about Pontatoc?" Ragnon asked. "It's only twelve miles down the road."

Leo Kranzky was shaking his head. "Never buy anything there. All they got's one little store, and they charge too much. Like cigarettes. Twelve bucks a carton. I can get 'em—"

But Tom Ragnon suddenly wasn't listening. He was staring at the ice cream receipt himself and remembering where he had seen it before: the Pontatoc General Store. He looked at Antone. "Jesus, John, I knew the damn thing looked familiar. Sometimes in this business you miss the obvious. I should have recognized it right away. I bought my groceries at that general store when I lived down here. A dinky, dingy, dusty place with an old-fashioned hand-crank register. And they use receipts like this!"

Antone looked back at Kranzky. "But this one says Rancho Malaguena on it, and this is Rancho Malaguena."

"It's not mine," Kranzky insisted. "I never bought nothing at that place before—ever!"

Ragnon had fixed his gaze on the watchman now. "You

better not be shucking us, Leo. Or if you are, you better come clean now. We're investigating a homicide."

"Homicide?" His eyes flicked again from one detective to the other. "I don't know nothing about no homicide, I swear to God I don't!"

"Nobody's been filming on this place in the last week or so?" Antone asked him.

"No. I told you, nobody's been here in the past year." But a quick shadow had flashed across his eyes, and the detectives caught it, wondering.

"How about kids?" Ragnon spat and got up slowly. "Anybody been around here lately with kids?"

"Kids? No. What's this about anyway? Maybe if you told me—"

"We're gonna drive around and look at those movie buildings, Leo," Ragnon said. "Anything else we ought to look at while we're here? A ranch house maybe? Guest houses?" Stooping, he slipped his pen into the neck of Kranzky's discarded wine bottle and carried it to the 4×4.

"Ranch house burned down three years ago and they never rebuilt it!" the watchman called after him. "I told you guys everything! There ain't been no murders around here!"

"Maybe not, Leo, but somebody bought ice cream around here, probably at the Pontatoc store, and put this place's name on it!" He looked at Antone, who had climbed behind the wheel. "C'mon, John, let's roll."

The Indian headed the Jeep Cherokee on down the road and over into the next valley as Ragnon cushioned the wine bottle on a blanket tucked between the seats. "If we can get his prints off this when we get back, maybe we can see if Leo is really who he says he is and no more."

"And I got the license number off the old car in back of his trailer," Antone said. "We can run that too."

"You're a man after my own heart, John," Tom Ragnon said. Then, as they came over the next rise, he pointed toward what looked like an old western town. "Looks like we just penetrated a time barrier."

Driving down the dusty main street between the false fronts of the pseudo-frontier town, Antone asked, "You get the feeling Leo Kranzky wasn't quite telling us the whole truth, Sergeant?"

"Nobody ever tells the whole truth, John, especially not to a cop. And especially not a guy like Leo Kranzky." Ragnon was getting a distinctly uneasy feeling about this place. His initial appraisal of Kranzky was not alarming in spite of his hog-leg, but there was sure something about this old ranch that had aroused his cop's instincts for trouble.

Swinging the Cherokee around, they drove behind the false fronts on one side, all of them empty, lonely-looking, weathered by time and neglect. And over the next hill a replica of a stockaded frontier fort reared against the sky, but it, too, proved false when they drove behind it. There weren't even any fresh tracks around except their own as Antone pulled up in front of the fort's log gate and stopped.

The wind was gusting more heavily now, and the sun was lower in the sky. They could hear the faint squeaking of the distant windmill. "Let's head on into Pontatoc and that general store," Ragnon said. "This has to be their receipt, and if Leo Kranzky's not in on it, there's at least got to be something he's not telling us."

"I don't know, Sergeant." John Antone was skeptical. "With a watchman like Kranzky, I get the idea *King Kong* could have been filmed on this place and he wouldn't know about it."

The general store in Pontatoc was a block from the sheriff's substation and across from the old Pontatoc Palace

Hotel. A bell clattered on the front screen door as they stepped into the gloomy interior, where goods of every age and description were stacked high on bulging shelves. More goods hung from the rafters under the high peaked ceiling. Open, barrel-shaped bins held beans and popcorn and flour with scoop shovels. The dry, dusty smell of the place was mixed with the scents of spices and onions and garlic and strings of drying peppers.

"Sergeant Ragnon!" the proprietor greeted them. He had square-rimmed spectacles; thick, curly sideburns; and a leather apron. And the detective introduced his partner to Calvin Riggs.

"Didn't expect to see you back in these parts so soon, Sergeant. They run out of Red Man up your way?"

"First case they give us brings me right back, Cal." He laid the receipt on the counter. "This yours?"

The grocer eyed it through the lower half of his bifocals. "You know it is. Gave you some just like it when you shopped here, didn't I? But you're all paid up. What's wrong with this one?"

"Strawberry ice cream," Ragnon said.

Calvin Riggs pushed on his spectacles, which had slid down his nose. "That's right. In my own handwriting. What about it, was it poisoned?" His grin exposed yellowed and missing teeth. "Or did you find it cheaper somewhere else?"

"Look closer, Cal. It's not mine. It says Rancho Malaguena, and we just came from there. Nobody around but a watchman named Leo Kranzky. He buy it?"

"That his name? Nah, I know they got a guy stayin' on the place, but he never comes in here. Gets his stuff in the city. Hear tell he's a wino."

"So who bought the ice cream, Cal? No date on it, but

should have been recent. Maybe sometime this past week?"

"Yeah, I remember. Young guy—late teens or early twenties. Husky, surly bastard. Muscle-bound, like he pumped iron. It was this week, but four, maybe five days ago. I remember his tight, faded blue jeans and a black T-shirt with the sleeves cut off at the shoulders. Long blond hair and a scraggly mustache and beard. Never said much, 'cept that he was staying over at the Malaguena Ranch, so that's the name I put down." He studied the receipt a moment more before handing it back to Ragnon. "Never thought anything more about it at the time, but it seems odd now, him saying that. Nobody's stayed over there for over a year that I know of, except that watchman."

"Did you happen to see what kind of vehicle he was driving, Mr. Riggs?" Antone asked.

"Yeah. Heard it. One of them noisy dirt bikes, with no muffler. Heard him drive up and then looked out the window as he drove off, raising a cloud of dust and noise, a real jerk."

"Did you notice the license plate, Cal?" Ragnon asked. "A number, or even the state?"

"Naw, I didn't look for nothing like that. The bike was blue, though, I remember that. Dark blue and white under the dust. What the hell happened, Sergeant? Who'd he kill?"

"We're just running down leads, Cal," Ragnon told him. "On an eight- or nine-year-old they found dead in a county dump."

"God, I saw that in the paper. They can't even identify him, poor little tyke. And you think this idiot biker did it?"

"We're working on the ID right now," Antone said. "I

don't suppose the biker had anyone with him, someone else on the bike. Like a kid maybe?"

"Naw, he was alone. Hell, he probably just saw the sign Rancho Malaguena on the gate as he drove by and used the name. Just a smart-assed kid himself."

"Thanks, Cal," Ragnon said. "If you think of anything else, call me. Looks like I may be moving back down here for a while."

"Yeah. Say, there is one thing strikes me as odd, don't it you?"

"What's that, Cal?"

"The ice cream. Ice cream melts pretty fast. If he wasn't staying with someone at Malaguena or someplace close, what was he gonna do with three half gallons of the stuff?"

SEVEN

"Maybe he's just an ice cream freak," John Antone suggested.

"Sure," Ragnon answered. "He just popped a wheelie around the nearest mesquite, then sat down and ate three half gallons all by himself. If you believe that, John, you'd wear an iron jockstrap in a thunderstorm."

After talking to Calvin Riggs they had crossed the street to the Pontatoc Palace, the only hotel in town. Inside the ancient red-brick gabled structure they had rung the bell at the desk and asked Cecelia Oates, a cousin of Cal's, about the kid on a blue-and-white bike. But she had seen no one like that, or heard him. She had reached up self-consciously and adjusted her hearing aid. In fact, she said, she hadn't had a guest of any kind at the hotel in a week, except for the Greyline bus tour on its way to the mining ghost towns, and they'd only stayed one night—all middle-aged couples.

They had checked then at the gas station, which was closed, and the Blackjack Bar and Red Stallion Lounge, as well as the local café, and come up with zip. Back at the sheriff's substation they drew mugs of fresh coffee and talked things over with Deputy Montoya, who hadn't even had a report of any noise or disturbance in the area by a biker. "The guy might not even have gone through town," Montoya suggested, "just turned around and headed back to Malaguena."

"Except the watchman denies seeing anybody." Ragnon was staring up at the old Seth Thomas, listening to its rhythmic, almost hypnotic tick-tock, tick-tock. Then he looked over at Antone, who was sitting in the wide window ledge, staring outside at the late afternoon shadows on the street and sipping his coffee.

"Maybe the watchman simply lied," the Indian said quietly.

The telephone rang loudly, overriding both the clock and their thoughts. Montoya answered and offered the instrument to Ragnon. "Your master's voice."

Ragnon took the phone and listened to the familiar impatient snorting of the walrus, who seemed to have a sixth sense as to when Ragnon was at the station. "So—you run down anything yet, Rags?"

"Found the source of the receipt, Chief. Right here in Pontatoc. Young white guy on a dirt bike, stranger in town. Bought the ice cream at the general store and disappeared. Watchman at Malaguena claims never to have seen him, but maybe he's lying. We picked up his wine bottle for possible prints, and you might run a make on his car. Arizona license Baker-Paul-Nancy 596. Nobody noticed the license on the bike."

"Okay. That's it?"

"It's almost five o'clock, Chief. We're gonna chow down a while and rest on our laurels."

"Not yet you're not. Your other partner's here, and she's got something."

"Ragnon?" Lucinda Crown's voice was a pleasant replacement.

"I hope you're doing better than we are, partner."

"I don't know, Ragnon. The deputies have run down a lot of dead-end leads—abused and missing runaways, throwaways, and plain disappearances, but not our kid. I'm still following up on children's dentists in this area, but coming up empty so far. And I haven't even been able to tie any of the known area chicken hawks in with this crime. There's a vast silence on the street."

"How's the computer artist doing on a match?"

"He's worked back to local nine-year-olds missing eighteen months ago, but he's knocked off for the day. Nobody here even thinks the victim *was* local."

"So the chief said you've got something. What?"

"Did you find a stable on that ranch?"

"No. Movie sets—a fort, a western town—all false fronts, but not even a phony stable. Just a watchman who sees, hears, and speaks no evil, but he's probably lying about something."

"Better find out what, Ragnon. I got hold of that Parker guy in the coroner's office and guess what. Not only was the stuff in the victim's hair definitely straw, but the dust and dirt under his nails all came from a stall or stable where horses were kept. If not Rancho Malaguena, where? And there's more. His injuries were sustained over a period of time, old bruises as well as new. Same with anal trauma—not just the one incident. So he's probably been missing a while, unless, of course, he's not missing at all and a relative did it who's not saying anything."

"We'll still have to ID him first to investigate that, but I'd say you done good, Crown, you done real good."

"And one more thing, Rags. Your ice cream receipt?

The contents of the victim's stomach, only partially digested from his last meal, was strawberry ice cream."

"Jesus, Crown, the receipt came from the store here in Pontatoc. Grocer remembers a young biker, about four or five days ago, which would be about right."

"Then there's a tie-in somewhere. Want me to come down?"

"Jesus," Ragnon breathed again, thinking about everything. Was it really coming together this fast?

"Rags—shall I come on down?"

"No. You're doing fine. Just stay with the computer imaging and the dentists—for now."

"Don't try to lose me on this, Ragnon." The sudden anxiety in her voice was real. "I mean it."

"Wouldn't think of it, Crown. Now put Old Iron Balls back on. Chief? Anything on that license?"

"Yeah, big fucking deal. Registered to one Leo Kranzky, P.O. box in Pontatoc. A DWI, he did some jail time. Nothing current except a couple of parking tickets and one for speeding, all unpaid. You gonna pick him up?"

"We're gonna go back and shake him a little. Catch you later, Chief." He hung up and looked at Antone. "Kranzky's got a couple of unpaid traffic tickets, and Crown is doing better than we are. No ID yet, but she got the coroner's man to go over the body again and got the stomach contents: strawberry ice cream."

"And the receipt's definitely from the Pontatoc store," Antone mused. "Of course, there are other ranches in the area, Sergeant."

"No." Ragnon tucked a pinch of Red Man in his cheek. "The biker told him Malaguena."

"Maybe the biker was lying too. He just saw the sign

as he went by. He was really at another ranch—an abandoned ranch?"

"Okay. We'll check abandoned ranches around here tomorrow. But for now let's grab some chow and then go back and nudge Kranzky again—about his outstanding warrants and other things. I think he's holding back something."

Leo Kranzky was having supper. They could smell the liver and onions frying as they pulled up in front of the trailer again and Antone touched the siren of the 4×4 in a brief howl.

Kranzky looked out the door, a long-handled spoon in his hand. Better than greeting them with his hog-leg, Ragnon thought, stepping from the Cherokee.

"You guys back again?" The watchman was his old surly self. "You better have a warrant this time or you can shove the fuck off. I'm busy."

"And here I thought you were gonna ask us in for supper," Ragnon cracked as he and the Indian walked up to the trailer door. "Thought you might want to talk about those unpaid traffic tickets they've got on you."

"Ah shit," Kranzky pouted.

"Course we'd rather talk about this place instead, and especially about a muscled young guy who likes noisy dirt bikes and strawberry ice cream. How about it, Leo? This guy must be crazy about strawberry ice cream. He bought three half gallons of it at the store in Pontatoc only four or five days ago, and you don't remember him?"

"Had that receipt with Rancho Malaguena written on it," Antone added, "so it had to be here."

Kranzky had stepped outside and was standing on the trailer steps, the spoon still in his hand and a puzzled, worried look on his face. "I still don't know what you're talking about, Detectives."

"But you haven't told us everything, have you, Leo?" Antone asked softly.

Ragnon spat. "He was here, wasn't he? The young guy, less than a week ago."

"No! No one but—" Kranzky was suddenly looking around, as if for help, and Ragnon was glad it was the spoon in his hand and not the hog-leg. He wasn't even wearing the holster. "Look. Maybe I forgot to mention something." Kranzky sounded almost apologetic.

"We thought you might have, Leo," Ragnon said, and spat again, waiting.

"But it wasn't no young guy on a bike. It was a couple—a man and a woman, middle-aged—that's all. And it *was* a week ago—maybe more."

Ragnon and Antone exchanged glances. "And maybe they happened to have a kid with them?" Ragnon asked.

"Kid? No, just the two adults. He was driving a big RV, a Winnebago it was, and she had a little blue Chrysler ragtop. No kids and no biker."

"And—?" Ragnon asked.

"They wanted to camp, that's all. Fifty bucks the guy gave me. I'm not supposed to let anybody camp, but fifty bucks—and they had their own rig so they wouldn't leave no mess."

"Two vehicles? A big Winnebago and a blue Chrysler ragtop?" Ragnon asked. "But only two people? And no kids?"

"Maybe the guy on the bike was with them?" Antone asked. "He bring them the ice cream maybe?"

"I told you, man, I never saw no guy on a bike—and no kids. Just the couple, and she stayed in the car. He gave me the fifty and I showed him a place to camp down by the dry creek bed."

"How long did they stay?" Ragnon asked.

"I don't know, a couple days—three maybe. I drove over there to charge 'em another fifty and they were gone."

"They leave anything? Any garbage? Anything?"

"No, nothing. The place was clean."

Ragnon looked at his partner. "What do you think, John?"

"I think he's telling the truth—now."

On the horizon the western sky had cracked in a blaze of gold and orange and amber under low clouds, an exquisite moment of truth and beauty that Ragnon knew in seconds would fade away. In minutes the drab grayness would take over, dissolving eventually into night, just like in life. Around them the wind rustled softly through the cacti and mesquite, and the smell of burning liver was coming from the trailer. "Better shut off your stove, Leo," Ragnon said, "and come show us. If everything checks out this time, we'll buy you a dinner in Pontatoc when you come in to the sheriff's office and sign a statement."

As they all climbed into the Cherokee, Ragnon turned to face Kranzky on the back seat. "What about horses, Leo? You still say there's no horses on this place somewhere?"

"Horses? Shit no, man, I told you, not for a year or more." He looked from Ragnon to Antone and back again. "Just an old abandoned stable," he added almost casually. "Down by the dry creek bed—where they camped."

EIGHT

A side road led over more hills and down to the dry, rocky creek bed. Ragnon clocked it on the odometer at 2.6 miles from the watchman's trailer, and estimated it about four miles in from the highway. An old mesquite log corral and a stable stood in the shade of a giant cottonwood rooted deep beside the rock-strewn wash.

"That's it," Leo Kranzky said. "Ain't been used in over a year. Used to be a bunkhouse around here, too, for the hands, but that burned down before my time."

Ragnon and Antone, leaving the watchman in the Cherokee, couldn't get to the stable doors fast enough. Sprung, and sagging inward on rusted hinges, they opened into a cavernous interior that was empty, its shadowy, gloomy, dusty environs lighted only by the fading daylight coming through a couple of broken, cobwebbed windows. No tack, no feed, no signs of recent occupancy; but in one corner a large pile of straw.

More dusty straw was scattered in the seven stalls on one side, and brown spots on some boards looked like dried blood. And while there was sufficient light, the detectives braced open the stable doors and began prying splinters from the blood-spattered wood and bagging samples of dust and straw from different parts of the stable. But they searched in vain for anything else that might disclose what had happened there.

Outside, Kranzky pointed out where the convertible had parked beside the corral, but any tracks it might have left were gone. But as Antone wandered beneath the shaggy cottonwood next to the bank of the wash he suddenly stopped and knelt, then called to Ragnon, "Sergeant! Over here!"

He was pointing as the senior detective ran over. A partial dual-tire print with a distinct pattern was imbedded clearly in a section of dried mud. "The wash was probably running a week ago," the Indian said, "during the rains."

Ragnon called up to Kranzky, who was standing with one foot braced on the front bumper of the Cherokee, smoking. "Where'd they park the RV, Leo?"

"Right about there, where you're standing!"

"And look here," Antone added.

Kneeling beside the Indian, Ragnon saw the small but clear indentation of a child's bare footprint in the dried mud. "Made the same time as the tire print?" he asked.

Antone nodded. "I'd bet my moccasins on it, Sergeant."

Both detectives stood there silently in the dusk beneath the old cottonwood, while above them its leaves flashed like tiny silver medallions and rustled in the evening breeze, a breeze that, though only cool, somehow suddenly brought a disconcertingly eerie chill.

It was almost nine o'clock by the old Seth Thomas on the Pontatoc substation wall. Deputy Montoya was gone, and the gooseneck lamp over the desk reflected on Kranzky's sweating features as he finished his statement and Ragnon shut off the recorder.

Leaning back in the old captain's chair, the detective crossed his boots on the desk and glanced at Antone, who sat in a chair tilted back against one wall, sipping coffee. "We've got a witness who can place the young biker *near* the ranch, John, and a witness who can place a middle-aged couple *at* the ranch, but no one to tie the two together or either of them to a child. So it still doesn't compute."

The old Seth Thomas bonged the hour softly.

"Can I go now, Sergeant?" Leo Kranzky asked sullenly, his valuable time intruded on enough.

"Yeah, go," Ragnon told him. "Sorry about your missing dinner, Leo, but the Pontatoc Café is closed, so we'll have to owe you one."

"What about those tickets they got me on—you gonna fix 'em?"

"Pay 'em, Leo." Ragnon spat into the wastebasket and brought his boots down noisily on the hardwood floor. "Be a good citizen and pay 'em." He closed his eyes, pinched his temples wearily, and yawned, then heard the door close behind the watchman and looked up as he climbed into his car outside.

Everything that could be done had been done, for now. They had some samples for the lab, and they had placed a couple of empty boxes over both mudprints and weighted them down with rocks for protection until they could get photos or plaster casts. But Ragnon knew it still wasn't much. Reaching over to the recorder, he played back Kranzky's statement.

"You think he did it?" he asked the Indian half seriously when the recorder clicked off.

"I doubt it, Sergeant. I don't much like the guy, but

that's not evidence of murder, is it? And his story's got a ring of truth to it now."

Ragnon looked around the empty office. "I'm gonna take tomorrow off, John. Go by the house and see my own kids, then maybe run up Prescott way, look in on the old man, and pick up my trailer on the way back. You might as well go home too. The chief's not gonna pop for overtime, and we'll have to wait for the lab reports on this stuff anyway. But I'm betting my last pouch of Red Man we'll get a match on the straw and dust. I think the kid was killed right there in that stable."

"And the killer long gone," Antone added, "but gone where?"

"I think we should call around to the RV campgrounds, John. Repair and accessory shops too. I know middle-aged couples in Winnies are like looking for sand on a beach, but how many are traveling with a Chrysler ragtop and maybe a young biker?"

"I'll take care of it tomorrow, Sergeant. I want to come back with the forensics team anyway and take my own pictures of those tracks."

"Bad habit, John," Ragnon spat, "working on a day off."

But Antone was deep in thought. "What if the straw and dust don't match, Sergeant? Or the brown stains aren't human blood, or a different grouping from the victim's? And with nothing connecting the couple with the biker—"

"Christ, bite your tongue, John." Ragnon got to his feet, stretching. "Our luck can't be all bad on this case. Something's got to match or what's a heaven for?"

John Antone smiled. "I see what you mean about hating a mystery, boss. It's getting too complicated for me."

"Me too, John. We're being pulled too many ways. Let's

go grab a beer or something, then head on in. I set my VCR to record the Phoenix-Los Angeles game on TV. If you want to take pot luck for supper and watch it with me, maybe it'll clear our heads."

The Phoenix Cardinals lost, 27 to 10, so misery had company. John Antone went home, never letting on he wasn't all that crazy about football anyway. And in the morning, as Ragnon drove to the tri-level house on Old Father Road that he had once called home, nothing was any clearer.

It had been three weeks since his last visit. He'd been isolated by his enforced assignment to Pontatoc. Now it looked like that would continue. But at least he had today, he thought gratefully as he turned his yellow Volkswagen Bug into the long gravel drive.

The landscape was varieties of cacti set amid crushed red volcanic rock, and it needed little care and saved a lot on water, but he could see the drip stain off the roof and knew the evaporative cooler had been overflowing again, probably needing a new float.

He also knew it was too early to be here—only 8:30, with Angie a nurse and on swing shift at the hospital—but he had no choice. When he was on a case, especially one that took him out in the boonies, he had to grab the time when he could, and he had called last night before the game and explained.

So here he was sitting in Old Yeller, his battered Bug, parked in the drive behind her shiny Olds Cutlass, waiting. But there was no sign of anyone being up and around, and he was reluctant to intrude.

The kids' bedroom was around to the back, and he got out of the car, thinking he might as well go throw some pebbles at their window. Brian was seven and Melissa five, her kids by her first husband, but he loved them like his own. And when the picture of the unknown victim came jarringly into his mind in full color, he pushed it away. Not today. He wasn't going to think about it today. That such a thing could happen to his kids was unthinkable, that it could happen to any child—then he heard the explosive cries, "Daddy! Daddy!" as they both stormed out the front door and attacked.

Scooping one up under each arm, he smothered them with kisses as he climbed the steps and was greeted by Angie at the door. "I'll bring you some breakfast out on the patio." She smiled. "They were both up early and insisted on waiting to eat with you."

Later, while the kids dressed to go to the park, Ragnon helped her scrape the plates and put them in the dishwasher. She smelled nice, he thought, in a new blue robe with her long black hair tied back in a ponytail.

"So they bring you back and dump an impossible case on you. Or is that *why* they brought you back?" The old sharp-edged criticism was there as always.

"That's part of it," he said.

"That poor little kid. And still no idea who he was?"

"Not yet. But my partner's working with a computer artist and pictures of missing kids. Depends on how long he's been missing, of course, but they might be able to project what he would look like now and get a match."

"Your new partner—Antone?"

"No. The Justice Department loaned us a specialist, a porno specialist. It looks like it's that kind of a case." He wondered why he didn't mention the specialist was a she.

"My God, Tom. Kiddie porn? I can't even understand something like that—sex with children. But then, I can't understand gays either."

Tom Ragnon shook his head. "It takes all kinds of

worms to make a world, and freedom of sexual preference is the new norm these days, isn't it? We're all a little kinky sometimes, depending on your perspective, so where do you draw the line?"

"I think you draw the line with children, Tom. You have to. You draw it at freedom of choice, which has to include the ability, the knowledge to choose, which children don't have."

He nodded. "I guess you're right, Angie, because there are also the others out there—the ones who turn on to cripples, to pregnant women, to old ladies in tennis shoes—even ones who turn on to killing."

"And they're the ones *you* have to deal with."

"In this business you meet all varieties of the human animal. Guess it's why they give us a badge and gun." He closed the dishwasher and turned it on, staring at her a moment as the machine hummed and readied its gears. "You look extra nice this morning, lady."

"Don't get any funny ideas." She actually blushed. "How are you doing, Tom—really?"

He shrugged. "I'm muddling through. I grew a mustache and shaved it off. I started jogging again and stopped. I'm adjusting to our situation. It's my dad I'm worried about now. He's getting worse. I've got to get up there to see him—maybe this evening."

"I don't see why they can't get him transferred to the V.A. facility in Tucson, where he'd be closer. You want me to go with you? I'm due some time off."

"No, thanks anyway. I—" The kids came bursting back into the kitchen, vitally alive, all smiling, wriggling bodies.

"The zoo, Daddy!" Melissa screamed. "Can we go see the alligators?"

"I like the Gila monster," Brian said somberly.

"Take it easy, munchkins," Tom Ragnon said. "It's our day. We'll see it all."

"All day, Daddy?" Melissa wanted to know. "Promise you'll keep us all day?"

"All day, till sundown—"

"If the creeks don't rise!" Both kids echoed the last familiar line with him in a laughing chorus.

Angie watched them pile into the ridiculous little yellow car and felt her heart lurch just a fraction. Why hadn't it worked out, she wondered. Tom certainly had his good points. And he had filled a void in her life after her first husband's death, a haven from the storm, the shock of grief. And he was a far better father than most men. So what was lacking? He was a good cop, and God knows somebody had to do it. But why did he have to stay in field work? Why such resistance to promotion, to getting ahead? Maybe it was like his socializing, or lack of it, an essential part of his makeup—he was a loner. Whatever it was, it had killed their relationship.

At about the same time Ragnon was heading for the city park with his kids, John Antone was moving the hose on his vegetable patch, sending the water gurgling down the long rows of corn and squash and beans. He'd bought the five acres southwest of the city three years before when he joined the sheriff's department, and it was located near the usually dry riverbed, but the desert land was fertile and he had a good well.

Behind him he could hear his daughter crying as Juana called him to breakfast from the screened porch of their three-bedroom mobile home. And as he entered, he picked up the baby from the cradle and held her while Juana tested the bottle on her wrist before handing it to him.

She tossed back her shiny blue-black hair and smiled as

she dished up his eggs and ham and the flat Papago fry bread that was his favorite. "Can you hold her and eat too?"

"I'll manage." He noticed two of his old deputy uniforms hanging freshly pressed in the doorway and asked a little irritably, "What are those for? I've made detective and I'm off probation. I told you I'm out of uniform for good."

"I just . . . wanted them all clean before I put them away."

But he knew it was more than that. She had fallen for him when he wore the uniform of a Papago Law and Order officer on the reservation, back before the tribe reverted to its original name of Tohono O'odham, "the people who emerged from the dry earth." She was prouder still when he'd been accepted as a deputy by the Mimbres County Sheriff's Department. Now, at twenty-eight, he had made detective and was wearing civvies, and it was something hard for her to accept—as if before he had been something special, but now he was like any other man.

Having to tell her that he was probably going to be away a lot now, even staying with his partner in his trailer in Pontatoc until they caught the killer of this child, wasn't going to help any. But, instead, she had her own surprise.

"I have to go home for a while," she told him. "Mama is sick again." Home was a Papago village called Coyote Sits. Nestled in the hills west of the Baboquivari Mountains, it was where her family was. His family, what was left of it, lived miles farther to the northwest across the reservation.

"Vincent's boy, Pedro, is bringing some baskets in tomorrow to sell," Juana explained. "He can get more for them in town than at the trading post, and I can ride back with him. Unless you can take us?" She gave him a hesitant sidelong glance.

"No. I've got to get back on the job. Take some photos at what we think is the crime scene. Pedro can take you." Vincent was her uncle and Pedro a twenty-two-year-old drunk. He drove his pickup over the reservation roads like a madman; but how could John say no? His eyes fell on his Redhawk hanging in its holster from a peg by the door. "I may be gone a while myself. It looks like a difficult case."

"The child that was killed?"

"Yes."

"I don't understand the murder of children."

"Neither do I." The baby was almost asleep in his arms. Handing the bottle to his wife, he burped his daughter and placed her gently back in the crib. Her hair was already long and black like her mother's, and he kissed her softly on the nose.

In the third bedroom, which he used as a darkroom for his amateur photography, he gathered up his camera and gear. The whole trailer was hung with his prize prints, mostly black-and-white and heavy with light and shadow. A few were in color. All were scenic panoramas or nature stills, stark and real; the ruins of an ancient Anasazi cliff dwelling in the north, a lonely, wind-twisted bristlecone pine, a collapsing mud and wattle menstrual hut once in common use on the reservation.

But photography was his hobby. He was a policeman first and foremost. Yet he wondered what he was getting into as a detective. It was what he had wanted, wasn't it? Homicide? But his three years in uniform hadn't prepared him for this. Nothing had prepared him for this, not courses in criminology in college, not years as a uniform cop. A detective not only looked at things differently, he looked at people differently, turning over each bloodied stone of an impassioned case and following it with Ragnon's bulldog tenacity to the bitter end. Maybe it was best not even to think about it. Maybe it was best simply to jump in with both feet and do it.

Back in the kitchen, he kissed his wife. "I wish I could drive you instead of Pedro. Take care. I love you both."

"There's a dance at White Horse Pass next Saturday." She smiled hesitantly. "You think we can go?"

"We'll see," John Antone said hopefully, knowing he would probably have to disappoint her there too.

NINE

The small basement room was dark except for the flickering white light on the movie screen, and silent except for the whirring of the camera projector above and behind them, its mote-filled beam displaying small, naked figures, all of them cavorting now around a swimming pool.

They had been watching for over an hour—short fuck-flicks, most of them in vivid color, some with sound and some without, but all featuring children, several as young as three or four years old. Males with females, males with males, females with females; children with children, children with adults—a cornucopia of raw kiddie porn, a pedophile collector's delight.

As the last one, titled *Kiddie Fun in the Sun*, went dark and the house lights came on, Tom Ragnon was shaking his head in sick disgust. "Jesus, Crown. And I always thought homicide was a nasty business." He had tried to focus on their little faces, their eyes, their expressions—trying to judge if they were drugged, frightened, or what. Mostly they seemed confused. In one, a large, hairy hand had kept interfering, positioning the children, slapping their bare behinds.

KINDERKILL

"Just thought you ought to see what we're dealing with," Lucinda Crown said beside him. "There's a lot more, if you want to see them. We've got some really juicy ones that deal not only with animals and torture, but excrement and urine—"

"No, thanks, lady. You don't have to rub my nose in it. I'm on your side. I've seen a lot of regular porn, but this stuff—it must be the lowest form of human sexuality."

"It's adults taking advantage of children's natural craving for approval and affection," Crown explained. "Most of these kids are the victims of bitterness, hostility, neglect, and most of all a lack of true affection in their lives—the kind most likely to become victims of pedophiles, who can almost smell out a vulnerable kid. And if they're not vulnerable enough, there's always drugs to insure acceptable behavior. And there's a large public for this stuff out there, Ragnon—a world market. Even national proponents for legalizing it. They actually say it's healthy, it's good for them, or that children really want it."

Tom Ragnon sighed heavily. "And one of them's out there somewhere right now—only on top of everything else, he kills."

"And we don't even know if it's part of a professional ring or some independents, maybe a family project—we just don't know."

Ragnon started to reach for his Red Man and stopped. He really should quit that, too, before he got tongue cancer or something. Jesus, he thought, it was only ten in the morning and already it was turning out to be a long day. He hadn't been able to get up to Prescott to see his dad the evening before as he'd planned, but he'd called and they'd talked a while. Because when he'd brought the kids back from the park late in the day, Angie had had a message for him from Crown. "She just called. A lady cop, huh?" She had smirked.

"What's the message?"

"Call her—as soon as—something about a match at the lab. Sounded like she was calling from home. I could hear Barbra Streisand singing 'Memory' on a stereo in the background. Here's her number if you haven't got it. You can use the phone in the kitchen."

But Ragnon had said a hurried good-bye and stopped at a public phone a mile away. It rang three times before being picked up, and Streisand was still singing in the background, but now it was "The Way We Were."

"Nice album," Ragnon said after Crown answered. "What's up? We get a match on the straw?"

"Straw, dust, almost everything, except the traces of blood weren't enough to type, and the footprint didn't match the victim's. It was a little too small. Probably left by some other family."

"At Malaguena? I doubt it, Crown. That ranch is not exactly a family park." He didn't like what it more likely meant. "They've got another kid still with them is my bet. Maybe more than one."

"You're probably right, but at least you found the site of the killing. Antone was down there all day with the forensic team, and I got Poole to send a police artist down to get composites from both the grocer and the watchman on their descriptions of the biker and the couple."

"And I suppose he wants us back down there too, right now."

"That's not quite the plan. Chief says you and I are to spend tomorrow going over everything we've got on the case. Then you can move your trailer down there and I'll follow. What's the Pontatoc Palace like?"

"It's not a palace."

"I didn't think so. Anyway, we're supposed to sit on the site, interview the cacti and roadrunners if we have to, till we come up with a fresh lead."

"Wait a minute, slow down, I don't—"

"Just meet me in the morning at the squad bay, Sergeant," she had told him. "Chief's orders. I've got some films I want to show you anyway. You can see what kind of sickies we're dealing with."

Well, he had seen the films, and it had made him a believer. And now it was afternoon, and they had spent hours more going over everything they had on the murder of a nine-year-old boy, and it still wasn't a hell of a lot, especially with no ID on the victim.

In the elevator going back upstairs from the cafeteria to the squad bay again at three P.M., he decided to ask her, "Any new leads on the victim's identity?"

"No, and we've about run through all the local dentists."

"And no results on the computer imaging either?"

"No again. They'll stay with it, but it's a tedious process, sorting out all the possibilities for different time periods and then aging each individually and matching him against the victim. It was a long shot anyway."

The elevator doors sighed open on the third floor and he held them for her. She had looked cool and efficient all day in her white duck jeans, white blouse, and matching Levi jacket. "And you agreed with Old Iron Balls that we should sit down there amid the cacti and roadrunners?" he asked her.

"I'm afraid I couldn't offer him anything better, and still can't."

"Well, maybe I can," Ragnon answered, reaching for

his Red Man with no restraints this time as he pushed open the door marked CHIEF OF HOMICIDE.

But Sidney Clayton Poole was adamant. "Don't bullshit me about hanging loose here in the city, Rags." He puffed out the words along with his cigar smoke as Ragnon sent a ringing shot of tobacco juice into his wastebasket. Even Lucinda Crown was lighting up one of her little brown cigarillos. "If that's where he was killed, you stay on the site till you come up with something. The deputies can handle anything that breaks back here—or send for you if it's important."

"Goddammit, Chief, those two bad negatives we found in the trash were shot in some sleazy motel or apartment, not on a ranch. And one profile shot even looks a little like the victim. So maybe they were here, in the city."

"Ragnon." Poole waved his cigar, making little trails in the air. "There's motels in every city in the country. They could have been anywhere. The papers in their trash showed they'd been traveling. If the ranch near Pontatoc was where the hit was made, pick up your leads there. In fact, I sent the Indian back down this morning, and I'm going down in about ten minutes to take a look for myself."

And in his heart of hearts Ragnon knew the old walrus was right. The thing to do was to go back down there and keep on digging, keep nosing around until something popped. Only he had just spent two months down there, and he had problems up here. But mostly he just felt Old Iron Balls was rolling over on him, and he didn't like the chief deciding how he should run his own case—even if he was right.

"Okay, I'll go," he said. "I'll borrow John's truck and haul my trailer back down there tonight, but only because I happen to agree with you."

"Thank you very much, Sergeant," said Poole, mashing out his cigar ferociously in his polished onyx ashtray.

But as Crown and Ragnon started for the door, Poole said, "Crown—stay. Ragnon—now that we've got the site pinned down, I want a homicide report from you on this case before you leave. That translates into today, so there's no misunderstanding."

Tom Ragnon nodded, exiting in sullen silence and using every ounce of his exceptional restraint to keep from slamming the office door.

When he was gone, Crown looked at the chief, puzzled, while he relighted the frayed stub of his foul cigar with his big horse lighter and puffed a moment to get it going. "Forgot it was my last one," he mumbled. Then he raised his voice. "Understand you're kind of cozy with one of our department lieutenants, Crown. McKittrick, in Vice?" Poole rested the fat cigar stub on his ashtray and met her eyes.

Lucinda Crown frowned. "I see him—socially. What's the point, Lieutenant?"

"He's just not the loveliest of guys, Crown. He's got a bad rep. Frankly"—Poole picked up his cigar and drew deeply—"he goes through women like shit through a tin horn."

"And is this just a friendly warning, Lieutenant, or do I detect jealousy?" She jetted her own smoke angrily through her nostrils.

Poole backed off a little, fidgeting with his cigar. "You're mine now, Crown—temporarily. Like Antone and Ragnon. You've been loaned to Homicide, not Vice."

Lucinda Crown smiled slightly. "I didn't get the impression Sergeant Ragnon belonged to anybody."

"He's a goddamned pariah!" Poole huffed. "But he's

loyal—to Homicide. And your loyalty is here too. McKittrick is known to be ambitious—even greedy."

"What you mean is that what I learn here stays here, is that it, Lieutenant?"

"I think you've got my drift, Crown." Poole smiled slightly, and his little walrus eyes twinkled. "Not that we don't cooperate. We track something that concerns Vice, we give it to Vice, and tit for tat. But always check with me. No bedtime stories out of school—got it?"

"Sure, Lieutenant, I think I've got it."

"And one more thing—Lucinda." A lecherous grin spread over his dumpy walrus features and she saw what was coming. "Maybe you and me could have a little drink sometime? Like maybe before you go down to Pontatoc, if you and McKittrick aren't busy—?"

"Why not?" She gave him just a shadow of her sharky smile in return. "In fact, it's a date—Sidney," she purred as she leaned over his desk and ground out the stub of her cigarillo right in the middle of his blotter. "The minute hell freezes over, I'll give you a call."

"Cunt," she heard him mutter as she went out the door, closing it not quite as gently as Ragnon had.

On the way down in the elevator she was still fuming. The old lech. She wondered if she should tell Ragnon, but decided to let it go. It wasn't that unusual, and he seemed to have enough problems with the brass without her giving him another reason to erupt, as somehow she felt he would.

Because she considered Tom Ragnon unusual, even for a cop. Really attractive in an odd sort of way, yet not at all like Jack McKittrick. And she sure as hell wasn't going to tell *him*. He'd probably laugh in her face.

Stepping off the elevator in the basement, she got her car out of the parking bay and headed home, still angry and a little hurt. The bastards always took sex for granted, always hit on her sooner or later, and she was sure Ragnon would be no different. He was just a slow starter. And Poole's awkward crudeness certainly wasn't surprising. Maybe it was his reference to McKittrick. Ragnon had pointed out the same thing about Jack's reputation. Evidently their affair was all over the department already, but they hadn't really tried to hide it. The man wasn't married. Never had been.

But Poole had raised in her now conflicting emotions about both McKittrick and Ragnon. Both were cops, but completely different men. Yet she was determined not to let it bother her. She had walked into the affair with McKittrick with her eyes wide open. They had met six months earlier at a law enforcement seminar in Phoenix, and she'd held out a month before going to bed with him. But the sex was good, damn good. She knew what kind of man he was, sensed it, and it didn't matter.

Ragnon was just the opposite, one of those freaks she'd only heard about—a truly deep-down decent guy. And she knew she'd probably end up in the sack with him, too, but for different reasons. Dammit, she thought, she never seemed to pick the "right" man, whatever that was. Maybe because she let them pick her. McKittrick was sexually stimulating. He certainly knew all the right moves. But he wasn't an easy man to know, and the hardness in him was bone deep and unforgiving. He frightened her sometimes, and she knew the fear was part of the thrill. But she'd never expected a lasting relationship, and was surprised it had gone on this long.

As for Ragnon, she felt their partnership would work out a lot better if they kept it on an official, impersonal level. But she was no longer sure that was possible. He, too, was hard to get to know, yet even harder not to like. Especially since he reminded her a little of her first love.

And remembering Ragnon's ex-wife's voice on the phone, she pondered what their relationship had been like. God, was she actually jealous?

Parking in the shaded carport of her apartment complex, she walked past the courtyard pool and rock garden and let herself into the climate-controlled comfort of home, regretting not a little that she was going to have to pack.

Kicking off her shoes, she got out the Jose Cuervo, tomato juice, and lime and mixed a strong tequila sunrise. She knew she drank too much, and wondered sometimes if she was an alcoholic. But maybe not. Not if she drank only at the end of a tiring shift and usually with other cops, instead of alone, like now. Well, she thought, changing into a robe and thongs, if she ever needed one to get started in the morning, then she would know.

Settling into a canvas sling chair on the small, balconied patio outside, she propped her feet on the rail, sipped her drink, and watched the sun slipping behind the distant mountains. She tried to put her mind back on the case, but everything was a blur. She thought Tom Ragnon was in the wrong business. He wasn't a cop. McKittrick was a cop. She was a cop. Ragnon was too nice a guy to be a cop. Yet this contradicted what she'd seen in his file: dedicated, stubborn, innovative, and self-reliant, with a good cop's intuitive instincts.

She finished her drink, mixed another, and was wondering why her professional life seemed always so under control while her personal life was an endless turmoil of emotions, when the phone rang.

"Crown?" It was Ragnon.

"Where are you, Sergeant?"

"Still at the office. Typing that goddamned report."

"Oh, Christ, I'm sorry. I forgot all about that. Want me to come down?"

KINDERKILL

"Yes. But not for that. Your computer artist just called."

"My God." She could hear the enthusiasm in his voice. "He got a match?"

"He thinks so," Tom Ragnon said.

"I'll be right there."

It was 6:45 and already dusk outside as Ragnon led Crown across the empty squad bay to his desk and switched on the lamp. Three enlarged pictures lay side by side on his blotter. The one on the left was a morgue photo of the victim as he looked now, the one in the middle a computer-enhanced image of a little boy who looked remarkably like him, and the one on the right the picture the image had been created from: a Child Find poster of a seven-year-old local boy reported missing twenty-six months earlier in Colorado while on vacation with his parents. The name on the poster was Christopher Alan Hannigan.

"He's nine years old now," Ragnon said softly, "and he'll never get any older."

Lucinda Crown was staring at the picture. "But it worked," she whispered breathlessly. "It's him!"

"Looks like him to me," Ragnon said. "Morgue photos can never look like a living person, but it is close. I think we've got it, Crown, but we'll still need a positive ID."

"Have the parents been notified?"

"Deputies are running that down now," Ragnon said. "Father is Charles A. Hannigan, an Air Force brigadier general, but the address at Child Find was no longer valid. They're checking with Air Force personnel and will call back with anything current."

The squad bay was quiet with the other duty detectives away at dinner or on assignments, and only a deputy at the switchboard down the hall. "Are we actually getting a break on this case?" Crown wondered aloud, lighting a slim cigarillo.

"Don't count on it. Not yet." Ragnon had walked over to the green slateboard and picked up a grease pencil. He turned on the overhead fluorescent. "What have we really got?" he asked. "A local kid reported missing in Colorado two years ago turns up killed on a vacant ranch forty-five miles away, and his body is dumped in a landfill here in the city." His grease pencil began making sweeping circles and ended with a big question mark as he looked back at Crown. "Where has he been for the past twenty-six months? Who has he been with? And most important—who was with him the last hours of his life?" More marks on the board as he continued. "Current newspapers from contiguous states found with the body indicate he was traveling, and we know where he was killed. But a child's footprint at the scene that doesn't match his? And a biker? And a couple in an RV and a convertible with no apparent connection to the biker? A mess is what we've still got, Crown." He finished with more big question marks on the green board, and then stepped back and stared at it.

"You know," he said after a moment of silence, "I'm beginning to have second thoughts about that watchman now. Maybe he *was* simply lying about seeing the couple in the RV and the Chrysler." He spat into the wastebasket and then turned to face her. "He could have made the whole thing up as a cover. What if he's a perpetrator instead of a witness?"

"But what about the biker and his Malaguena receipt for the ice cream? Did the grocer make that up?"

"How about the biker as an accomplice of the watchman?"

"In which case, why didn't the watchman disappear along with the biker?"

"Maybe because the watchman—"

"Don't sweat it, Rags," a familiar voice said behind him. "We've already nabbed him." And they both turned to find the chief and John Antone standing in the squad bay door. "The Indian and me," Poole said, smiling broadly, "we got the perp."

"Who? Kranzky?" Ragnon looked at Antone, who nodded, but seemed slightly embarrassed.

"Picked him up at his trailer slick as you please," Sidney Clayton Poole announced. "He's safely locked away in the Mimbres County Jail." He was leering triumphantly as he slowly peeled the cellophane from a fresh cigar. "We'll get a warrant and toss that trailer of his inch by inch till we find something that ties him in."

"Leo Kranzky?" Tom Ragnon repeated, dumbfounded.

"Well, it sure as hell ain't Peter Rabbit," Lieutenant Poole said, still smiling.

PART II
Hannigan's Child

TEN

Less than a hundred miles away the same dusk was settling into the high desert canyon of an old Apache stronghold still thick with stands of scrub oak and juniper. It was now a federal desert park, and there weren't a lot of visitors on next to the last day of September, the season being still too warm for most winter campers even under the spotty shade of the stunted trees that nestled among huge boulders.

Except for some aging hippie types in their homemade camper at the far end, and one old couple in a station wagon, the only occupants of the park were a big Winnebago RV with a dirt bike racked to the rear, a closed green van with tinted bubble windows on each of its rear sides, and a late-model baby-blue Chrysler LeBaron convertible.

The latter three vehicles had just arrived, lumbering along the narrow, rocky road up the ravine and into the campground. A middle-aged woman was behind the wheel of the convertible as it pulled up in the deepening shadows and parked beside the RV and the van. In the fading daylight an older man stepped from the driver's side of the

RV. Wearing a crushed straw hat with a wide feather band, dusty hand-tooled leather boots, and a red satin western shirt tucked into designer jeans, he watched a long-haired, muscled youth in faded Levis and a sleeveless black T-shirt emerge from the van.

The three of them met on the wooden planks surrounding an old iron pump, where the youth gave the long handle a few dry, rasping yanks before the water gushed clear and cold from the Artesian spring below. Ducking his head under the flow, he let it stream over his straggly blond hair and neck, while behind them, from the rear of the van, came the muted sounds of children crying.

"Better see to the kids, Billy Ray," the woman said in a low, husky voice as she stepped up to her turn at the pump. "It's time for their sweetheart pills." Dampening a handkerchief, she began dabbing at her face and wrists.

Billy Ray, stepping from the platform, bent to pull his T-shirt over his head and began drying himself with it, rubbing his straw-colored hair vigorously and then wiping his bare chest and armpits, his muscles moving silky as snakes over his smooth back and shoulders, his only adornment a small tattoo of a green marijuana leaf over his heart. "They'll keep a few more minutes," he told her, looking at her with heavy-lidded eyes that were colorless and dull as stone. "How long are we gonna be here anyway?"

"Depends," the older man said, washing his own hands at the pump now and rinsing his face, and then cupping a drink of the cold spring water. Removing his hat, he ran his fingers over a bald pate fringed with gray-streaked hair that hung down to his collar. "Why don't you take the kids over there to the facility, and then give them the rest of those sweet rolls. It'll be a while till supper."

The woman had pulled a red bandanna from her neck

and was drying her face and hands. Her hair was long and dingy brown, and tied back severely with a black ribbon. Her cheeks, heavily rouged, seemed coarse and puffy. She wore a white cotton shirt and blue jeans, and western boots that matched the older man's. "I think this should be as good a place as any for a while, Pudge," she told him. "At least until it begins to fill up later on. Then maybe we can find another ranch, or one of those picturesque ghost towns. That last place was perfect except for the damn watchman."

Peter Judge grunted. "I know." He was watching Billy Ray as he sauntered over to the van, opened the back door, and led three kids off toward the stone privies built some seventy yards down the hill. "But what are we going to do about him, Carmen?" he asked.

Carmen Jones was uncertain, too, about Billy Ray Lee, remembering the opera festival in Aspen, Colorado, two summers before when they'd met him. He'd seemed the ideal partner they'd been looking for. Then they'd left him with his van and the kids while they went into Denver to meet a buyer. When they'd gotten back, he'd claimed one of the kids had run off. It could happen. They'd accepted that. But two days later a child's body had been found in an alley in Aspen, raped and murdered. No picture in the paper, but the description had been close and they'd wondered about it. Especially when the same thing had happened again this summer at the opera in Santa Fe, and again he'd claimed only that one of the kids had gotten away from him.

The first time they'd known Billy Ray only a few weeks, and hadn't really thought anything about it. He'd grabbed a replacement out of a park and they'd left town. The second time, in Santa Fe, they'd been suspicious but unsure. Now it had happened a third time, and only a week before, after they'd left Billy Ray and the kids at that Malaguena Ranch and gone to meet a buyer in the city and pick up the van, which was being repaired.

Billy Ray had brought the RV later and rendezvoused with them at a KOA campground. But again one of the kids was gone. "He just slipped away," Billy Ray had grumbled testily. "I can't watch the little pricks all the time."

But Peter Judge no longer believed him, and neither did Carmen Jones. Catching up on the newspapers, they had seen the story of the boy found in the dump the day after they'd left Billy Ray at Malaguena. Now, cupping a match to her cigarette with hands that were large but carefully manicured, Carmen whispered hoarsely, "He's wastin' those kids, ain't he, Pudge?"

"I think so," Peter Judge muttered. "Yes. It's too much to be a coincidence." He had removed his feathered hat and was fanning himself in spite of the cool breeze that was rustling the trees around them. "But I'm not about to confront him with it."

"Then we'd better just ditch him," Carmen said regretfully. There was still a boyish immaturity about the twenty-four-year-old—hard-muscled with faint golden hairs on his smooth, blemish-free skin. She enjoyed his company at times, if not his hard rock music tapes.

"Maybe not," Pudge said. He was carefully filling a pipe. "I've been thinking. Maybe we can use him instead."

"Use him?" Carmen ejected a stream of smoke petulantly. "How can we use him?"

Pudge was lighting his pipe. "I've been giving something serious consideration." They watched Billy Ray lead the three kids from the toilets over to the big RV, where he left them waiting by the steps while he went inside.

"What have we always wanted to do? A kiddie snuff film, right?"

"But, Pudge—"

"Think about it. He's gonna kill again anyway. Why not persuade him to kill one on camera? They can only gas him once, my dear."

"But what about us? We'd be accessories!"

"We'd plead temporary insanity—if we were caught. Or he tricked us. Or we'd trade our testimony for a reduced charge. There are excellent lawyers to preserve our rights. But don't worry. With luck we won't be caught. And the money for a snuff would be fabulous."

Carmen Jones watched as Billy Ray emerged from the RV with a carton of ice cream instead of rolls, and then led the kids back to the van. That's the way he was, she thought, stubborn and contrary, never following instructions to the letter, but always doing things a little different, as if for spite. "Maybe," she said to Peter Judge, tempted, though still not completely convinced. But Pudge was always good at turning a potentially bad situation into a profit. "Maybe," she repeated. "But we'd have to be extra careful. He's always been so damned unpredictable."

In the van, Billy Ray left the rear doors open for some fresh air while he sprawled on thick cushions on the carpeted floor and turned on the stereo, filling the confining space with mind-pounding hard rock while the three kids settled around him, each with a spoon and a dish of strawberry ice cream, seemingly oblivious to the harsh sounds.

Billy Ray loved the music. He didn't know how Pudge and Carmen took all that heavy opera shit. While he moved with the beat and spooned up his own ice cream, he watched the kids closely—especially Jeanie, the oldest at seven and the one he now liked best.

Jeanie was blond and had a sad little smile. Sharon was

six and had brown hair and dark, elfish eyes, but Billy Ray didn't like her as much. Freddie was the newest and youngest at five. They'd snatched him at a shopping mall in Pueblo, Colorado, only a couple of weeks before, and he was still a little bewildered by it all, but he'd learn. They all learned, sooner or later, who their real friend was.

Then his thoughts turned darkly to the one who wasn't with them anymore. He didn't even remember what his real name had been—Christian or Christopher—Chris, that was it. But they'd renamed him Kip. They renamed them all. It was better that way. It made for a lot better control. But sometimes Billy Ray lost control. It had happened twice before, and now again. Kip had been with them since Billy Ray had first met Pudge and Carmen over two years earlier, had even become his favorite. As the months passed, the little boy had grown completely dependent on his love and care. He had punished him frequently, sometimes severely, but had always followed punishment with affection. Until Kip, too, had finally grown rebellious and had failed him, like the others.

Billy Ray was so certain each time that he could maintain control of both himself and the kids. But he had a long hate list and was angry most of the time anyway. And the kids were never perfect, and when they failed him once too often—that was when they conveniently "got away." He didn't think Pudge or Carmen really believed it, but then, he didn't much give a shit about that either.

Reaching over, he gave some of his ice cream to the blond little girl, who gave him her pitiful smile in return. He stroked her arm. Jeanie they had named her. Yes, he thought, Jeanie was his favorite now. . . .

Hearing a sound beyond the pounding vibes of hard rock, he looked around and saw Pudge standing at the back of the van, holding an electric lantern high and shouting at him. Sullenly he turned down the volume.

"Either keep the damned thing low or use your earphones!" Billy Ray could hear him clearly now, even above the rumble of the portable generator over at the RV. "Why don't you lock the kids away for a while, Billy Boy. Carmen is fixing steaks for supper, and I've got an idea for a new feature-length video. Even a tentative title—*Barefoot Boy with Cheeks*—how's that grab you?"

"Okay, I guess," Billy Ray answered dully. "But I ought to put the New Mexico plates on the vehicles now."

"That'll keep till morning, when it's light." Pudge didn't like the way Billy Ray's heavy-lidded eyes never looked directly at him when he talked. "C'mon. After supper we'll smoke a little pot, then maybe put on some Wagner and shoot some stills of you and Freddie there in the RV. He's the freshest and youngest. Start getting him broke in."

Billy Ray looked at Freddie, whose wide eyes still held the terror of the unknown. Pudge always played that damned German shit for the sessions with the kids, claimed it turned him on. "He said a while ago he was sick, Pudge. That's why I got out the ice cream. Thought it would make him feel better, but he ain't even eating it."

"You get him well, Billy Boy," Peter Judge responded soothingly. "Freddie's headed for stardom, so you get him well."

ELEVEN

Tom Ragnon, watching an oversized, demonic-looking fish in an undersized aquarium swim lethargically through the mirrored gloom behind the bar, listened to Tony Bennett leaving his heart in San Francisco while he waited for their beers and hot quesadillas. By the time he was carrying the order over to a corner table, where even John Antone was ready to indulge in one of his rare cold brews, Tony Bennett had moved on to a more soothing "Shadow of Your Smile."

It was 11:00 A.M. and the lounge had just opened. Even the waitress hadn't gotten it together yet, but the three of them had gathered for a private sit-down. "You mean there was no new forensic lead tying Kranzky to the killing?" Lucinda Crown was asking, biting into her cheese-filled tortilla. "Just Poole's suspicion, and the fact that the watchman was near the scene at the time?"

"The privilege of rank," Ragnon grunted, sipping his beer.

"I felt bad," Antone said, "picking him up like that. He was passed out in his trailer. Took us twenty minutes to get him on his feet so we could get him cuffed and moving."

"Did you arrest his hog-leg too?" Ragnon asked unkindly.

"Lighten up, Rags," Crown said. "Old Iron Balls ordered it. What could John do?"

Ragnon thought about it, taking a long swallow of beer. "So maybe it is worth another look. See if we can tie the biker to the watchman. And who knows, if Poole sweats him, maybe he'll spin a tale even God could believe."

Crown looked at him over her arm as she reached for a napkin. "You really believe in God, Ragnon?"

Tom Ragnon nodded. "In God, yes. It's formal religion I've got no faith in."

"At least he's keeping us on the case," Antone noted. "Because I've got a feeling the killer isn't sitting in the Mimbres County Jail. He's still out there—somewhere."

"The biker?" Crown asked, eating and drinking slowly.

"He's a lot better bet than the watchman," Ragnon said. He was remembering Poole's words back in the squad bay last night when he'd announced the apprehension of Kranzky: "Looks like we're close to putting a lid on this one, Rags." And his little walrus eyes had glared through his cigar smoke at the confused shambles of markings Ragnon had on the slateboard. "Kranzky doesn't look like much of a hardball to me, and he can't afford a good shyster."

"You had no grounds for an arrest," Ragnon had told him.

But Poole had laughed. "We 'detained' him under that new ruling, while we 'diligently pursue the investigation.' We'll sweat the little bastard a while and he'll talk."

Now Ragnon was taking another bite of his own quesadilla and looking across the table at Antone. "When did Old Iron Balls show up down there?"

"Just about the time I was ready to come back."

"And he tied it all to the watchman, just like that?"

"Kranzky was there, wasn't he? The only one at the scene. That seemed to be enough for the chief. And if they charge him, it just might stick. Like the chief says, he can't afford a fancy lawyer."

"Oh, I don't know." Ragnon reached for a napkin. "A couple of those young public defenders are sharp."

"Aren't we getting off the point, gentlemen?" Lucinda Crown asked them.

"What's the point?" Ragnon asked, draining his glass of beer.

"The point is, did he do it? Or was it one of these?" She indicated the three composite drawings made from the grocer's description of the biker and the watchman's of the middle-aged couple, which John Antone had laid out on the table in front of them when they came in.

Ragnon studied the three faces again. The young biker's dull, hooded eyes, the full lips, the scraggly mustache and beard. And the couple, looking oddly alike: square faces, soft chins, eyes widely spaced; differing mostly because the man's brows were full, shaggy, while the woman's were plucked to a thin line. But even her face was hard, like a man's. He glanced up at Antone. "Are these being distributed?"

"All over the Southwest, Sergeant."

"Remind me to increase it to contiguous states." Jesus, he thought, the older guy, with his bald pate and shoulder-length hair, looked like Benjamin Franklin without his spectacles. He looked up again. "I guess Kranzky could have done it, maybe with one or more of these as accomplices, but why?" He looked at Crown. "You're sure it wouldn't be a snuff film?"

"There's still nothing on the street about one. And there would be. They make them to sell."

Ragnon looked at the Indian. "What do you really think, John? Did we miss something?"

"Not if we're still on the track of that biker."

"You mean we can forget about the RV and the convertible and the middle-aged couple?"

"I don't think we can forget about anybody yet, Sergeant."

Tom Ragnon agreed. Because they didn't even have a confirmed ID on the victim yet. They had spent the morning in the squad bay going over the reports from Child Find with the deputies who had tracked down General Hannigan and his wife. Divorced a year earlier, about fourteen months after the disappearance of Christopher, Christine Hannigan had been awarded the house and furniture and car, and custody of their older son, Danny, now twelve. She had sold the home and moved to an apartment in Phoenix, while the general, pursuing his duties as a regional fiscal officer, lived in bachelor quarters at various bases around the western U.S.

But currently he was on leave, and they had reached him at a summer place he had retained in the red-rock canyon country of northern Arizona, outside Sedona, which he was closing down for the winter. The general had also explained why Crown had been unable to find a local dentist for an ID through dental records. The work on Christopher had been done in Sedona the summer he was six. The general was having the chart sent down. Yet, oddly enough, he had refused to come himself. Instead, Mrs. Hannigan was due at the coroner's office at noon, where Crown was to meet her for the official ID of the victim.

Ragnon had thought about that too. A man's refusal to come down and even try to ID the body of his missing son bothered him more than the detention of Kranzky. So, while Crown interviewed Mrs. H. and hopefully got a positive ID, Ragnon had decided he and Antone would make the four-hour drive up to Sedona and chat with the general.

The fact that Prescott was only sixty miles from Sedona and he could drop over and see his dad had nothing to do with his decision, he had assured the chief, but Old Iron Balls had reluctantly agreed only when Ragnon had volunteered to use his own car and gas. And thinking about it now, he had to admit the trip was more an excuse for the Prescott detour than anything else. He didn't expect to get much out of a reluctant general, who maybe just didn't give a shit about his kid.

John Antone said as much later in the afternoon as they began the climb out of the desert into the mountains. The higher elevations of northern Arizona were like another state, with balmy summers amid forested lakes and streams, but brutal winters. "Is this something like the mountain going to Mohammed?" the Indian asked as Ragnon guided his battered yellow Bug around the curves.

"Not quite, John. But if it wasn't so far out of the way, I think I'd let you drop me off in Prescott and go interview the general by yourself."

"You really think the trip will be that useless, Sergeant?"

"Does a bear fornicate in the woods? We'll have the mother's verification, and the dental record should clinch it."

"And if they don't?"

"Then so much for computer imaging, John, and we'll be back on square one."

By four in the afternoon the clouds—great, billowing white headers—banked the vast sky above the red-rock canyons as Ragnon drove through the tourist town of Sedona, where a touch of fall was already in the air. The normal afternoon crowds had already thinned, either moving inside the bars and cafés and curio shops or on north to Flagstaff.

They found the road, and a mile out of town was the Hannigan mailbox, with a long red-earth drive leading to a modern ranch-style house, all glass and stone and with a panoramic view of the canyons. "Looks like even divorced generals don't hurt too bad financially," Ragnon remarked as he eyed the chain-link-fenced yard which contained a vicious-looking Doberman.

The dog began growling ominously as they drove up and parked in front of the gate. "Did you tell him we were coming?" Antone asked a little anxiously.

"I never tell 'em I'm coming, John. You always get a better reading with a little surprise."

They sat in the car while the dog's snarling and growling became more and more vociferous, until the door in a long, screened side porch opened and a man looked out. Then Ragnon picked up a manila envelope from between the seats and got out.

When he walked up to the fence, the dog advanced to meet him, its expression and manner becoming even more menacing, until the man whistled low and sharp, causing the sleek brown animal to retreat slowly and reluctantly, whimpering, as if it had been denied a meal.

"General Hannigan?" Ragnon called out.

"What do you want? Are you lost?" The man came off

the porch, signaling the dog to sit. He was dressed in blue denims and a gray sweatshirt with U.S. Air Force stenciled across the chest. He came striding down to the gate like a man who brooked no nonsense from intruders.

"I'm Sergeant Ragnon," the detective said, introducing himself, "Mimbres County Sheriff's Department." He held up the leather holder of his shield and ID. "Are you Brigadier General Charles Hannigan?"

"Yes. Wait a moment." A curious expression had crossed his face as he turned and whistled with two fingers, and they watched the dog trot obediently beside him, allowing itself to be interned in a wire cage.

The general came back to the gate, a short, square bulldog of a man with a full head of graying black hair and a salt-and-pepper mustache. Crow's feet tracked the corners of his hard blue eyes, and Ragnon judged him near his own age. Close up, his sweatshirt looked as if it hid a slightly developing paunch that reminded Ragnon unpleasantly of his own. "You're a little far from your jurisdiction, aren't you, Sergeant?" The general had made no move to open the gate.

The Indian had walked up to the gate now and stood beside Ragnon. "This is my partner, John Antone," Ragnon said, "and we're investigating the death of a nine-year-old boy that *is* in our jurisdiction. The one we think might be your son—Christopher. Missing for two years?"

General Hannigan's look was almost vacant. He said nothing.

"General?" Ragnon tried again. "Your wife—ex-wife—is going to try to make the official ID, and we'll see if there's a match with the dental records you sent. But would you at least look at this picture of the victim?" He held up the manila envelope.

"I . . . told the policewoman who called . . . I didn't

want to come," Hannigan answered stiffly. "My reasons are private. My choice."

You pompous bastard, Ragnon thought. "Wouldn't it be better to know for yourself?" he persisted. "One way or the other, General? Wouldn't that be better than wondering?" He withdrew the picture from the envelope.

But Hannigan had seemed to shrink, becoming somehow less than what he was. He avoided looking at the picture, and made no move to open the gate. "No," he insisted, even taking a step backward. "My wife can make the identification. I told them that. He's gone. I accepted it months ago."

"Did you love your son, General?" Ragnon asked brutally, still holding out the picture to the closed gate.

It raised a spark. "Of course I loved him! What kind of a question is that?"

"Then look at the picture and tell me if it's him."

"All right, I'll look." He still didn't open the gate, but took the picture through the gap between the gate and the fence post.

Hannigan stared at the morgue photo wonderingly, then blinked and shook his head, handing it back through the fence. "I'm . . . not sure. He was only seven then. I think so, but I can't be certain. Not after so long." He looked away.

"Thank you," Ragnon said, putting the photo back into the envelope. "Of course it'll take the dental records to be conclusive. I'm sorry."

The general didn't ask how he died, or how they'd managed to trace his identity. "I'd ask you in . . . gentlemen," he said instead, "but . . . you understand."

"Of course. We've got to go anyway. And you have our condolences. But if I could ask one more question, General? Do you recall when you saw your son last?"

"Certainly. The day he ran away. In Colorado."

"He ran away?" Ragnon glanced at Antone.

"Yes. I was on leave and we were all at a summer opera festival in Aspen. There was a family argument—an argument with me mostly—and he ran away. We didn't report it until that evening, arguing ourselves about it, but I really thought he'd come back to the hotel on his own. It's a small town. When he didn't, we reported it to the Aspen police and went looking ourselves. We stayed there three weeks, looking, until the police finally found a boy who'd seen him getting into a van in a park in downtown Aspen the same day he ran."

"What kind of a van, General?"

"A late-model Ford, I think. Dark green with bubble windows, they said."

"But no license?"

"No number. Just an out-of-state plate. Maroon with white numbers. Probably Arizona. Then nothing. No more word, no new clues, nothing—till now. I gave his picture and statistics to Child Find after we got back home, and also reported it to the police there." He shook his head. "Missing in Colorado two years and he turns up dead not fifty miles from home. I don't understand it."

"What about the driver of the van?" John Antone asked.

"The witness didn't see the driver. Not even if it was a man or a woman. Just the van. I'm sorry, but—"

When someone called out from the porch, Hannigan looked around. A small boy had come to the screen door, a boy about twelve. "I can't find the film!" he called.

"Your other son, General?" Antone asked.

"No. Danny's with my wife. That's Jeff, a neighbor's boy. I'm closing up the place, and he's helping me pack. Go back inside, Jeff! I'll be finished here in a minute!" He looked back at the detectives. "Thank you again, Sergeant. You too." He reached through the gap in the gate and shook hands firmly with them both. "If I can be of any further help, I go back on duty next week. You can reach me through the CO at Luke Air Force Base in Phoenix."

On the drive southwest through the mountains toward Prescott, Ragnon was chewing thoughtfully as he asked, "Well, John, what kind of reading did you get on the father of Christopher Alan Hannigan? Relief? Disinterest? Fear? What?"

"A strange combination," John Antone said. "Surprise and resentment at first—we were intruders. Then curiosity, and yes, relief. Fear only toward the end—when that boy appeared on the porch."

Ragnon spat out the car window, the tires protesting as he took the turns on the steep mountain road a little too fast. "Yeah, that boy. What'd he say—a neighbor's kid? Not a relative's or a friend's. But I didn't even notice any neighbors up in that canyon, and no bike or cycle for transportation, only the Lincoln in the double carport."

"The general may just miss his own kids, Sergeant."

But Ragnon wasn't so sure. It was another irritating complication that would have to be resolved. "Remind me to call Aspen when we get back and get a copy of that two-year-old police report." Then he let the Indian take the wheel at a rest stop, and while he dozed, the winding turns down out of the mining town of Jerome were negotiated a bit more safely.

In Prescott, at six in the evening, he left his partner eating a hot dog in the park while he went to the hospital. He found his father asleep and he stared down at him—a pale and wasted man, his gray mustache growing over his lips. Never a large man, he was down to one-hundred-thirty pounds or so, and Ragnon sat by the bed in silence, watching, remembering; thinking of runaway kids, abused kids, murdered kids, all the wasted lives.

He had never been close to the man dying on the bed. His parents had divorced when he was six and he'd lived with his mother as an only child, seeing his father just at Christmas and during the summers. And he'd joined the navy right after high school. Now his mother was dead and this strange man was dying, too, and Tom Ragnon felt he had been a disappointment to them both.

His mother had always wanted him to be a lawyer. She had seen him as a corporate attorney, like an uncle in San Francisco. He didn't think his father had seen him as much of anything. He'd sent support money off and on for his only son, but Harry Ragnon had pretty much belittled everything Tom had ever done, including his police work. "Still taking bribes, kid?" was his favorite joke, and Tom's retort was always "Making a fortune, Pops." But deep in his gut the accusation hurt. Harry didn't much believe in cops. "Half of 'em are on the take, and the other half practicing to be" was the way he liked to put it. If it hadn't been for a loving, caring grandfather, Ragnon wondered . . . Then he became aware that his father was awake and staring back at him with watery red eyes. "They taking good care of you, Dad?" he asked.

"Bunch of dipshits run this place," the old man croaked. "When you gonna get me outta here?"

"Soon, I hope. Still working on it." He dared to take the gnarled, blue-veined hand that lay above the cover and hold it. Because he didn't know if the move would be soon enough. And he knew his father would find dipshits wherever he went now anyway. "You need anything? I brought you a couple of *True Crime* magazines." His father liked them—the gorier the better. Yet he had never seemed to connect such crimes with his son's work in homicide.

"I had a dream last night," the old man whispered. His voice seemed raspier, weaker, his breath was foul. "I was back at Monte Cassino on the Italian boot. The Big War, remember? I told you about Monte Cassino. Well, I was still trying to get out from under that goddamned mule. The pain was killing me. I think they gave me a shot."

Tom Ragnon remembered the story of the besieged abbey on the Rapido River in central Italy the winter of 1944. All his father's memories seemed to be going further and further back now. He couldn't remember what he had for lunch, but he could remember World War II: wounded in battle when the German defenses bloodied the Allied advance on Rome, a twenty-two-year-old sergeant with an ammunition train of mules ambushed by Krauts and lying pinned under a heavily laden dead mule for two days and nights before the medics found him. If that didn't give a man time to think about the evil of his ways, Tom Ragnon guessed nothing did.

When his father drifted off again, he used the pay phone in the hall to call Poole. "Chief? We're in Prescott, visiting with my dad."

"How is he, Rags?"

"The same. Weaker maybe. More disoriented."

"Sorry. Maybe if you want to take some time off, Crown and Antone—"

"No. I'd rather stay busy. We talked to the general. I'll tell you about it later. Kid disappeared in a van in Aspen, Colorado, but no description of the driver. Anything new down there?"

"Crown got a positive on the ID before Mrs. Hannigan fainted. And the dental charts matched."

"Good. At least we're no longer riding a horse with no

name. Call the Aspen police and ask for their report on the victim, missing twenty-six months ago. There's something about this general we're gonna have to nail down."

"And we're still sweating Kranzky," Poole said, "but nothing new, and his prints came back clean. Probably release him for lack of evidence. But there is something else."

"What—?"

"I can't find Crown."

"What do you mean, you can't find her?"

"After interviewing Mrs. Hannigan and her boy she just checked out and disappeared. I'm betting she's shacked up somewhere with McKittrick," Poole added spitefully. "They say he's checked out too."

TWELVE

The fading afternoon sunlight, filtered through thin, dingy curtains, made odd patterns on the cracked ceiling over their heads. Lucinda Crown was sure the room, with its stiff plastic and metal furniture, stained carpet, and worn cotton bedspread, rented by the hour. Especially in the afternoon. Though for a Vice lieutenant it was probably "on the house."

Leave it to Jack McKittrick to take her to the better places. She swore she could hear voices from the massage parlor next door—even above the clatter of the room air conditioner—but mostly it was McKittrick's heavy breathing in her ear and his sweaty, naked body moving rhythmically with hers that distracted her from her own needs. That and remembering what Ragnon had said about McKittrick jumping the bones of a corpse. She shuddered.

Suddenly she cared where McKittrick took her, how he treated her. Before, it hadn't mattered. His insensitivity, his rough ways—it was what she had wanted in a man. She had wanted to be used. Not abused. She never let it go that far. But McKittrick had no manners, no class, and she reveled in it. He was a hairy, hard-assed barbarian and she loved it. Not him—and she realized it for perhaps the first time—she certainly wasn't in love with the man. She just enjoyed sex with him. Or had. What had changed?

Gripping his hairy back hard, she lunged and pushed and pulled, but she was conscious of every other tiny thing around her. She just couldn't get it off as she heard him moan in release and then roll away from her, the sweat-wet hair matted to his chest as he sighed and threw an arm over his eyes. "Jesus, Mary, and the Constitution, but you're a world-class fuck, babe." He hadn't even noticed it had been all one-sided this time.

Reaching over him to the nightstand, Lucinda Crown groped for her cigarillos and thin pencil lighter and they shared one, passing it back and forth as they lay side by side still naked on the bed. She could hear the muffled sounds from the massage parlor clearly now as the air conditioner shifted to a lower cycle. A radio was bouncing a hard-rock song against the wall. "What's wrong, babe?" McKittrick asked. "You working your kiddie case too hard?"

"Not hard enough." She exhaled and handed the cigarillo back. "The case is moving, but in all different directions. We're skating around like hogs on ice."

"You and Prince Valiant—what's his name, Ragnon?"

"And John Antone. They're both good at homicide, Jack, but time is slipping away, even for them."

"I've heard a lot about Ragnon. A good cop but no ambition. A real bonehead when it comes to sucking up to the brass. It's a wonder he ever made sergeant. Hey." He raised up on one arm to look at her. "You're not getting the hots for *him*, are you? You seemed a little cool with me just now."

Reaching up with one finger, she smoothed his thick

blond guardsman's mustache. "How's your promotion looking, Jack?"

"Better all the time, babe." He mashed out the stub of their cigarillo in the ashtray on the stand.

"You play all the angles, don't you?" she asked.

"It's the only way to fly, ain't it? Let's get a shower. I've got a meeting tonight with the county supervisors. They want more sweeps around the outskirts of the city. Too many working girls moving down from Phoenix, giving our area a bad name. They even want to arrest the johns now, and put their names in the paper."

They were in the shower together, scrubbing each other's back, when she brought up what had really been on her mind all afternoon. "I interviewed the victim's mother this morning, Jack. A Mrs. Hannigan. After she'd ID'd her son."

"And—?"

"Something interesting came up in your line. Remember the scandal at the Air Force Day School a couple of years ago?"

"Child abuse by the operator and employees? Sexual abuse? Sure, but most of it was dismissed for lack of evidence. They weren't allowing kids to testify on video then, and you know what it's like to put 'em facing the perpetrators in open court. The parents wouldn't allow it and the case folded."

"Well, Mrs. Hannigan says her husband was involved in it."

"And they're divorced, right? So what else would you expect her to say?"

"Somehow I got a ring of truth out of it. She wasn't just a vengeful ex. And he's a one-star general. He was a bird colonel then."

McKittrick turned off the water and whistled sharply as

they stepped out, reaching for the towels. "A fucking general, huh?"

"Mrs. H. says it was hushed up, and he wouldn't even talk to her about it."

"How was he involved, for Christ's sake?"

"She didn't know, but there was more. Her older son has never come right out and said it, but he's hinted at sexual episodes with his father. Even hinted it was the real reason his little brother, the victim, ran off. But he won't actually talk about it, even now. She also found some pictures afterward. Children—boys—not naked but posed suggestively."

"Did she confront him with them?" They had moved back into the bedroom and were dressing.

"No. She said probably because she was afraid of what she'd find out. Their own sex life had never been that active. She suspected other women, even other men, but not children. Not until now."

"Goddamn." McKittrick laughed roughly. "A general who's a chicken hawk—if that don't make a pretty picture. What do you want me to do?"

"See if your people can dig out any more on the day school scandal, especially anything concerning Hannigan. The case is in your jurisdiction."

"Shit, you don't think the general offed his own kid?"

"I don't know what to think. Like I said, our case is going in too many directions. We need a handle, a firm one. Hannigan himself might just be it."

"The case is closed, babe, it'd take—"

She came up to him. "Don't give me any official bullshit, Jack, just do it—unofficially. You've got the balls, right?" She reached down and gave him a gentle squeeze.

Jack McKittrick grinned broadly. "You just said the magic word, babe."

KINDERKILL

* * *

This time the phone was picked up after the first ring.
"Lucinda?" Ragnon asked, relieved but still suspicious.

"Yes—Ragnon?" She sounded a little out of breath.

"I called from Prescott, but no answer. Chief said you'd checked out but not where. What happened?"

"Nothing. I had an interesting talk with Mrs. Hannigan. I think I got something. What happened with the general?"

"He was interesting too."

"And your dad?"

"No change there. We just got back at eleven. John's gone home." He hesitated. "I suppose you've had dinner?"

"Not really—more like a snack. Why, are you inviting me?"

"Looks like it. I know it's late, but the Char-Broil Lounge serves a great steak, with wine and candlelight, the works—my treat. I guess it'll be like a date, Crown. Only not a real date, of course." The lounge was a popular cops' hangout a block from headquarters. "Meet you there in half an hour, okay?"

"Sure sounds like a date to me, Sergeant," Lucinda Crown said.

By the time she joined him at a corner table, it was nearly midnight and the place was packed. He had already picked out their steaks for broiling on the hooded mesquite grill built into the center of the room, and ordered a decent red wine. "I asked for two medium rare. Shall I change yours?"

"Medium rare is perfect, Sergeant." The red-checkered tablecloth, red candle in red-netted globe, and the reddish overhead lamps all combined with the flickering red glare from the coals in the open grill to give the place the hellish look of a steel foundry. Her look was perfect, in a white blouse open at the throat, with dark blue slacks and dangling white earrings. In fact, Ragnon thought her dangerously alluring, but after the way she'd carried on about no dickless tracy jokes and no personal involvement, he wondered if it was really going to be this easy.

"So," she said, sipping her wine. "What about our General Hannigan?"

Ragnon described the rather strange encounter.

"You say there was a boy on his porch? Not his son?" Crown asked.

Ragnon nodded. "Said he was a neighbor kid, helping him pack."

"But he never did invite you in?"

"No."

"What did this Hannigan look like?"

Ragnon described him.

"Then he couldn't have been the male composite of our middle-aged couple with the RV—even disguised?"

Ragnon thought about it. "No. The face wasn't even the right shape. The composite was square, fleshy; the general long-jawed, strong. No, I don't see how—why would you think that? You don't think he did it?"

"Or maybe had it done?" She told him the details of her meeting with Mrs. Hannigan and what she had said about her older son and ex-husband and the day school scandal.

Ragnon was pensive as the waitress brought their steaks. "That does put an extra wrinkle in things, doesn't it? We'd better check it out."

"I already am—having it done."

"Oh?" Ragnon frowned. "McKittrick?"

"It's where I was this afternoon." She chewed a bit of steak carefully. "With McKittrick."

"The chief mentioned you were both unaccountably missing—'shacked up' was the term he used—but I assured him it was just a coincidence. I guess not, huh?"

"He's a Vice lieutenant, remember? I told him about it, asked him to reopen the case, unofficially, see what he can find."

"As a favor to you—"

"Yes, dammit. For us, our case."

"I don't think I want any favors from McKittrick, especially you owing him. And why do I get the feeling there's more?"

"What do you mean more?"

"You took all afternoon to tell him about this possible link with Hannigan? Where did all this take place, at his apartment or yours?" Ragnon knew he should bite his tongue. A sudden schoolboy rush of irrational jealousy was ridiculous. It was none of his business.

That's even what she said. "It's really none of your damn business, Sergeant!"

Before they could come to blows, the waitress appeared again with a message that Ragnon was wanted on the phone. "Your headquarters."

The wall phone was near the kitchen and Ragnon had to plug one ear to hear. "Yeah, Chief, I know it's after midnight. I'm not a kid and she's here with me. We're having a late dinner." There was still a little leftover anger in his voice, and he knew it carried through the line to Poole.

"You're supposed to be on a case, Rags, not a fucking date. Anyway, here's your partner. He's got something he thought was worth bothering me for. Let him bother you."

"Sergeant?"

"What the hell, John, I thought you went home."

"Juana and the baby are still on the reservation, so I thought I'd stay and do a little checking. I ran everything we've got on our three suspects through the regional computer."

"And—?"

"Looks like it turned something on two of them."

"Jesus, John, which two?"

"The young biker and the middle-aged man."

"Then they're a team?"

"No. Not even a connection shown with each other. Just two separate IDs, but both of them interestingly criminal."

"But nothing on the woman?"

"Not a damn thing on her, Sergeant."

"We'll be right there, John," Tom Ragnon said.

THIRTEEN

"At least we scored twice," John Antone said. "I requested sex-crimes data and fed everything we had into the regional computer, and these two popped out." He had laid them on Ragnon's desk and turned on the lamp: mug shots side by side with the two artist's sketches of the young biker and the middle-aged man with the RV, along with their rap sheets.

Tom Ragnon whistled at the likenesses and glanced at Lucinda Crown. "What do you think?"

Crown was studying them closely and nodding. "We should mix the photos with some others and see if the watchman and grocer can still pick out their man, just to be sure. But it's them. I'd bet on it." She looked at Antone. "I wonder why nothing came back on the woman."

Nobody had an answer for that, and Ragnon tucked a pinch of Red Man in his cheek as he sat on a corner of his desk and studied the sheets on the two they had. "Billy Ray Lee, a.k.a. Billy Lee Ray." He spat into his wastebasket. "Cute. Born Billy LeRoy Raynes twenty-four years ago in Socorro, New Mexico. Five-eleven, one hundred eighty-five pounds, blond hair and dark eyebrows. Occupation: fry cook.''

Ragnon stared at the narrow, feral face, the ice-hard pale eyes beneath heavy lids, the ragged growth of wispy blond beard and mustache, and read on: "Distinguishing marks: appendicitis scar, mole on inside of left wrist, tattoo of green marijuana leaf on chest over heart." He glanced up at the others. "And he's been a busy boy, our Billy. In and out of various juvie detention centers and foster homes since age thirteen; arrested suspicion child molestation at eighteen in California; served first sentence on a felony at nineteen for burglary and grand theft auto; released after nine months and picked up six months later in Utah, violation of parole. Two years later vandalism and sexual assault in molestation of a five-year-old, charges dismissed for lack of evidence." He glanced up again. "And get this. Picked up three months ago in New Mexico, suspicion of murder in another child molestation; released for lack of evidence. Jesus, what have we got, a serial killer of children?"

"Maybe two," Lucinda Crown said. She had picked up the other sheet. "Peter Leon Judge, nickname 'Pudge.' He looks like an older version from the same mold. Age forty-nine, five-nine, one hundred seventy pounds. No distinguishing marks. Bald on top, long-haired fringe, but known to wear a salt-and-pepper beard at times, and occasionally a toupee. Portrait photographer by trade. Previous occupations: children's photographer, clown, day school supervisor." She looked up at Ragnon and Antone. "All jobs dealing with children. He even ran a summer camp for boys in Colorado."

"And look at his rap sheet," Antone said.

"Sentenced seven to fifteen in California after child molestation dropped in exchange for a guilty plea to a reduced

KINDERKILL 119

charge. Paroled four years ago. Arrested again last year in Colorado, child molestation; charges dropped when parents refused to allow child to testify." She looked up. "No outstanding warrants on either of them, and neither was on the known pedophile list."

"Okay, what have we got that's so goddamned hot?" Lieutenant Poole came striding into the office chewing on a cigar and obviously ticked off at having been dragged away from the late movie on TV.

"Looks like John caught a couple of brass rings, Chief," Ragnon said, moving aside so the lieutenant could view the desk.

Poole, the cold cigar clamped in his jaw, stared down at the pictures and records. "What about the woman? No known associates of these two?"

"Computer didn't turn any. Maybe she was just along for the ride."

"Yeah," Poole mused, reading through the records. "And no current addresses on either of them. Last known addresses are two years old and in different states. Even the one picked up three months ago had a General Delivery." He tossed the reports down. "So looks like pulling the mug shots on these two pricks ain't exactly the same as catching 'em. By the way, Aspen called confirming Hannigan's story about the green van, but nothing new. It's still in their pending file."

"At least we've got enough for warrants now," Ragnon said, spitting into his wastebasket, "and an APB."

But Sidney Poole had already turned on Lucinda Crown. "And where the hell were you all afternoon?"

She colored slightly, and before she could respond, Ragnon answered for her. "She was with McKittrick, Chief. Getting him to follow up on something we might have picked up on Hannigan."

Poole scowled. "You mean *he* might have done it? A fucking general?"

"It takes all kinds, Chief."

"It's not too likely," Crown said, "not with what we've got on these two here, but something was going on, and McKittrick agreed to look into it."

"In exchange for what?" Poole challenged her cruelly.

"Let's just say he owed me one, Lieutenant," Crown answered, her voice like ice.

"So what's next?" Poole turned again to Ragnon.

"We go back down to Pontatoc, show the mug shots to be sure we're on track, and start the hunt from there like we planned. My trailer's already on site."

"Finally," Poole said. "But you still don't have anything putting this Pudge and Billy Ray together. Or anything at all on the woman."

"We'll get it. Sorry to have dragged you away from your TV."

"Shit. Now that I'm here, maybe I can catch up on some of my own paperwork—yeah, I got it, too, Rags. And where the hell's that first report on this case?"

"In your basket, Chief, under the rest of the garbage. Surprised? I got it in yesterday, before we went to Sedona."

"Well, pull it out and add this stuff to it—before you leave." And they watched him disappear through the frosted glass door into his inner sanctum.

Ragnon looked at the wall clock and then at his partners and shrugged. It was 1:15 A.M. "As you can see, working with the chief is about as much fun as playing leapfrog with a unicorn."

"So how are we going to play this?" Crown asked, lighting one of her cigarillos.

"John and I may as well move on down to my trailer

in Pontatoc now. In the morning we'll run a photo lineup by the grocer and the watchman just to make sure they still want to jump through the same hoops. Then we'll show the pix around town, just in case they jog a memory that was faulty with the sketches, or we missed someone."

"Like the only gas station in Pontatoc," Antone said. "It was closed the day we were there. But the suspects had to gas their vehicles somewhere."

"You're a partner after my own heart, John."

"What about me?" Crown asked impatiently.

"You too, lady, but right now get some sleep. Then I want you to stay on the Hannigan thing. There's something there that doesn't click. Go on up to Sedona if you have to, but at least talk with Mrs. H. again—see if she can give you any more goodies. And see what else you can dig up on the general's life—his military background, public records. Even the local news morgue may have something or other. Anything, okay?"

Lucinda Crown snubbed out her half-finished cigarillo in the glass ashtray on Ragnon's desk. "And the angle McKittrick's working on for us, the two-year-old day school scandal?" She gave him her sharky little half smile. "I might have to check with him about it."

"So check with him," Ragnon snapped, poker-faced.

"Sergeant," Antone said, interrupting them, "I just remembered something else during our interview with Hannigan—what that kid on the porch said. He couldn't find the *film*, remember? The general said the boy was helping him pack, and the kid said he couldn't find the film, I'm sure of it."

"Jesus," Tom Ragnon said, "you're right. I remember him saying film too now."

* * *

It was nearly 2:00 A.M. by the time they pulled out of the underground parking garage of the Sheriff's Department Building and headed southeast on the freeway in the Jeep Cherokee. John Antone was driving. "We're still being pulled different ways on this, aren't we, Sergeant? Something's not right with Hannigan up there in Sedona, and our witnesses down here can't place either of our two suspects together, and there's nothing at all on the woman. So where's it all taking us?"

"Hopefully not down the garden path, John." Ragnon had been using a penlight to study the mug shots of Pudge and Billy Ray, but his eyes just quit focusing and he flicked off the light and slipped the photos back in his pocket along with the other mug shots they would use for a lineup. Settling back in the seat, he tilted his hat down over his face and folded his arms. Beneath the brim he could barely see the milky glow of the moon edging upward high above the horizon. "You're right, John," he said, "the case is going nowhere."

They had stayed only long enough to bring the crime report up-to-date and slip it back in Poole's basket, but that's what it really added up to. "So far, a nowhere case. But it's gonna work, John," Ragnon promised him. "We're gonna make it work."

John Antone smiled in the darkness. "And you're gonna show me how."

Tom Ragnon tucked a pinch of Red Man in his cheek. "Remember the towns from the newspapers they trashed? Pueblo, Albuquerque, Las Cruces—then they swung west into Arizona. They were coming down out of the high country into the warm winter desert of southern Arizona. I'm certain now they weren't going on through to California, or north again—not with their records in those other states. And if that's true, the key as to where they are now is there in Pontatoc or on Rancho Malaguena. The chief's right about that."

"You mean the biker and his ice cream receipt."

"I mean all of them, John—all bloody goddamned three of them—the woman too."

"But nobody saw anybody in Pontatoc except the biker."

"And he bought the ice cream." Ragnon rolled down the window and spat. "Enough for several people. Several kids? I'm betting he took it back to Malaguena, to the others. Remember the child's footprint that was made the same time as the tire print but didn't match the victim's foot?"

"But the watchman never saw the biker, just the other two. And no kids."

"The watchman never saw a green van either, but it could have been there too, somewhere. Kranzky stuck close to his trailer after getting his fifty bucks, right? You said yourself *King Kong* could have been filmed on the place and he'd have missed it. It was what—two, three days later before he went back to that stable looking for them and they were gone?"

"But who saw them all together?"

Ragnon spat again. "That's what we're going back to Pontatoc to find out."

"You do hang in there, Sergeant." John Antone was smiling again.

"I try, John. I surely do try."

"But that still leaves us with Hannigan out in left field in Sedona, doesn't it?"

Ragnon grunted. "Crown and what's-his-name can take care of the Hannigan part of this story."

"His name's McKittrick, Sergeant. How well do you know him?"

"Only by reputation. Met him once at a Vice-Homicide bash. As I remember it, we were both pretty sloshed and didn't hit it off too well. I think he knocked me ass-over-elbows into a swimming pool. He's smart but rotten. He also makes a lot of Brownie points with the brass. And he's got narrow eyes."

"What?"

"I think that's what I really don't like about him, John—his fucking narrow eyes."

"Sure—and the fact that he's going with Lucinda Crown."

"Does it show that much?"

"You're not getting stuck on her, are you, Sergeant?"

"No—goddammit, John, I've got enough on my plate without getting stuck on Lucinda Ann Crown. Now, can't you kick this thing in the ass a little? I'd like to get there before the dew is off the lily."

At the trailer Ragnon had set up on a slab behind the volunteer fire station in Pontatoc, they both found themselves still too strung out for sleep, and Ragnon brewed them some hot chocolate. He even slipped a cassette into the VCR, but watching Mike Hammer tie up *his* murder in a neat bow proved too discouraging and he turned it off.

They even tried playing a little backgammon—then both found themselves staring at the clock: 3:45. It seemed like it hadn't moved in fifteen minutes. "You think maybe Hannigan was doing his own kid—sexually?" Antone had finally asked what was on both their minds. "That he's doing that kid we saw on the porch?"

"That's been bothering you too, John?"

"Maybe we're chasing shadows down here with this

Pudge and Billy Ray—unless he hired them to make the kill."

"I don't know what to think, John." Exhaustion was beginning to claim them both. "Maybe we'll find out something tomorrow—today. Maybe Crown and McKittrick will find something. And maybe not."

"I just don't understand sex with kids—any kids, but certainly not your own kids. To sacrifice a child like that . . ."

"Crown showed me some choice movies back at headquarters while you were down here at the ranch shooting the tracks. They were nasty stuff, yet she says they've got stacks of films and videotapes and magazines full of sex with kids—a warehouse full of confiscated stuff. And not just from this country. It seems we don't make enough of our own to satisfy the market. We have to import more of it from places like Holland and Denmark, who claim the good old U.S. of A. is the biggest kiddie porn market in the world."

"I guess children have always been sacrificed, Sergeant, by different peoples, in different ways. Even among the ancient Sand Papagos there was sacrifice. You know, there's still a shrine on the reservation where believers leave trinkets and change in memory of the children. The legend says that even in the desert there was a great flood, so much water pouring forth from a vast hole that it threatened to destroy all the people.

"Their songs and dances had been useless; their sacrifice of sacred fetishes had failed. Then an ancient wise man suggested the greatest sacrifice of all, the most prized offerings the village could give—their children. Four were chosen, two boys and two girls, the strongest, prettiest, painted and dressed in their finest clothes and placed with great ceremony and sorrow into the hole to drown. And it worked. Slowly the rush of water stopped, the flood went down, the people were saved." John Antone stared at Ragnon. "But this kind of sacrifice of children . . ." He shook his head in disbelief.

Ragnon was glancing over his shelf of paperback novels racked above the couch, mostly old westerns and sea stories. "You ever read Alistair MacLean, John?" he asked.

"You mean like *Bear Island* and *Guns of Navarone*?"

"Yeah, those too. But you know, I think his greatest novel was one you probably never heard of: *H.M.S. Ulysses*."

"No, I never heard of that one."

"I think it was his first—a story about sailors on a British cruiser trying to guard convoys from deadly German U-boats in the freezing North Atlantic during World War II." He looked at his partner with resignation. "They had an impossible job too."

FOURTEEN

They had been shooting the scene for nearly an hour in the dry, boulder-strewn wash, with the recorded music of Wagner booming off the canyon walls around them. Then Peter Judge called a halt, and it was suddenly quiet. The three kids sprawled, still naked, on the sand in the shade of a huge boulder, while Billy Ray steadied his ghetto blaster on a rock nearby, found a hard-rock music station, and filled the canyon with the electric thunder of heavy metal.

Pudge lit up a joint for the kids and let them pass it back and forth between them, while he packed up the portable video camcorder and then began fumbling with his pipe. No one even tried to talk above the noise until Carmen Jones walked over from the big RV parked under a tree and turned the volume down on the radio. "Give that rock stuff a rest too, Billy Ray," she said huskily. "Or put on your earphones. It's giving me an Excedrin headache."

Billy Ray Lee, pulling his jeans back on along with his cut-off sweatshirt, made a sour face. "Do I complain about your long-haired opera shit?" Then he told the kids to get dressed too, and picking up his radio, he headed for the RV himself.

"A fairly good session," Pudge said, puffing on his pipe to get it going as they watched Billy Ray disappear inside the RV. "But that new kid, Freddie, is still a little too stiff and moody. Didn't Billy Ray 'talk' to him?"

"Didn't you notice? His little butt's still bruised from the strap. Maybe some take a little longer to mellow out." Lighting a menthol cigarette, she watched the three kids, who were beginning to dress slowly. "At least those big amber pills seem to keep them calmer than the blue ones. Did you mention the possibility of a snuff to Billy Ray yet?"

"I asked what he thought." Pudge had struck another match and was sucking fresh fire into his pipe.

"And—?"

Peter Judge smiled. "He said, 'Sure, why not?' Just like that. He wants to snuff Freddie."

"When?"

"Now." Pudge shook out the match.

"Now—? We can't just—"

"I know, I told him, it's got to be carefully planned, and we've got to get feelers out for a buyer. But soon. He wants to do it soon."

They had been filming in the seclusion of a ravine on the far side of the still nearly empty campground, but even that was too risky. They needed complete privacy—especially for a snuff. "I think those aging hippies are getting curious," Pudge said. "One of them approached me at the water pump yesterday, bummed some tobacco, and tried to strike up a conversation. And that young couple just arrived this morning in their camper. We'd better move out now, before it gets crowded and someone talks to the kids."

"But where can we do a snuff?" Carmen ground out her menthol under her boot heel. "Where can we find a place that's really private?" Her head still throbbed and she wondered if she'd gotten too much sun.

"That Malaguena Ranch would have been perfect," Pudge said, "without the watchman. But we'll find someplace like it, somewhere completely isolated." He pulled a roadmap from his back pocket and spread it on a boulder, still keeping his eye on the kids while he talked. "I even found a possibility this morning. See this string of old mining towns? Harshaw, Duquesne, Washington Camp—all mostly deserted, but still partially occupied or visited frequently by tourists, so they won't do. But there's one I've heard about—it's not even on the map—called Perlyville. Only a couple of miles from the Mex border, about here." He put a nicotine-stained finger on the spot. "Not even much in the way of roads down there anymore, but we can make it. And there's old rusted machinery and tumbledown shacks we can frame scenes around. And when we're done we can dump the body down one of the old mine shafts."

Carmen Jones rested a heavy hand gently on the inside of Peter Judge's thigh and squeezed. "It's exciting, Pudge, but scary, isn't it? And I'm still not sure we can control Billy Ray like we should. He's good at managing the kids, but he's really dangerous, isn't he? The way he fools around with his guns, always cleaning and oiling them and taking them apart. I don't like guns, Pudge, and when he practices firing, it really frightens me."

Pudge put a comforting arm around her shoulder. "Isn't that really part of the excitement, my dear? The danger? It's what's going to make the snuff film such a winner. Look." He knocked out his pipe on the limb of a tree. "Why don't we go ahead and finish this one this morning, then move on down to Perlyville? I'll mark the directions for Billy Ray, and we'll let him get on his bike and put the word out about a snuff to see who might be interested. Then he can meet us there. We can tow his van behind the RV."

"All right, Pudge." She watched him fold away the map, then call to the kids, "Okay, get outta your clothes again, kiddies! We're gonna shoot one more session before lunch!" Then he turned toward the motor home. "Billy Ray!" He had to call three times before Billy Ray stuck his head out the open door. "Get the chains outta the van, boy! We'll go ahead and do the bondage scene and wrap this one up while Carmen fixes some sandwiches! I'll take the kids over there by those rocks and cactus, and afterward we'll let you go scouting for a buyer of that snuff!"

Billy Ray Lee had grudgingly turned down the volume on his radio so he could hear Pudge. It was his favorite group, Iron Maiden. He hated being ordered around so much anyway. Like the old fart was his father or something. And Carmen sure as hell wasn't his mother. But they had been acting more and more like parents the past few months.

He barely remembered his real father, a drunken, violent, emasculating zealot who disappeared when Billy Ray was seven or eight. His mother hadn't been much different, only weaker, and he could fight back. Until the succession of boyfriends who had finally driven him off on his own at thirteen. He'd been making his own way ever since.

But making kiddie porn sure beat cooking for a living, which was the only thing he seemed to have any talent for, other than hustling kids. And he remembered his resentment of the greasy hash houses where he'd gotten back at shouting, domineering bosses with little things, like spitting in the soup when no one was looking—just hawking up a big goober and stirring it in while smiling secretly, getting back at people and feeling good. Billy Ray Lee hated people, and animals too. In fact, he found he hated most things, including himself.

He'd joined up with Pudge and Carmen only because they had the know-how and equipment for making the kiddie porn that brought in such big bucks, bucks that had bought him the van almost as soon as he'd met them. Even this—and he hefted the weapon he'd bought from a mail order catalogue while they summered in the woods near Santa Fe. A semiautomatic 9mm carbine, it lacked only a minor alteration to make it fully automatic again, and he'd picked up the conversion kit at a swap meet in Albuquerque.

He'd never had much experience with guns—had even been turned down by the fucking army—and he hadn't practiced a lot with this one. But he didn't feel he needed much, because once it was converted to fully automatic, he knew it would spray a lot of lead very fast, and in any direction he pointed it.

"Billy Ray!" Pudge called again. "C'mon!"

"Coming, motherfucker," he muttered. "Don't get a tight asshole." And he laid the weapon carefully aside for now. They treated him like a kid himself, he thought—especially that creep Carmen. And it was him that handled the kids, seduced them in the first place and kept them docile and easy to handle. Well, he knew it wouldn't be long before he cut loose on his own again. Just take his guns and the van and the kids and go. He'd taken their shit for two years. All he was waiting for now was to do the snuff. That would mean not only excitement but the biggest bucks of all. Even the thought of it set him tingling, and he wondered why it hadn't occurred to them before. He was already planning how he wanted to do it. Slow—it would have to be slow.

He'd worried a while about the last kill. It was careless leaving it in the dump with the trash like that. A mistake. Yet how could they ever trace it to him? No way. It was a nothing kid, and he'd done it twice before and escaped detection. Still, this time, he'd be more careful. He'd finish the snuff and then, surprise—maybe he'd just waste Pudge and Carmen, too, before he split, depending on how he felt at the time.

Because feelings were important to Billy Ray. He had strong feelings about everything, but especially about killing. And he'd killed a lot of stray animals—cats, dogs, even a stupid cow once. He even remembered his first kill, when he was only four or five years old. It was only a cat, not a human, but he still remembered the thrill of drowning it in a bird cage, dipping the cage into the old cistern and raising it to watch the cat going crazy with fear, and each time holding it under a little longer, until finally the terrorized, squalling, clawing cat was reduced to a lump of soggy, silent fur in the bottom of the cage, lifeless.

The pleasure of its dying had been like waves of limpid warmth washing over him. And now, when the feelings got too strong, when his control slipped away and he killed a kid, the sheer joy of the experience was indescribable. And he trembled with the knowledge it would soon happen again—this time deliberately.

FIFTEEN

"That's him—you got him right there." The grocer at the Pontatoc General Store slapped his hand with certainty on the mug shot of Billy Ray Lee that was mixed in with four other mugs of youths, all with long blond hair, all laid out side by side on the counter.

Tom Ragnon nodded, gathering up the pictures. "Okay. And he was riding a blue-and-white dirt bike. But you're sure you never saw any of these? Look again." And he moved over to the mixed mug shots of balding middle-aged men, Peter Judge among them. "Try picturing them now with a hairpiece."

"Nope." The grocer shook his head insistently. "Never saw any of these guys."

It had been the same with the others around town—repeated trips to the hotel and café, the bars and curio shop and bank—even the little real estate office that sold forty-acre plots of subdivided ranchland.

Now at the store, Ragnon looked over at John Antone, who was busy trying to choose a candy bar. "Back to square-one time, John. The watchman picks out Pudge but can't ID Billy Ray, and it's just the reverse with Cal here.

So we still can't put the two of them together. And no kids seen by anybody."

The grocer was shaking his head sadly. "Sorry, Sergeant. Wish I could've been more help. But at least you got them two."

"We've got pictures is what we've got," Ragnon said. "We've got no idea where they might be."

"There's so many of them big RVs rollin' around this part of the country, Sergeant," the grocer said, taking Antone's money and ringing it up on the old cash register. "And most of 'em with middle-aged couples."

"But hopefully not many traveling with a bike and convertible and maybe a van."

Antone was looking at his watch. It was nearly 10:45. "What time did you say the gas station opens?"

"Whenever old man Johnson feels like opening it." Calvin Riggs was tamping down the tobacco in an old briar. "Sometimes he'll open on Sundays or holidays and close in the middle of the week." He struck a kitchen match. "Wife died last year, and he gets a sudden surge of fishin' fever and just takes off for the lakes in the high country. Sometimes he has a young guy working for him—"

"I remember him," Ragnon said. "Joe Ramos. But I don't think I ever saw Johnson the whole time I was stationed down here."

"Even Ramos ain't that reliable. Locals know to keep their tanks topped off, and maybe an extra five-gallon can around."

As Antone pulled the Jeep Cherokee in under the overhang beside the pumps, they found the station still locked up tight, though the OPEN sign in the window had never been turned. The station had been their first stop, and was now their last—a long shot at best, but it had to be covered. The grocer had given them directions to Johnson's home, and to Ramos's. But as they sat there a moment in the shade, Ragnon wondered if that was going to be a waste of time too.

"Crown says these pornographers always make their deals in cash and with no contracts, so there's nothing on paper," Ragnon mused aloud. "And they move around a lot out of necessity, but usually only short distances. Except that around here there *are* no short distances."

"Where do they film these things in the city, Sergeant?"

"Motel rooms, old warehouses, abandoned buildings. Why?"

"Then if they film out here in the country they still have to have privacy, right? Out-of-the-way places—"

A battered Chevrolet pickup with an over-the-cab camper had pulled up alongside the station behind them, and a white-haired old man got out and went to a side door. "Johnson?" Ragnon wondered aloud, interrupting his partner.

"Or a reasonable facsimile."

The old man came out the front door of the station, unlocked and swung up the double doors to the grease racks, and then, wiping his hands on a rag, ambled over to the gas pumps and began unlocking them while he squinted at his visitors. "You boys ain't from around here. Where's Deputy Montoya?"

"Over at the station house," Ragnon answered. "We're just passing through. You Mr. Johnson?"

"That's right." He cocked his head to eye Ragnon's shield and ID as it was held close to his nose. "I heard about the trouble, but I never seen no people like the ones you're a-lookin' for. On the other hand, lots of people like that come through here on their way to one place or the other."

"Take a look at these anyway, will you, Mr. Johnson?" Ragnon held out the two mug shots of Pudge and Billy Ray.

"Naw, never seen either one." He glanced up. "Why don't you ask him?" And he pointed to the young man who had just ridden up on a bicycle and was parking it against the station wall.

As the youth walked curiously over to the Cherokee, Johnson said, "Joe Ramos, my neighbor's boy. Helps me out sometimes. Joe, take a peek at these. You ever see these guys around here?"

Joe Ramos nodded at Ragnon, then took the pictures one at a time and studied them each for several moments before handing them back. "Sure. Two—three days ago," he said. "They stopped to gas up. I was by myself and it took a lot to fill three vehicles."

Ragnon almost held his breath as he glanced at Antone and asked Joe Ramos, "What kind of vehicles?"

"A big motor home, a little blue convertible, and a dark green van."

"Jesus Christ." Ragnon reached for his Red Man. "Two or three days ago. They're still around, John!"

"And you're sure it was these two?" Antone asked.

Joe Ramos looked again. "Yeah, it was them. Only reason I remember is the old guy was dressed like a drugstore cowboy, and the young guy was all muscles. A mean-looking dude—had spooky, sleepy-looking eyes.

"You didn't happen to notice the plates on the vehicles?"

Joe Ramos shook his head. "No reason to."

"And who was driving what?" Ragnon asked carefully. "You said three vehicles."

"The old guy was herding the motor home and the young guy the van."

"And I'll bet a woman was driving the convertible," Ragnon said.

"How'd you know that?" Then his expression changed. "Only I'm not sure she was a woman."

"What do you mean, not a woman?"

"I don't know—seemed too mannish-like, you know? Husky voice, hard-looking—and ugly, man."

Ragnon had taken out his notebook and was scribbling fast. "What else do you remember about them, Joe?" he asked.

"Nothing much. Never talked much, any of them. Old guy paid in cash. Young guy took the kids to the toilet."

"Kids—?" It was getting better all the time. "How many kids?"

"Two—no, three. Little kids. Young guy got 'em out of the van and took 'em into the men's toilet."

"Boys or girls?"

"I dunno, man. Two girls and a boy, I think."

"How did the kids act? Did they say anything? Did they act happy? Scared? Confused?"

"Shit, man, I don't know. I was filling their tanks. The young guy just hustled them into the john and then back in the van. They wasn't crying or nothing."

"You're doing fine, Joe," Ragnon said. "Now tell us more about the woman who looked like a man."

"She was just strong-looking—tough-looking. Wore a dress and had long hair but didn't look like a regular woman. Like she almost needed a shave. She only got out of the car once, and went into the motor home, and then back to the car."

"You said she had a husky voice. What did she say?" Antone asked.

"I don't remember, man. I finished gassing them up and the old guy paid in big bills. I was afraid they were gonna be counterfeit." He looked over at Johnson. "You remember the two big bills?"

"Yeah. Fifties, I remember that. When I came back I took 'em over to the bank next morning, but they was okay."

They went over the story with Joe Ramos twice more, until they felt sure they had everything. Then, just as they were about to leave, Joe said, "There is one more thing that might be important, Sergeant."

"What's that?" Ragnon asked.

"They had a state map, and the young guy asked directions to the old Apache stronghold in the Dragoons." He pointed toward the distant range of mountains far across the miles-wide desert valley to the northeast.

The only stop they made was at the sheriff's substation to make a call. "I could give you some help," Montoya said, "but the other two deputies are both on an accident run—a three-car pileup on the turnoff from the freeway."

"It's okay, we'll handle it," Ragnon said, picking up the phone and dialing headquarters in the city. "Put me through to the chief. It's me, Ragnon. Chief? We found a witness who can place all three of them together, along with their vehicles and three kids. And a lead as to where they went from here—Cochise's old stronghold in the Dragoon Mountains. We're heading there now."

"Better take some backup, Rags," said Poole, "a couple of deputies anyway."

"They're out on an accident, Chief, and we can't wait. It's a good forty miles across the valley, and it was two or three days ago. Send Crown down to take a statement from the witness—kid named Joe Ramos at the gas station. Then she can wait for us at the hotel."

"I haven't seen her, Rags. Haven't even heard from her."

"I suppose she's with McKittrick?"

"Who knows?" Poole's voice was full of wise-ass sarcasm. "She's *your* partner, Rags. You're supposed to keep track of her."

"Terrific. Okay, we'll get the statement later. And Chief, one more thing. Run the info on the third suspect, the woman, through the sex-crime computer again. Only change one thing: her gender. She may be a he."

"Christ—a transvestite?"

"You guessed it. See you."

"We couldn't be that lucky," Tom Ragnon said.

"How's that?" Antone answered. Behind them a thick cloud of reddish dust boiled out on both sides of the speeding Cherokee as the dirt road took them closer and closer to the ragged peaks that seemed to float under the cloud shadows riding on the heat haze.

"Lucky in that they'll still be there—all three of them. And the kids."

As the road wound around and into the foothills and began to climb, a dry wash appeared alongside, a wash that could turn in minutes to a raging torrent of flash-flood waters with only a small concentration of rain high up in the peaks. "We don't want the lights and siren, do we, Sergeant?" Antone asked, shifting to a lower gear as the canyon road narrowed and grew increasingly steeper.

"No, John, we're not coming on like Rambo. Maybe they'll think at first we're just a couple of smoky-bear rangers—at least until they recognize the sheriff's star on the door." But as they pulled into the campground they found it disappointingly empty—or nearly so.

They passed an old homemade camper rig and several aging hippie types who waved but still watched them suspiciously as Antone downshifted again and drove slower, deeper, into the campground, and finally pulled in among some trees. He braked at the sight of a second vehicle, parked almost out of sight under a big juniper—a Winnebago motor home. Ragnon even reached behind him to be sure his gun was handy. Then a young couple and two children came around from the rear and walked up to them.

"We're looking for some people in a Winnebago," Ragnon told them. "Probably have a van and convertible with them too. Have you seen them?"

The man shook his head. "Haven't seen anybody like that. Nobody at all really except those guys in that old camper rig back there. But we just got here an hour ago—looked nice and deserted, the way we like it. Is that Apache chief really buried somewhere around here?"

"In at least four different places around here," John Antone said, smiling. "All the locals will swear to it."

They drove on over to the well, and while Ragnon held the cloth-sided canteen they carried slung in the back of the Cherokee, Antone worked the iron handle to bring up the rush of cold spring water.

"We'll take a look around anyway," Ragnon said, taking a long drink and handing the canteen to the Indian. "Then on our way out we'll see if the hippies saw anything." His disappointment was strong but not unexpected. And it was mainly disappointment with himself, that it had taken them a week to track them here.

"Looks like you can ask the hippies now," Antone said, pointing to a middle-aged man with half a dozen canteens dangling about his shoulders as he approached them under the trees. Long-haired and bearded, he wore a leather headband, a shell necklace, and knee-high fringed moccasins. He also wore a smile that revealed white, even teeth. His gentle blue eyes were smiling too. "You minions of the law wouldn't mind sharing some of that water, would you? We're heading out today, so you don't have to worry about us overstaying our welcome."

"Help yourself," Ragnon said. "The water and air are still free. It's the campsites they charge for these days."

"I guess nothing lasts forever," the man said, unslinging the canteens. He held one up to the pump's iron muzzle and began jacking the handle noisily.

"You been camped here long?" John Antone asked him.

"Little over a week. But we can't pay, if that's what you're getting at."

"We're not the ones charging," Ragnon said. "Looks like you've had the place pretty much to yourselves anyway."

"Winter crowds will be arriving soon," the man said, setting aside one canteen and placing another under the flow as he continued to pump the handle. "It's starting to cool off. That couple in the Winnie just pulled in, but another older couple stayed only one night. Still too warm for them."

"That's it?" Ragnon asked cautiously. "Nobody else in a week?"

"Only another big Winnie that was here two or three nights. Stayed off to themselves—young guy and a pair of mid-lifers."

Ragnon's pulse quickened. "Just a Winnebago—that's all they had?"

"Hell, no, they had it all. Bike racked on back of the Winnie, a big green van, and a convertible, if you can believe that, a Chrysler LeBaron."

"We can believe it. Any kids?"

"Yep. Three little ones." He held another canteen under the flow. "But they didn't really seem to fit somehow."

"What do you mean?"

"Don't know exactly." The man tilted back one of the canteens and took a long drink while Ragnon watched impatiently as water dribbled down the edges of his beard. "Never saw any of 'em up close except the older guy. Just strange somehow." He wiped his mouth. "I tried to strike up some talk with him here at the pump, but he wasn't real friendly, you know?"

Ragnon showed him the mug shot of Pudge. "That him?"

"Hey, that's him—old Ben Franklin!"

"When did they leave?"

The man glanced at the sun. "I don't know. I'd say a good hour or so ago—just before noon."

Jesus, Ragnon thought, glancing at Antone. They had missed them by a goddamned hour? But even on dirt roads they could be forty miles away by now. More if they simply returned to the highway. "Where'd they camp?" he asked.

"Right over in there—by them boulders."

The two detectives forced themselves to search the campsite slowly, methodically—even turning over the trash barrel and spreading out the contents, but finding nothing incriminating or even significant. Even the tire tracks were too crisscrossed and messed up to be of any help.

An hour later they drove down out of the canyon, waving to the hippies as they passed. As they cleared the outer slopes of the foothills, with the desert floor spread out in front of them in another miles-wide valley and the mountains ranged against their backs, Ragnon had Antone stop the Jeep and he got out. "See if you can raise Pontatoc from here, John," he said. While the Indian put the radio mike to his lips, Ragnon lifted the binoculars and gazed out across the empty landscape. There wasn't even a dust cloud rising in the distance. "They're out there somewhere," he murmured to himself. "God, we were close!"

"Got 'em, Sergeant!" Antone called from inside the Cherokee. "Deputy Montoya!"

"Have him get out a fresh APB and see if we can have a flyover. And have him tell the chief to notify the sheriff's offices in both Santa Cruz and Cochise counties—see if they'll have their deputies check all the border campgrounds in this part of the state."

Half an hour later they were twenty miles out in the valley, with the sun still high and the desert stark and empty beneath it, when a single-engine Piper Cub swept low over them wagging its wings. Antone stopped the Jeep and made contact on the radio, while Ragnon got out and swept the desert with his binoculars again. But the response was negative. "No sign of anything like our three, Sergeant," he reported. "But they're going to sweep south again along the border."

"Damn!" Ragnon cursed his mistake. "We should have requested that flyover before we left Pontatoc."

"Hindsight, Sergeant," Antone said as Ragnon climbed back into the Jeep. "They were two or three days ahead of us, then. Now they're only two hours. We're closing."

Tom Ragnon smiled. "My partner, the eternal optimist." He shook his head. "Maybe if we hadn't wasted time searching the goddamned camp . . ." But that was behind them now and the hunt was still ahead. But which way? He sat a moment, feeling the breeze through the open Jeep window against his face. It was the first day of

October, the violent thunderstorms of summer over, the more infrequent rains of a desert winter yet to come. The nights and early mornings were already chilly, yet the heat of afternoon seemed to be lingering longer this year. He gazed the thirty-odd miles across this valley to the Chiricahua mountain wilderness beyond, then south toward more barbed hills and low ranges trailing into Mexico, the whole land once dominated by roving Apache bands.

Now dopers and illegals and gun-runners came and went with near impunity. And pedophiles too, he supposed. In many ways the wide-open border country was seemingly unchanged by a hundred civilizing years of modern human intrusion. They could be anywhere out there now. An RV, a convertible, and a van. If they kept to the back roads . . . He looked at the Indian, who was gazing silently across the vastness himself. "Visions, John?" he asked.

"Gas stations," John Antone said quietly.

"What—?"

"Even with oversize fuel tanks, Sergeant, they'll have to gas those machines again eventually. I told Montoya to have the deputies alert the gas stations all across the southern border."

"Very good, John. I'd forgotten about that." He wondered what else he'd missed today. He couldn't help the sudden, overwhelming sense of helplessness. It was a big country, and they had come so close. Now the bastards were gone, like Apache raiders of the past, vanished in the dust and shadows as if into another realm.

It made his jaws ache just thinking about it.

SIXTEEN

Lucinda Ann Crown was curled up on the couch in her apartment, her shoes kicked off and her feet tucked comfortably under her. Sipping a piña colada she had mixed herself, she tried to empty her mind and simply absorb the sounds of "Hey Jude," which was playing softly on the stereo, not quite drowning out the rhythmic bonging of the noon hour by her glass-covered pendulum clock.

It had been a long day already and it was only half over, but she had stopped by the apartment just for a breather. She was wondering how Ragnon and Antone were doing verifying the mug shots down in Pontatoc, when the phone rang, its harshness obliterating both the song and the clock.

It was McKittrick. "Luce—how'd you do?"

"Hello, Jack. I'm not sure. Something. Not much at the news morgue. Hannigan was mentioned in an article about child abuse on a Little League ball club. Not accused, though. And his wife didn't know anything to add. The boy did have something new—it seems to keep coming out a little more each time—not about the ball club but about his father's sexual abuse of himself and the victim. He claims the general had a secret room at the Sedona residence that was like a shrine. Says it was in the basement behind the workshop bench. The mother knew nothing about it, so no corroboration. Any luck on the day care thing?"

"Not enough to reopen it. He did spend an unusual amount of time there, causing suspicions, rumors, even accusations. But some of the older kids were found to be lying, so the whole thing was dropped. But your mention of a shrine at Sedona is *beaucoup* interesting, Luce. I had someone mention that, too, on tape."

"What—?" Crown put her feet on the floor and leaned forward. "What do you mean?"

"Where're your partners—off chasing rainbows?"

"In Pontatoc, verifying the mug shots and looking for leads. Now, what about the shrine? Someone else knows about it?"

"Nothing to do with your case. She didn't kill the kid."

"She? Jack, who else saw a shrine in Hannigan's basement?"

"Believe it or not, a whore."

"A whore? I don't believe it." She reached for her cigarillos and slim pencil lighter.

"Described it just like your witness—"

"But how is that possible?"

"One of my people showed your victim's Child Find picture around. The whore recognized him."

"She'd seen him?"

"Not him—a picture of him. Seems she went with some others to a stag party a while back. No names, but military types in a fancy house near Sedona, all flagstone and glass. Belonged to this newly made general. No wives attending, just the party girls. But it seems the general didn't want to play himself. Listen, I'll put the tape on. The whore's name is Jasmine."

"—up north near Flagstaff. I forget the name of the place." The girl had a twangy Midwest accent. "Funny name, lots of red-rock canyons around it."

"Sedona?" McKittrick's voice suggested.

"Sure, that's it. Big house, all glass and fancy rock, and this wild party. All military big shots, but no uniforms. Everybody was in civvies—then skivvies, of course." She giggled.

"I'll get to the good part," McKittrick cut in, running the tape forward.

"—I came on to this older guy," the girl's voice continued. "He was pretty sloshed—somebody said he was the general—but he wanted no part of it. Just wanted to take me downstairs, show me 'his real treasures,' he called them. There was this room that opened up behind a workbench in the basement. I've seen weird, but this guy was the pits. The place was full of pictures of naked kids—*little* kids, mostly boys, but some girls, too, all grouped on the walls around a kind of shrine—"

"She says she almost puked." McKittrick had shut off the tape. "The general took her back upstairs, but he never did screw her. And she picked Hannigan out of a group Air Force picture I rounded up. Swears he's the one. Shall we get a search warrant, then go on up to Sedona and tickle your general a little, see what makes him tick?"

"A search warrant on a whore's testimony?"

"That combined with the other kid's story—the victim's brother, and the old day care case. Plus Ragnon and the Indian spotting a strange kid on the premises—all that should do it, Luce. Besides, I know a judge owes me. How about it?"

"God. Sedona. It's a four-hour drive."

"Relax, I can get us on a department chopper heading

for Flagstaff in an hour. And they'll pick us up on the way back."

She stared a moment at the rainbow prism of light reflected through the crystal dolphin on her window ledge. Its back was arched forever in a suspended leap and its shining clarity of form was somehow soothing, something right with the world. She sighed.

"Luce—?" McKittrick's voice on the phone. "How about it?"

"Okay, Jack. I'll shower and change and meet you in an hour."

"That's my girl. I'll call ahead to the Coconino sheriff's office and arrange to meet a deputy to serve the warrant."

* * *

"You people all that sure about what you've got?" Deputy Donald Coburn was skeptical as he turned the Coconino county sheriff's car off the highway onto the road leading to Hannigan's. "General's been coming up here for years—even after his divorce. I can't really believe this."

"Stop before we get to the house," McKittrick told him. "Somewhere we can walk in and get a look-see with your binoculars."

A couple of minutes later the deputy pulled off the road and parked among some trees. Taking his field glasses from the case, he led the way up into some rocks overlooking the huge stone-and-glass home. He handed the binoculars to McKittrick and pointed. "That's Hannigan's. That's his station wagon in the carport."

"Looks like we're just in time," McKittrick said. "He's packing to leave." He handed the glasses to Crown, who watched the general loading boxes and suitcases into the back of the wagon.

"No sign of a child." She handed the binoculars back

to the deputy. "Or anyone else. Just the dog Ragnon mentioned." The big Doberman was confined in a cage.

"Let's go," McKittrick said, and led the way back to the deputy's car.

When they pulled up to the open gate, the deputy blocked the exit with his car and they all got out. The dog was barking ferociously now and clawing at the cage. Hannigan, emerging with two garment bags held by the hangers, seemed surprised but not unpleasantly so. He quieted the dog with a sharp whistle.

"Hello, Donald," he greeted the deputy, nodding at the other two. "What's going on?"

Coburn introduced McKittrick and Crown as detectives from another jurisdiction. "It's the investigation into the death of your son."

"That's odd." Hannigan proceeded to hang the garment bags on a rack in the back of his station wagon. "Two detectives were here just yesterday. I told them what I knew."

"We've got a search warrant, General," McKittrick said, watching for his reaction as the deputy handed it to Hannigan a little sheepishly.

"A search—" He looked up at McKittrick, and from him to Crown and then to Coburn. "What's this all about, Donald? I didn't have anything to do with my son's death."

"It's not exactly about his death, General. It's something else. Sorry, but the warrant's good."

As Hannigan read it his face blanched and then reddened. He stared at McKittrick and Crown. "This is outrageous—you're both insane. But go ahead—look. I'll wait on the porch."

"We'd like you to accompany us, General," Crown said.

They followed Hannigan through the main parts of his

home almost casually, disturbing nothing, saying nothing. Then McKittrick paused at a door off the kitchen. "Where does this lead?"

"The basement," Hannigan answered curtly.

"And what's down there?"

"Nothing. The usual: a furnace, storage, a workshop, and a darkroom. I develop some of my own pictures as a hobby. Take a look if you like." But his tone had tightened, as if the words almost stuck in his throat. "There's some people who are going to hear about this—"

"I'm sure there are, General." McKittrick opened the door, switched on the light, and descended the stairs, followed by Hannigan, Crown, and the deputy.

It looked like an ordinary basement, with a curtained-off corner that served as a darkroom. Crown drew back the curtain, but the place was clean. No strings of film drying, no negatives, no finished prints lying around. The workshop was a table and bench joined, with a rack of tools jutting up from its back, and it was flush against an inside wall. "You see?" Hannigan said softly. "Nothing."

Jack McKittrick walked to one end of the worktable and hefted it, testing its movability and weight. Then he stared straight into Hannigan's horrified eyes as he lifted and moved it slowly outward, opening a section of the wall behind it.

McKittrick could hardly believe it himself as he reached in and felt for the light switch, illuminating the windowless chamber in a soft fluorescent glow. He had almost begun to doubt the validity of both informants, but here it was. He looked around at Hannigan, whose face was ashen, whose stature seemed to shrink and shrivel even as he stood there. "This your hobby too, General?" the Vice cop cracked viciously. "Your little sandbox? Your playpen?"

Crown had stepped behind the table now and was peering into the room as McKittrick turned to the deputy. "We found what we're looking for. If the son of a bitch moves, shoot him."

Coburn looked with bewilderment at Hannigan, who had sunk into a straight chair beside the workbench, his head in his hands.

Inside the room the fluorescent tubes shone on a cloth-covered table set with unlit red candles that was uncomfortably like an altar. But it was the dozens of photos displayed on three walls around it that really caught their eyes—in both black-and-white and full color—large individual blowups and small group shots—and all of children. Some looked as young as five and six, none more than nine or ten. All were naked and in sexually explicit poses.

Crown was already at the cloth-covered table, opening albums with pictures of more naked children, and dragging things out from shelves beneath it: books and pamphlets with titles like *Show Me* and *How to Have Sex with Kids*. She looked at McKittrick. "Underground publications," she said. "And look at these." She handed him two pamphlets, one titled *Where the Young Ones Are* with lists of 7-Elevens, Circle Ks, and video arcades in both Phoenix and Tucson that were good hunting grounds for vulnerable youngsters.

McKittrick tossed the pamphlets down and looked again at one of the pictures on the wall. "Isn't that your victim, Crown?" he asked, pointing at the full frontal view. "His own kid?"

Crown stared. Both Hannigan boys were in the picture, naked. She looked more closely at some of the other photos now, and found two more of Christopher, the victim. In one he was alone; in the other he was postured with a little girl who looked about six or seven also.

McKittrick, checking the lower shelves under the cloth that hung from the table, pulled out more things, including a scrapbook of clippings showing kids in their underwear. "Christ. Looks like sections from a Sears catalogue." And there were real catalogues, too, of available X-rated videotapes of children engaged in sex, and a mailing list of other collectors from all over the U.S. McKittrick held it up. "Wait till the postal inspector gets his hooks into this."

They stepped back into the basement workshop and McKittrick nodded to the deputy. "Take a look in there if you like. Get educated. See what turns a creep like this on."

As the deputy ducked into the hidden room, McKittrick and Crown stood looking at Hannigan, who was shaking his head and wringing his hands. "You're quite a collector, General," the Vice cop said. "A real prick of a chicken hawk. I'd've never believed it."

"They're only pictures," Hannigan whispered so low they weren't sure they heard him.

"What?" McKittrick asked.

"I said, they're only pictures." His voice was a little louder, but cracking. "I would never do anything to hurt a child." His head was down, his eyes on the floor as he clenched and unclenched his hands. "Especially my own. I—love children."

"You what?" McKittrick snapped. "You *love* children? You sure as hell do, you bastard. And I suppose this crap isn't hurting them? At least mentally and emotionally if not physically? You are one sick son of a bitch, General." And he began reciting the Miranda warning.

"I understand," Hannigan said as McKittrick finished,

and for a moment they thought he wasn't going to say any more. He looked up at them both, and then over at Deputy Coburn, who had returned to the open doorway of the room and was staring at the general in disbelief. "I think I know who killed my son," Hannigan said quietly.

McKittrick and Crown exchanged glances, and the Vice cop started to speak, but Crown gripped his arm for silence as Hannigan went on. "I told the other two detectives that the last time I saw Christopher was in Aspen, Colorado, two summers ago at an opera festival. I told them we'd argued and he'd run off, and that we found out later he'd gotten into a green van that same night and disappeared. And that was all true. But that's *all* I told them. I couldn't talk about any more of it because of my own involvement."

"But you want to talk about it now," Crown said softly.

Hannigan nodded. "I'd met another collector earlier that day while with my sons in a park. He was driving the green van. We exchanged pictures, catalogues, things like that."

"Describe him," Crown said.

"Young guy, muscular, long blond hair and a frazzled mustache. He was wearing a fishnet undershirt, and I could see some kind of small tattoo through it, on his chest. He was interested in my younger son—in Christopher. I could tell, being like him myself. An older man was with him, but he stayed in the van."

"This look like the young guy?" McKittrick stuck the mug shot of Billy Ray under the general's nose.

"Yes, that's him. I remember the hooded eyes."

"Was there a woman too?" Crown asked.

"A woman? No, no woman. Just those two. I bought some still photos and they left. Three weeks later, when the police told me they'd found a boy who saw Christopher getting into a green van that same night of the festival, I knew."

"Jesus Christ," McKittrick muttered. "And you didn't *say* anything?"

"I couldn't. God, don't you understand? I couldn't get *involved*, not with the police. If I'd even said I remembered seeing two such men and their van in the park, they would have questioned me. I might inadvertently have—" He choked up. "I didn't know they'd keep him—kill him." He looked from McKittrick to Crown, his voice pleadingly pitiful, no longer a general, no longer a man. "I thought they just wanted to—use him and let him go—like me."

"But, General," Crown almost whispered. "They *did* keep him. They probably had him the whole two years!"

"You're a goddamned piece of shit, Hannigan!" McKittrick suddenly exploded, and kicked the chair leg from under him, tumbling the general to the floor.

"Jack!" Crown yelled, and helped Hannigan to his feet. "There was a boy here yesterday, General," she said softly, soothingly. "The other detectives saw him. You called him Jeff. Was he a local boy? We'll need to talk to him now."

"A neighbor boy," Hannigan muttered, standing now. "From town. I never harmed him. I never harmed any of them."

"Of course not, you bastard!" McKittrick growled. "You just used them!"

"I don't want to say any more," Hannigan whispered hoarsely, talking to Crown. "I just want to call my lawyer."

SEVENTEEN

"Now—I think I got this all straight when you called last night," Ragnon said, "but let me run it by you again. Hannigan is a secret pedophile himself and had pictures of his own kids, including the victim, in this basement room. And you're saying he actually talked to Billy Ray on the day his son disappeared in Aspen and never reported it?"

"Described him right down to the tattoo on his chest," Crown answered, sipping her chilled wine cooler. "Though he couldn't quite make out the design through a net shirt. But he ID'd the mug shot."

"The sorry son of a bitch," Ragnon murmured.

"That's what Jack called him to his face. He also kicked a chair out from under him. Other than that, Jack showed remarkable control."

"I'll bet." They were both sitting on the couch in Ragnon's trailer in Pontatoc. The fading daylight through the windows was the only illumination, and the detective was nursing a beer and watching the shadows creep across the Remington and Russell western prints that were the only

155

adornment on his walls. Crown had eased off her shoes and stretched out her stocking feet on the coffee table.

"We missed the chopper flight back and had to rent a car," she said wearily. "Then I spent most of today at headquarters. He's charged with five counts of child molestation. If we're lucky, he'll plead guilty or no contest to one or two and they'll drop the others."

Ragnon's eyes had left the western prints. Crown was wearing a dress now, and he saw she had great legs. "The charges should stick," he said, "and there's mandatory sentencing now."

Crown nodded. "Jack and I found the neighbor boy you saw. He corroborated everything, but his mother is still in shock, so we don't know if there'll be a witness there or not. Hannigan's also got a high-priced lawyer."

"Jesus. Hannigan still could have killed the kid himself, or had it done."

"No. I checked that, too, this morning. He was on an inspection tour with three other officers all that week, just before he went on leave. And I don't think he had Billy Ray kill him. You had to see his face, hear him tell it. We had him cold turkey. He was telling the truth."

"But I don't understand these guys. Why?"

"It's a thing with true pedophiles, Ragnon. They evidently can't help being the way they are, feeling the way they do, like gays. Only they're attracted to children instead of adults. Something in their sexual makeup never grew up, like a glitch in their personality. Instead of a mature sexual relationship, they turn on to children. They may be perfectly normal in every other way." She took a long sip of her wine and set the glass down. "And it's apparently not something that's curable. But they're also not helpless. They evidently can control their actions, most of them, even limiting it to collecting pictures and videos.

But some of them need the real flesh of a child and go after it."

"And some of them have a need to kill."

She nodded. "The ones like this Pudge and Billy Ray have additional aberrations. Billy Ray is probably sociopathic."

It was dusk outside now, and Ragnon switched on a lamp. He offered her a refill on the wine, but she shook her head. "No thanks. You have anything stronger?"

"No, sorry. I can go—"

"Never mind. I shouldn't have any more anyway." She leaned back. "You should have seen the damn pictures," she continued as if mesmerized by the experience at Hannigan's. "Dozens of them, all around this lighted altar that was like a shrine." She suddenly smiled at him sadly. "I'm glad you don't keep anything stronger around, Ragnon. I'm really a much nicer person sober." She reached for her cigarillos. "Where's our partner run off to?"

"Went into the city at noon. Running down a report on our third suspect, who's evidently not a woman."

"Not a woman? A transvestite?"

"Looks like it. The report's from Deaf Smith County, Texas. John's also checking two more reports from sheriff's offices in New Mexico and Colorado on Billy Ray and Pudge."

"Billy Ray's my bet as the killer of Christopher," Crown said. "Either he was through with him, or just tired of him, or maybe just got angry enough to off him. And these types that have done it before tend to do it again." She met his eyes. "He will, Ragnon. He'll kill again. Unless we stop him."

Ragnon was rolling his empty beer bottle slowly between his hands. "And we almost had them in that campground in the Dragoons yesterday. Then even a flyover couldn't spot them. And reports have been coming in all day from deputies checking campgrounds all across the southern border—nothing." He sighed and gave her a thin half smile. "Luckily I thrive on failure. John will be back first thing in the morning and we'll go out again. He figures now they'll stick to the ghost towns and old mining camps, places they could maybe do filming in private, of which there must be only hundreds scattered all along this border."

"And if they cross into Mexico?"

"Don't be a party-pooper, Crown. Think positive." He smiled again. "Like me." Getting up, he slipped a cassette in the stereo, and the strains of Dionne Warwick's "Déjà Vu" filled the trailer.

"Right now," Crown said, "I'd rather not think any more at all. And that's my kind of music. Can we talk about something besides the case? I'm really beat."

"You want me to take you over to the hotel?"

"God, no." She looked around the tiny living area, at the western prints, at the dark shag carpeting, at the shelves of books that were mostly paperbacks, and wondered when he found time to read. He wasn't the neatest housekeeper in the world either, but there was a simplicity and comfort in the trailer that she liked. She even noticed that they both liked dolphins. His was on a shelf by the door, smooth, dark-grained polished wood, arched as if leaping from the sea.

"Your dolphin." She nodded. "I've got one like it, only crystal."

"Great minds," Ragnon said. "That's ironwood, hand carved by the Seri Indians of Mexico. It's authentic. There's a lot of beautiful reproductions around since they became popular. The Mexicans jump on anything that sells and mass-produce it. And they're good at it. Metalwork, wood, leather, polyester serapes now instead of wool, genuine 'antique' guns and swords—the shops in Nogales are full of the stuff.''

They were quiet a moment and then Ragnon tried again. "How about TV? Maybe there's a good whodunit. I love it when they catch the bad guys. Or I've got cassettes . . ."

But Crown was looking down at the couch they were sitting on. "Does this thing make into a bed? If we're going to get an early start tomorrow, I'd just as soon stay here tonight."

My God, Ragnon thought, the sky is falling. "If you like." He tried to sound like Mr. Cool. "It's comfortable enough. So—what'll we talk about?" he asked. "McKittrick?" And he bit his tongue.

"What about McKittrick?" There was a sudden edge in her voice. Was she going to put the sky back up?

Ragnon decided to take the plunge. "How serious are you and McKittrick? How involved?"

She smiled her sharky little smile and sighed. "What you're really asking is are we screwing, right?"

"Well, yes—or words to that effect."

"It's none of your damn business, Ragnon."

"No, I guess not."

"But the answer is yes. Satisfied?"

"I think I'm sorry I asked. But I'm tough." He managed to smile again himself. "I can take it."

She laughed. "You're not tough, Tom Ragnon." She was lighting one of her brown cigarillos. "McKittrick is tough. And he's a good Vice cop, like you're good at homicide. But you're two completely different types. He's viciously ambitious, and dishonest. He'll go as far as it takes to get what or where he wants, do whatever he has to. You'll go only so far and draw the line. Because you've got a fatal flaw, Rags. You're basically a nice guy, an upright citizen, a decent human being. And I'm afraid you'll draw the line too short sometime and find yourself standing on the wrong side of it."

"Thanks for the keen analysis. I think I can skip my shrink this week."

Her smile was sharky again. "Maybe I just had too much of your wine cooler, Tom Ragnon. I'm being too honest myself, too blunt. I apologize. So why don't you just take me to bed now? Maybe some of that nice-guy, human-being stuff will rub off on me." And she ran her fingers lightly along the stubble of his jaw, making him wish he'd shaved as Dionne Warwick launched into "After You."

At that same moment John Antone was standing in darkness at the shrine of the flood children near the village of Gu Achi on the Tohono O'odham reservation. He had been there since sundown, when the whole western sky had settled into a blaze of gold and orange, tinting the underbellies of the boiling white clouds above. In the golden desert stillness, only the wind had stirred the greasewood and palo verde around him as the day gave way to dark and he stood before the heap of conical-shaped stones surrounded by long piles of thorny ocotillo stems, with openings in the four directions.

Behind him, it wasn't far to the road where the Jeep Cherokee was parked. Yet it was centuries away in time, and he knew the mixed emotions of his roots as he placed an offering of tobacco and a bright shiny bullet from his Redhawk on the shrine, and asked I'itoi, Elder Brother, for the Power and the ability to use it well.

He spent most of the night there with the flood children, who were still believed by some to be happy and playing deep underground after their sacrifice. He didn't really know what part of it he believed, or what part of him felt the presence of I'itoi here, but he passed the hours in prayer under the high, bright desert stars, chanting the ceremonial hunting songs to keep awake and stroking the tuft of eagle down he wore on a thong at his throat.

In the darkness before dawn he left, his spirit renewed, and stopped by his great-grandfather's village, where he took down the old Winchester saddle gun from its shelf of honor, borrowing it and a dozen brass cartridges. In the kitchen an old woman sat at a table, kneading flour for fry bread beneath a naked light bulb dangling on a cord. "I'm taking the rifle for a while, Grandmother," John Antone said, his hand stroking the scarred, darkly oiled stock of the heavy lever-action weapon.

"Hunting?"

"Hunting men."

"Bad business," the old woman said.

"Yes, Grandmother, bad business."

Because he had the confidential reports now—from Deaf Smith County in Texas, Pitkin County in Colorado, and Santa Fe County in New Mexico—and he knew the breed of man they hunted—a defiler of life, a killer of children, a conscienceless being who murdered without feeling, without remorse.

Outside, in a dark corner of the ocotillo-fenced yard, he paused where the basket containing an ancient Apache scalp was buried. His great-grandfather had been an enemy slayer and had gained much power. Now he and Ragnon had their enemies, too, enemies as cruel and ruthless as any Apache had ever thought of being. And he prayed again, to whatever gods still ranged this awesome land.

And then he headed for Pontatoc. Not even stopping at his five-acre plot to see his own wife and child, who had returned from the reservation—there was no time. Ragnon was waiting for the reports, and for the hunt to resume. And while he drove he reviewed in his mind the new information on the three they hunted.

From Deaf Smith County sheriff's office in Texas: Carmen Jones, born Herman Henry Spears in Bayonne, N.J. Known to wear women's clothing and frequently pose as a woman. Known to deal in pornographic materials. Known to frequent summer opera festivals in New Mexico and Colorado. No known addresses, but believed to be traveling in company with one Peter Judge, occupation, photographer. Current destination possibly New Mexico or Arizona.

From Pitkin County sheriff's office in Colorado: Peter Judge, nickname Pudge. Ran a day care center 1982-1983. Closed down by county authorities after child abuse accusations. Subject disappeared and no charges filed.

From Santa Fe County sheriff's office in New Mexico: Billy Ray Lee, a.k.a. Billy Lee Ray. Suspected of child endangerment and firearms violations. No charges due to lack of evidence. Psychiatric profile: possible psychotic personality, considered dangerous. Last known address a post office box in Santa Fe, now closed.

EIGHTEEN

Her panty hose lay on the floor, entangled in his shorts. It was the first thing he saw when he awoke, their underclothes entwined and illuminated by a pale band of early morning sunlight that streamed from a crack at the bottom of the window shade. A fly, trapped somehow between the screen and the glass pane, buzzed angrily.

Blinking, he focused on the digital clock beside the hide-a-bed: 6:32. Turning, he felt her warm, firm flesh beside him and remembered. "Crown? You awake?"

"I think you can call me Lucy now, Rags," she whispered, her hand moving around him, her fingers tangling in the hair on his chest. "You're good for what ails me."

But was he as good as McKittrick, he wanted to ask. Wisely he bit his tongue. "It wasn't bad, was it?" he said instead.

"It was terrific—is that the right time?" She had raised herself on one elbow and was looking over his shoulder at the clock.

"If it's not," Ragnon said, yawning and stretching, "it'll do till the right time comes along."

"I'm just glad you came along, Tom Ragnon."

"You mean I'm good for your libido?"

"You're good for me, period, partner. And I don't find a really good relationship that easily, believe me. I think I've been wanting you ever since that first day in Poole's office."

"Yeah, I remember how eager you were," he said sarcastically. "I could hardly keep you off me." But he pulled her close. "Besides, I thought you had a relationship with McKittrick." That name kept slipping in between them.

"I don't know what I had with Jack," Crown said. "Whatever it was, it wasn't all that substantial." She reached over him for her pack of cigarillos and scooted up to a sitting position on the bed. Lighting one with her pencil lighter, she sent a stream of smoke toward the ceiling. "Maybe I should tell you, Rags. I was sexually abused myself as a child."

"Jesus, Lucy, who—your father?"

"An uncle. My parents divorced when I was five or six. I never saw my father again, and lived with my mother in Seattle. And this uncle came to stay a while. I was seven when it started, and almost nine before it finally ended with him moving to Wyoming. I went through it all, the guilt and fear and shame. Typically my mother wouldn't even believe it when I finally got up the guts to tell her. I heard he died the year before I became a cop, but I've always wondered how many other little girls he got to. Anyway"—she mashed out the cigarillo viciously—"good sexual relationships with men have never been easy for me. Not even with my husband."

"What happened to him?"

"Dead—in 'Nam. He was a twenty-three-year-old pilot when he went in over Hanoi in sixty-nine and was shot down. No parachute, no body, no nothing. his plane ex-

KINDERKILL

ploded in midair. His wingman saw it." She looked at him. "Were you in 'Nam, Rags?"

"Not quite. I was in the navy—destroyer escort duty for the carriers, plowing furrows in the South China Sea. Fortunately I never even got shot at."

She smiled. "So you became a cop to increase your chances."

"I became a cop because that's what I always wanted to be." He threw back the sheet that covered them and reached for his clothes. "Now, how about breakfast? I make a great French toast, but that's about the extent of my culinary talents."

"Sorry, I never eat breakfast, but I'll take a cup of coffee, and then I've got to get over to the hotel and shower and change."

"Okay, but you can shower here."

"I need clean clothes, dummy. Unless you've got an assortment of ladies' undies hidden away?"

"That I can't provide." He had moved into the kitchen and put a new filter and fresh water in the coffeemaker. "You take sugar, cream?"

"No. Black, thanks."

With the coffee brewing he opened the bread box. "How about toast or a stale Danish—you can dunk it."

"Just the coffee, Rags." When she was dressed she added, "I've got something to tell you that you're not going to like. It's why I saved it till now."

He paused with the coffee container poised over two white mugs. "You and McKittrick are secretly married?"

"No." She laughed. "Nothing quite so juicy. I'm going undercover on this case."

"You're what?" He splashed coffee over the side of the mug.

"Just shut up and listen. Another of Jack's informants

got word on the street that a kiddie-porn snuff video is to be made in southern Arizona and will be up for bids. So I put the word out under an assumed name that I'm interested, price no object, but with one stipulation: I want to meet the child while he's alive and have sex with him."

"Jesus, Crown, are you nuts? Besides, you're a woman." He handed her a mug of coffee.

"There are female pedophiles too, Ragnon. Not nearly as many as men, but some just as strong for kids. My street contact will put me in touch and vouch for my cover."

"And who vouches for him? He could set you up."

"No, he's on parole now and I've got him in a bind on another charge. It's me in and out safely, or evidence will show up on the Attorney General's desk that will put him away for good. It's a chance I couldn't pass up."

"No." Ragnon was adamant. "It's too risky. And what makes you so sure it's our three anyway?"

"I'm not. But the odds are pretty good, considering, don't you think?"

A knock on the door interrupted them, and Ragnon opened it to admit John Antone. "Sorry, Sergeant." The Indian looked uncertainly at Lucinda Crown. "I didn't mean to intrude—"

"You're not, John," Crown said. "In fact, you're in time for breakfast. Rags is making French toast." She turned her sharky smile on Ragnon. "Isn't he?"

"What have you got, John?" Ragnon asked him, pouring another mug of coffee and handing it to the Indian as he eyed the large manila envelope in his hand.

Antone spread out the latest reports on their three suspects on the kitchen table and waited while they read them. He didn't mention his sleepless night spent in prayer at the children's shrine on the reservation. But Ragnon sensed there was something more. He saw the bright intensity in the Indian's eyes. "So," he said, "we've got the three of them now in one slimy package. And they do get around, don't they? What else?"

John Antone smiled. "Hopefully they may not be moving around for long, Sergeant." And he laid the additional arrest warrant on Carmen Jones, a.k.a. Herman Spears, on the kitchen table beside the reports. "I picked this up on the way down this morning."

"Great, John. Now all we have to do is talk Crown out of *her* cockamamie idea." And he told Antone about the charges against Hannigan, his tie-in with their suspects, and Crown's plan to go undercover.

The Indian was thoughtful. "You know, she could be right," he said. "It just might work, if her contact is solid."

"Wonderful." Ragnon shook his head in disgust. "You're taking *her* side. John, it's not a matter of working. It's a matter of her safety. There'd be no backup close by. She—"

"What about the safety of the kids they've still got with them?" Crown asked pointedly. "If we don't get to them soon . . . Look, Ragnon, I've been undercover without backup before. I do this kind of thing, it's my job—it's what I do, dammit!"

"Not my partner, not while I've got anything to—"

Another knock interrupted them, and they glanced questioningly at each other as Ragnon reached over and turned the knob on the door.

Lieutenant McKittrick's heavy frame filled the doorway as he stooped to enter. "Jack—?" Crown exclaimed.

"Who'd you expect?" the lieutenant growled ominously. "The Tooth Fairy? Or maybe Evelyn and Her Magic Violin?" He glared around at Antone and Ragnon.

"What the fuck's going on?" Then his gaze settled back on Crown. "I tried to get hold of you all night. Where you been—here?"

"Here, Jack—in Pontatoc. I've got a room at the Palace."

"Try again, Luce," he said bitterly. "I called the fucking Palace—every hour on the hour, till three o'clock, when they took the goddamned phone off the hook."

"Oh," Lucy Crown said.

"How about a cup, Lieutenant?" Ragnon offered gallantly. "And I'll put on some eggs—"

"Cut the bullshit, Ragnon! She was here, wasn't she? All night—with you!" He glanced uncertainly at Antone as if wondering if maybe she had serviced the both of them.

"She's a big girl, Lieutenant," Ragnon said tightly, still holding out the mug of coffee to the hulking Vice cop.

With one sudden sweep of his big paw, McKittrick knocked the mug out of Ragnon's hand, sending it crashing and the hot liquid splashing across the table and onto the tile floor and the door of the refrigerator. "I don't want your fucking coffee, Sergeant! I want you to lay off of Crown!"

A moment of tense silence settled over everything while the dark brown liquid trickled down the refrigerator door. No one moved. It was so quiet they could hear the hum of the electric clock on the kitchen wall. Finally Ragnon said very softly but very clearly, "Fuck you, Lieutenant." Then he glanced at Crown and shrugged. "Looks like it wasn't the best time to start a romance."

"You son of a bitch!" McKittrick had balled his fists.

"Stop it!" Crown shouted. "Both of you! If you two macho bulls want to rut and snort over me, I sure as hell don't have to listen to it!"

"Where the fuck you going, Luce?" McKittrick snapped as she opened the door.

"Back to my hotel!" And she slammed the door shut behind her.

Ragnon looked at McKittrick and smiled sarcastically. "Does this mean we don't get any more cooperation from Vice, Lieutenant?"

"It means you're going to get your ass kicked, Ragnon! You're going to get your fucking balls busted if you don't stay away from Crown!"

"And how can I do that—even if I wanted to? She's my partner."

"Not anymore she ain't," McKittrick sneered. "You've got your suspects and warrants. All that's left is to catch 'em. Lucy's been pulled off the case. You can ask Poole. She's going to work with me, gathering evidence against Hannigan in a separate action. That's what I came down to tell her—and to make sure she comes back now."

"Okay." Ragnon felt a sudden relief along with his regret. At least she wouldn't be pulling her dumb undercover gig. "But she doesn't need an escort, Lieutenant. So why don't you just shove off?"

"Let's step outside, Ragnon," McKittrick said. "We'll settle this now. No rank here, just you and me." He glanced at Antone, who had been standing quietly beside the refrigerator, watching it all. "Stay here, redskin, you don't want to see this."

John Antone smiled without mirth. "Can't do that, Lieutenant. He's my partner."

"Stay out of this, John," Ragnon warned him, already picturing himself being hurled out of his own trailer by this hunk of hard-boiled, overgrown beef. At six-two and 220 pounds, McKittrick had at least forty pounds on him and four inches.

"Yeah." McKittrick's narrow eyes looked even more dangerous as he sized up Antone's squat, muscular build. "You on probation or what, injun? I can have your fucking badge if you interfere."

"He's still my partner," Antone said calmly. "You take him on, you take me too. And you may whip my injun ass, Lieutenant, but you'll bear some scars for it, I'll double-damn guarantee it. Then we'll see whose badge gets yanked."

"Why don't we just go talk to Crown, Lieutenant?" Ragnon asked reasonably. "Tell her she's off the case. Then ask her if she wants to follow you back. I'll even concede you could probably throw both of us through the side of this trailer. But we're busy, we've got a killer to hunt down before he kills again. So let's talk to Crown. Either that, or start swinging and let's get it over with."

McKittrick, muttering obscenities, turned and went out the door with Ragnon calling after him, "We'll meet you at the hotel in five minutes, Lieutenant!"

Watching the Vice cop drive off in his unmarked car, tires spitting gravel, Ragnon looked back at Antone. "Jesus, John, what was all that crap about taking on the lieutenant? That big son of a bitch is meaner than two wet cats in a burlap bag. They say even the Raiders cut him as a rookie linebacker when they were at Oakland because he was too damned mean."

"It wasn't crap, Sergeant." Antone smiled with genuine affection now. "I meant every word of it."

"Shit, you probably did. And thanks, but it would take more than the two of us to tame that turkey." Ragnon was wiping off the refrigerator door with a damp dishrag. "We'd've probably had to shoot the bastard. I sure don't see what Crown sees in him."

"Women just see with different eyes, Sergeant," John

Antone said, still smiling as he knelt to wipe the coffee off the floor.

Minutes later, mounting the stairs of the Palace Hotel, they could hear McKittrick's booming voice as he shouted at the desk clerk. Once they were inside, he turned, still fuming, and thrust a note at Ragnon. "Look at this! She's gone! The goddamned bitch has checked out!" And he stormed out the front door and down the steps to his car.

Tom Ragnon stood there, staring at the note in his hand and its terse message: "I won't be fought over like a piece of raw meat—you guys work it out. There was word waiting from my contact, so I'll be undercover."

"Aw, shit," Ragnon moaned.

"That's right, Rags," the chief said, confirming the news. "She's off the case. Not only that, but I just got word the Hannigan part of this thing's been federalized."

"What do you mean federalized?" Ragnon was at the pay phone in a corner of the hotel lobby with Antone standing beside him.

"It's what the feds do when they take over a case and sit on it—in this case our air force general. If he was a spy or stealing weapons or something else that's just unpatriotic, maybe they'd go ahead and crucify him. But something personal and nasty like a general buggering little kids is too touchy to publicize. Instead, they'll have a very private investigation, probably slap his wrist, transfer him, and sweep it all under a rug, bury it in a broom closet, whatever, okay?"

"Goddammit, they can't—"

"They have, Rags. It's already done. So where's McKittrick?"

"On his way back. But I still think it stinks, Chief."

"So does bullshit, but we put up with a lot of it, don't we, Rags? So what about your three perps?"

"We've just about got 'em cornered. John figures they'll be camped somewhere along the border, someplace remote, isolated."

"Sure, Rags, cornered. Somewhere in southern Arizona, right?"

"Chief—"

"Just tell Crown to come on in—now. With her off the case, it's up to you and Antone to find 'em. You've got the warrants."

"Crown's gone," Ragnon said, "disappeared."

"What do you mean—disappeared?"

Ragnon told him about her plan to go undercover. "She's setting it up all on her own with a snitch."

"With no goddamned backup? Jesus H. Christ, Rags, she's off the case! You tell her! I don't want her cold dead ass on *my* books. There'd be no end to the fucking paperwork!"

"Thanks for the sentiments, Chief. I'll tell her as soon as I find her."

"You goddamned well better, Ragnon—she's your responsibility!"

"Tell me about it," Tom Ragnon said, and hung up.

PART III

A Dog and Pony Show

NINETEEN

The town had once been Perlyville. Mined for gold and silver at the turn of the century, its surrounding hills were covered with greasewood bushes and prickly pear, and pitted with tunnels and shafts and heaps of slag and rusted machinery.

It wasn't even on the map now. And there were no streets. Just a thick mesquite grove, the trees growing up through a few scattered, roofless, adobe-walled ruins and clapboard shacks, with sunlight leaking through the cracks and rusty nail heads jutting from wood long dried and warped by a relentless desert sun. The buildings barely stood at all, sagging through the long, empty years, home only to lizards and snakes and tarantulas, ground squirrels and roadrunners and a family of javelinas. A place where men and women had once fought and loved, lived and died, or moved on.

Now Perlyville was alive again. With human maggots. A big Winnebago RV was parked alongside a green van under the thorny branches of a huge old mesquite. Nearby, a dusty powder-blue Chrysler convertible was pulled inside a dilapidated adobe structure, the only one in the deserted town with at least half a roof, a wind-warped sheet of rusting corrugated iron.

The side door of the Winnebago opened and Peter Judge stepped out, grumbling, "He should have been back by now, dammit. He's been gone two days." He knocked his pipe against the doorframe, spilling the ashes into the dust at his feet. "He knows the kids need looking after. It's his job."

Carmen followed him out, carrying a tray of bologna sandwiches and mugs of Kool-Aid. "Maybe he got lost."

"No way. I marked it plain enough on the map, and he's not stupid."

"Well, he *is* unreliable," Carmen whined. "And now he's got that awful-looking gun he picked up in Santa Fe this summer. What does he need with an automatic weapon, for God's sake?"

"But for all his faults, you've got to admit he can handle kids," Pudge said, "and find them. He's like a Pied Piper." He unlocked the back door of the van and opened it.

Inside, the three children were huddled together in a far corner of the carpeted interior, one of them clutching a Cabbage Patch Kid doll. "C'mon." Pudge motioned them out. "Chow time, kiddies."

They ate hurriedly, sitting cross-legged on the ground by the van, wolfing down the sandwiches and Kool-Aid like little animals while Pudge and Carmen watched. "Maybe he's found another kid," Carmen suggested, lighting a cigarette as Pudge punched fresh tobacco into the bowl of his pipe. "Or maybe it's taking him longer than we thought to put out feelers about the snuff."

"Maybe." He scratched a kitchen match on his thumbnail, held the flame to the bowl, and puffed slowly, thinking. The sun was low in the afternoon sky, and the breeze that had sprung up had a chill of fall that made him shiver and wish he'd put on his sweater. "Somehow things aren't turning out as well this year," he said.

"What do you mean?"

"I'm not sure. Maybe it's a mistake trying to make a snuff with Billy Ray. Maybe . . ." They both heard the low, distant growl of the dirt bike almost at the same time, and looked in the direction of the weed-grown trace, where a dust cloud was rising above the trees.

"Here he comes now," Carmen said.

Billy Ray's bike came thundering between the mesquites and deserted buildings and braked to a stop a few feet away. Pulling off his polished black helmet with its dark visor, he slung it on the handlebar and grinned wolfishly. "I've got good news and bad news, folks," he said.

Pudge looked at Carmen. "Lock the kids back in the van. We'll party later and maybe shoot some night scenes." He turned to Billy Ray, who had pulled off his leather jacket and hung it over the bike. "So what's the bad news, Billy Ray?"

"I'll tell you the good news first—it's why I took so long. We've got a possible buyer for the snuff."

"Already?" Pudge frowned. "That's awful fast, Billy Ray."

Billy Ray shrugged. "Some things are meant to be, Pudge. My contact says she's lookin'. She wants to meet and talk."

"She? The buyer's a woman?"

Billy Ray nodded. "He says it's a she. Says she wants something unusual along with the video—she wants to meet the kid and bed him before we shoot."

Pudge was thoughtful, puffing his pipe. "She assumes it will be a boy?"

"I put the word out on a boy. Freddie, right? Anyway,

my contact's checking out her contact. If the deal looks legit, it oughta be good for big bucks. But just to be sure, I'm meeting her away from here."

"Where—when?" Carmen asked, locking the back door of the van.

"Tomorrow at noon, over in Arivaca at the bar on Main Street."

"You taking the kid in the van?" Pudge asked.

"Naw, I'll ride over there this evening on my bike so I'll have plenty of time to scout out the place. Then I'll call my contact. She's supposed to bring front money if she's serious. Then she can meet the kid."

"So what's the bad news?" Pudge wanted to know.

"My contact also says the cops are onto us."

"What—?" Carmen gasped. "All of us?"

"Looks that way. Me and Pudge anyway. Mug shots and descriptions going around, questions being asked." As he lit his own cigarette, Billy Ray's wolfish grin devoured them like it was a great joke. "Maybe you better start wearing your wig again, Pudge."

"What cops, where?" Pudge asked.

"County detectives, sheriff's deputies, all sniffing around after that kid they found in the trash. They want to pin it on us."

"My God," Carmen almost screamed, "they probably *can* pin it on us!"

"On you, Billy Ray," Pudge said quietly. "You killed that kid—he didn't just run away—like you killed the others."

"So you guessed. It's why you asked me to do a snuff, right? Only this time it'll all be planned in advance. You can write the snuff right into the script and I'll give you one."

"But we can't do it now, Pudge!" Carmen was aghast.

"And you can't meet this woman," Pudge said. "She might be a cop."

"Stay cool, the both of you. I told you I'm having everything checked out. And Arivaca's a fly spot on the wall. If anything even looks dirty, I'll split."

"It's crazy," Carmen whined.

"It's money, sweet meat, and it's exciting." He laughed and blew her a mocking kiss. "Even having cops on our ass is exciting. Now"—he flicked away his cigarette and rubbed his hands together—"I'm hungry. What's to eat?"

"We already ate," Pudge said, "but Carmen'll get you a steak out of the freezer, and there's a pot of beans on the stove. Kids ate, too, but you better take them to the latrine. We're letting them use the big rocky wash back there through the trees." He pointed as Carmen turned toward the RV.

Billy Ray stared after her with his stone-dull eyes. "Why didn't she do it?" he asked angrily. "Why am I always the fucking baby-sitter? I'm getting tired of that bitch-stud always—"

"Easy, Billy Ray, easy," Pudge said, soothing his ruffled feathers. "I already fed them, and it's just that you can handle them so well—they trust you. But I still think we ought to lay off the snuff project—just for now. Lay low for a while. We've made too many waves."

But Billy Ray shook his head stubbornly with a sneering smile. "You got no fucking balls, Pudge, you never did. Now, Carmen, I can understand her gutless pussy attitude, but you—at least I'll meet with this cunt, get some bread, check her out. Then maybe we can move across the line into Mexico to shoot the scene, out of these cops' jurisdiction. Those bean eaters down there won't give a shit what we do as long as we slip 'em a little *mordida*."

There was obviously no arguing with him, and Pudge

relented. "Okay, meet with her, and *maybe* we'll do it—in Mexico. Now go look after the kids, and by the time you get back, Carmen will have your steak ready."

But as he unlocked the back of the van and motioned the kids out, Billy Ray was convinced of only one thing. Once they'd done the snuff and got the money, he'd kiss this pair of shitheads good-bye. And one other thing he hadn't mentioned to Pudge: He wasn't afraid of a confrontation with cops. In fact, now that he had his carbine converted to automatic, he was looking forward to seeing a dozen or so of the pricks over his gunsight.

TWENTY

Tom Ragnon sat in his battered yellow Volkswagen in front of the house on Old Father Road, too enervated to even move. Around him the dawn, a pale golden glow against the mountain that rose to nine thousand feet just beyond the city, painted the scattered cloud strata a pinkish hue. The propeller on a wind vane he'd mounted on the carport two years before was motionless, and he watched a papergirl come down the curving street on her scooter, the rhythmic putt-putt of its two-cycle engine the only sound disturbing the morning stillness.

He heard the paper hit the drive and the scooter fading away, and he glanced at his watch: 6:05. Scratching his sandpaper jaw, he considered the past twenty-four hours. He'd gone unshaven and sleepless and unfed, looking for Crown. It felt like desperation time.

"Rags? What are you doing out there?"

He looked up toward the house, where Angie was standing in her robe in the drive, the paper in her hand. She waved him in. "Why didn't you ring the bell, for God's sake? You know I'm always up early unless I've got the late shift."

"To tell you the truth, Angie," Ragnon said, mounting the porch steps behind her, "I didn't even remember what shift you're on."

She put a mug of steaming coffee in front of him, and two whole wheat muffins in the toaster-oven. And while he settled into the breakfast nook and stared out the window at the patio, she continued her admonishment. "You look like—what is it you say—shit warmed over."

"I lost one of my partners," Ragnon told her.

"What? Killed?"

"No, not that." And he told her about Crown—and McKittrick. At least part of it.

"I'm sorry, Rags." She buttered a muffin and handed it to him. "But at least she isn't dead."

"She could be soon if she gets among the philistines." And he told her about their three suspects and the kids.

"That's awful. What are you going to do?"

"Find them—all of them—Crown too." He got up, the muffin half eaten. "Can I use the bathroom?"

"Sure. And you'd better change clothes. There's still some of your old things in back of the closet. But why don't you get some sleep first—at least lie down a while and close your eyes."

"Can't. Wasted another day already." He turned toward the hall. "Just a shower and shave and then I've got to call the chief, and my dad." He paused in the doorway. "Kids still asleep?"

She nodded. "I'll get them up before you have to leave." She looked at him. "You sure you're okay, Rags?"

"I'll be fine." He was patting his pockets. "I don't suppose I left any Red Man lying around?"

"No. Isn't chewing almost as bad as smoking?"

"I know, and I'm going to quit that too—right after this case."

While he showered and shaved, he thought about the damned case. It was beginning to infect his soul. It got that way with some of them. He was becoming obsessed with finding these people before they killed again. He was also obsessed with finding Crown. Her going undercover alone only aggravated the situation, and he took that personally, too, his emotions about all of it tangled and tormented, his anguish real.

Forty minutes later he was back in the kitchen doorway in a dark blue sweatshirt that said WILDCATS across the front and a pair of old corduroy pants. "I called my dad on the upstairs phone," he said.

"No change?"

He shook his head.

"I'll fix you some eggs with green chilies, the way you like them."

"No—thanks, but I'll take another mug of coffee and a muffin. I've still got to call the chief." He picked up the wall phone and dialed downtown. It was 7:25 by the clock on the stove. "Chief?"

"Where the fuck you been, Rags? Have you found Crown?"

"No. I'm at Angie's. I checked Crown's apartment but she hasn't been there, and her car's still in the carport. No luck with her description at the car-rental agencies, but McKittrick's keeping his people on it. She's using a pseudo ID and probably disguised. I think she's somewhere on the border looking for a meet, but I don't think we'll find *her* now till we find *them*."

"Shit! Okay, Rags, stay with it. And call Antone at his place. I just talked to him and he's got a new lead on Billy Ray. He wants to roll."

Ragnon hung up and dialed. "John? Ragnon. What have you got?"

"Deputy Montoya called me from Pontatoc. They just got word from a gas station attendant in Arivaca. A guy answering Billy Ray's description gassed a dirt bike there about closing time last night, paid in cash, bought some cigarettes and candy inside the store, and left."

"Arivaca's only ten or so miles from the border. No sign of anybody else? No other vehicles?"

"None. But they must be in the area."

"Unless they already crossed over. Call Montoya back, John. Ask about Crown."

"Already did. No sign of her either."

"Have you had any sleep?"

"A little."

"Good, that's twice what I've had. I'll be at your place in half an hour. We'll take my Bug and you can drive. And grab us some rations. There won't even be a Burger King where we're going." He hung up and looked at Angie, thinking about his two kids sleeping upstairs. "I'd like to stay a while but . . ."

"I know." She smiled weakly. "The battle never ends. Maybe next time."

At John Antone's, Ragnon parked his yellow Bug in the circular drive, beeped the horn, and got out. Walking to the front of the car, he opened the trunk as Antone came out on the screened porch of his mobile home. Ragnon watched him kiss his wife and baby good-bye, then walk out to the car lugging an old lever-action Winchester in a leather boot, along with his sleeping bag and duffel. He stuffed everything but the rifle in the trunk with Ragnon's gear, and closed it.

Ragnon nodded at the heavy .30-.30 saddle gun as Antone stowed it behind the front seat, its stock pitted and scarred and rubbed to a shine with linseed oil. "You fixing to do a little big-game hunting?" he asked.

"You never know, do you, Sergeant?" The Indian smiled. He was wearing a green plaid flannel shirt under a Levi jacket, and faded blue jeans. "I'll bet my best moccasins you changed from standard loads to hollow points in your Cobra."

"How'd you guess? I also picked up a couple of flak vests, just in case." He waved to Juana on the porch, then got in on the passenger side while the Indian kicked the oversize tires and then slid in behind the wheel.

"You think this'll do it, Sergeant?" he asked as he fired the ignition and the noisy engine roared to life.

"It'll go where no man has gone before, John, and hopefully bring us back. Because we need to keep a low profile on this little trip, and that big Cherokee of yours is just too visible. Besides, this little yellow devil burns a lot less gas. We just won't be as comfortable." He looked over at the Indian. "You bring your Redhawk too?"

Antone opened his jacket to expose the butt of the Magnum in his shoulder holster as he steered the car down the drive and past the patch of head-high corn that was almost ready for harvest. "Everything else we need is in the duffel bag."

"I hope you put a coffeepot in there too," Tom Ragnon said.

"Also a canteen, beef jerky, and cans of peaches and beans and some fresh tortillas. We're ready for anything, Sergeant."

"We better be," Ragnon added soberly, tucking a pinch of Red Man in his cheek. "Like I told you, John, I've got a bad feeling about this one." And pushing back his sweat-stained Stetson, he tried to get comfortable for the ride to Arivaca.

TWENTY-ONE

Billy Ray Lee, rolling his sleeping bag up tight, strapped it to the back of his bike with a bungie cord and pulled on his helmet. The morning was clear, the temperature in the low sixties. By the angle of the sun, he guessed the time at close to ten o'clock, and he looked around at the mashed-down grass beside the cemetery fence on the outskirts of Arivaca, where he had spent the night.

He had gassed the bike the night before and scouted the town, finding nothing suspicious. He had checked in with his contact, who reported the buyer appeared safe, and the meet had been moved up to 11:00 A.M. at the bar on the main drag. She'd be wearing a red scarf and matching cloth cap.

Now, walking the bike out to the road, he still saw nothing out of the ordinary—no cops, no suspicious-looking people or vehicles, in fact, very few people or vehicles at all—and mounting the bike, he fired it up and headed for the café for some eggs and hash browns and hot biscuits. Billy Ray Lee never liked doing business on an empty stomach.

* * *

Nine miles away, on the two-lane road leading to Arivaca, Lucinda Ann Crown had just finished changing a flat tire on her rental car, a pale green Plymouth sedan. Lowering the wheel on the jack, she gave a final tightening turn on the lugs with the wrench, then threw the tools back in the trunk along with the flat tire. Slamming the lid shut, she leaned a moment against the car, getting her breath back and blotting her brow with the red kerchief she had brought to wear for recognition. Then she looked at her watch, glad now she had allowed plenty of time. According to the odometer, she was eleven miles in from the Arivaca Junction with the freeway. She was getting close to the town, and it was only ten o'clock.

Lighting one of her slim brown cigarillos, she took it easy driving the remaining nine miles, trying to lose herself in her cover and prepare for the meeting to come. She wondered if he would show. And if he did, would he come alone? A friend who worked in cosmetics at a local department store had helped her with her makeup—a mask so thick she wondered if she'd overdone it. The effect had aged her at least ten years.

A baggy blue jump suit, dark glasses, and a red cloth cap completed her outfit, along with a floppy cloth handbag which was close beside her. In it was her pseudo ID: a driver's license, credit card, and a Maricopa County voter's registration card; even a grocery list scribbled on an old envelope which was addressed to her alias, Norma Hughes, with a matching Phoenix address. And five thousand dollars in a tight rubber-banded roll. Also in the bag was her .25-caliber Beretta with a round in the chamber—she could shoot right through the cloth if she had to. It wasn't much of a gun, but deadly at close range if used properly, and at least she was confident she could do just that.

Even so, she didn't feel comfortable. Nervous tension came and went in waves, but that was normal for her. She knew she wouldn't really settle down until they were face-to-face. Even when she had a backup on undercover, she never felt really at ease. The fear got all knotted up in her stomach, her appetite gone, her need for booze stronger than ever. She wondered sometimes if she was on a nonstop train to margaritaville.

Now, alone on this one, she was already wondering if it was all a big mistake. It had happened so quickly, and she still wasn't sure if she really had enough leverage on her contact to be certain he would vouch for her, and not just set her up.

Snubbing her cigarette in the ashtray, she turned on the radio, found a soothing soft rock station, and let her thoughts drift back again to Ragnon and McKittrick. They were difficult men to handle separately. Together they were the pits. Emotionally torn by both of them, she wasn't sure she'd had her cop's cap on straight when she'd made this move. Maybe she'd gone undercover solely to put some distance between herself and them, and not because it was an especially smart move or something she really believed would work. And she certainly hadn't expected it to happen so fast. But the opportunity was there when she'd returned to the hotel in the form of a message from her contact, and she'd grabbed it.

Drawing cash from her own savings for the front money wasn't real smart either, she thought, but she'd had to avoid any contact with the department if she was going in alone. And she was committed now. She wanted these scum in the worst way. Hannigan had been bad enough, but these three would kill again. And the knowledge that they probably wouldn't hesitate to kill her, too, if she had made a mistake made her all the more uneasy as she pulled into the dusty little one-street town of Arivaca and dropped her flat tire off at the shade-tree garage for repairs before going on to the bar.

As she came in from the bright sunlight, her sunglasses clutched in one hand and her floppy bag in the other, her eyes were slow adjusting to the dimness of the long barroom, which was narrow as a boxcar. She thought maybe it *was* a converted boxcar. It even had electrified railroad lanterns at spaced intervals along the back, the low-watt bulbs making a diffused red glow that reflected off the glasses and bottles and a gilt-framed mirror.

The bartender was a middle-aged woman who served her a beer cheerfully, but Crown made it plain she wasn't there for conversation and the woman retreated gracefully. Crown searched the back mirror for other customers. Only three at this hour—no, four. She spotted a man at the far end, keeping him in her peripheral vision and avoiding looking directly at him while she sipped her beer.

A neon beer-ad clock behind the bar flickered: 10:45. She was early. Maybe he was early too—if it was him. She lit a cigarette, took a long, deep drag, and let it out slow. She was wearing the red scarf and matching cap, so it was up to him to make the move. She let her head turn slowly, looking without staring, but his face was still in a shadowy red gloom. The big hand on the clock had moved three spaces, to 10:48. Was he going to make his move or wait till the appointed time? Was it even him? And was he alone?

Two of the other customers got up and left together, calling to the barmaid by name, as if they were regulars. That left the third customer behind her, sitting alone at a table along the wall, but in the dimness she had no sense of his appearance, or even if it was a he.

Then the one at the far end made his move. She watched him in the mirror as he came along the narrow aisle. It was the young guy in the mug shot, but his picture didn't do him justice—he looked even slimier in person. And her hand moved almost imperceptibly closer to her bag.

Then just as suddenly she settled down, her stomach calmed. She mashed out the cigarette in a shiny copper ashtray and finished her beer. The thing was going down. The die was cast. She was about to meet Billy Ray Lee or Billy Lee Ray or whatever—thickly muscular, long blond hair worn loosely, dressed in a gray sweatshirt cut off at the waist to expose a hard, bare midriff, gray jogging pants, and sneakers. "Hello, Norma," he said quietly, his voice like a pseudo-lover's but with a peculiar cutting edge. She got a whiff of stale breath and body odor, and felt a quick and sudden sense of nausea.

He ordered two more beers while she got up the nerve to turn from the mirror and face him. His smile slid off to one side of his face. His scraggly blond beard and mustache seemed phony and out of place on a long angular face. Her eyes fixed for a moment on a gold chain at his throat, and then she found his eyes: slightly hooded and like gray stones, empty and unsmiling, yet boring into her. For an instant she thought his look would melt the makeup right off her face, exposing her identity, laying her bare, making her vulnerable and dead.

But he only scooped up the two sweating bottles the barmaid brought and motioned her to one of the little tables along the wall. She hadn't even heard the third customer leave as she clutched her bag and followed him, but except for the barmaid now, they were alone.

Cozy. Her blood was racing. Sitting across from a baby-raping, child-killing degenerate by a thickly curtained window that barely let in enough light to see his face. His eyes still cold and hard and emotionless as granite, and desolate as an empty campground in the rain.

He was gripping his beaded bottle with both hands, hands that were thick-fingered with large knuckles. She half expected to see HATE or FUCK tattooed across them. "To what?" he toasted, raising the bottle now. "The movies?" He gave her his mirthless smile, exposing surprisingly clean, even teeth.

She motioned with her own bottle, surprised that her hand was steady. "To business," she said softly. "Let's get down to it."

"Sure thing, lady." He took a deep swig and wiped the foam from his lips on the back of his hand.

"It's like this," she whispered huskily. "You're making a special video. I'm in the market. But I want to meet with the subject first, alone."

Billy Ray didn't even blink. "That might be arranged." He took another swig of beer. "It'll cost you."

"How much?"

"To meet the subject, or for the finished cassette?"

"Just the meeting—now."

"How much did you bring with you, lady—now?"

She swallowed. "Five thousand—front money—payable when I meet with the kid."

"Where is it?" He stared across the table at her, fish-eyed and unreadable, then nodded at her bag. "In there?"

She nodded. "Cash."

"What else? ID maybe? Or a recorder?" His smile was more of a leer now.

She opened the bag and took out her wallet. Unfolding it, she pushed it across the table. He studied the driver's license and fingered the matching credit card and voter registration. He even turned over the grocery list and then poked through the thirty dollars cash in the wallet, then handed it back. As she took it he suddenly grabbed her wrist in an iron grip. The pain reached to her elbow, and with it not only a sense of his strength, but of the depth of sheer malevolence within him. He turned her wrist to read the inscription on the ID bracelet she wore. "Norma," he muttered, and let her go. "So I still haven't seen the money, Norma."

She took a deep breath, rubbing her wrist and glancing at the barmaid, who was busy washing glasses, then reached in the bag and flashed the roll of bills. It seemed to satisfy him. "I've also got a gun," she said. "You want to see that too?" And she thought of the long steel needle she wore concealed in her hair under her cap, a weapon she wore only undercover and as yet had never had to use.

Billy Ray grunted, patting the bag, feeling the contents, then tossed down the last of his beer and sat back. "It doesn't feel like a very big gun," he said, smiling.

"Big enough," she said, and waited. He seemed to be thinking.

"Payable when you meet the kid, right?"

She nodded. "And time alone with him."

"Right. Okay, why not? You can meet him now, Norma, if you want to make the trip."

"Yes—now," she answered tightly. "Is it far?"

"Let's go," he said. "I'm on a bike. See if you can keep up with me."

Outside again, she put on her sunglasses and got into the car, watching Billy Ray as he donned a black helmet with a tinted visor, fired his bike, and roared out of the parking lot, slinging gravel. As she followed him down the main street of the town, she couldn't believe it was going to be this easy. He was evidently taking her to the kids, and probably to his accomplices too, unless he just wanted to get her alone and make a try for the money. Then she spotted the yellow Volkswagen Bug pulled up at the gas pumps in front of the general store and almost froze.

Time seemed to slow to a crawl. Tom Ragnon was there in a a dark blue sweatshirt, gassing the bug and watching the pump. Half turned, he had only to move his head a fraction and he'd see her, but she resisted the temptation to scoot down in the seat. The car was a rental, and with her makeup and sunglasses—no way. And then she was past him and accelerating to catch up with Billy Ray, who had gunned the cycle and was already putting distance between them.

Yet for an instant she had been tempted to stop and call out or signal—something—like it was a last chance, but she'd steeled herself. This was why she had left, to separate herself from Ragnon as well as McKittrick. And if she did stop, all they would have would be Billy Ray. And if he didn't choose to talk? No, in a way it was a relief to have Ragnon so near, but she'd find the others first, and the kids. Then there'd be time to call in the marines. She hoped.

TWENTY-TWO

Tom Ragnon, holding the nozzle in the gas tank of his Volkswagen and concentrating on the gallons ticking off on the pump as he topped it off, was only vaguely aware of the bike going by on the road behind him. Either his brain was in idle, or his senses dulled by lack of sleep and the fact they'd already checked three bikers on the way down, but it didn't even register that the sound he heard might be *their* biker still hanging around Arivaca.

And he glanced only momentarily at the green Plymouth sedan as he put away the hose. Some part of his mind registered a female driver, and instinctively his eyes swept over the license plate, but later he would remember it only because of an odd coincidence. The plate almost spelled out his ex-wife's name and birthdate: ANG-349.

Screwing the cap back on the tank, he watched John Antone come out of the store, waving the manila envelope containing the mug shots. "He's positive Billy Ray is the one who gassed up his bike here last night," Antone said. "Says he wouldn't have paid any attention except the creep tried to stiff him on the change."

"And no one with him?"

"No, he was alone. And he's not sure which way he headed when he left."

"Terrific," Ragnon said. He wished he'd brought a picture of Crown.

They spent a while showing the mug shots around town then, but there were no takers until they got to the café. A young guy like that had been in and demanded breakfast after the morning shift. They even had a sign, NO BREAKFASTS SERVED AFTER TEN A.M., but it was close and he seemed like trouble, and since they had no other customers, the cook decided to humor him.

"Jesus, John." Ragnon glanced at his watch. It was almost noon. "The son of a bitch was here overnight!" But nothing unusual had happened at the café, no meeting with anyone, and not even any funny stuff with the change—unless he'd gotten away with it. They hurried out, the trail getting warm, and struck pay dirt at the bar.

"Sure." The barmaid nodded, canting the mug shot to get more light from the red lantern behind her. "I'd say that's him. Picked up a woman—or maybe knew her—it was hard to tell. Couldn't overhear anything. They talked low, and neither of them was very friendly."

"How long ago?" Antone asked.

She shrugged, glancing at the neon beer clock that said 12:10. "I dunno, maybe an hour, probably less."

"Can you describe the woman?" Ragnon asked.

"Hell." She laughed. "I don't pay attention to the women. The guys, sure, like him—young and hard-muscled. No, she was maybe fortyish, cheap-looking, like she'd been around the track a time or two. Wore a red cap and scarf and blue jump suit, I remember that. Seemed nervous too. They talked a while at that table over there and left. Why? What'd they do?"

"Nothing yet, I hope," Ragnon said. "They leave in a car?"

"Guy had a bike. I heard it. I don't know about the woman."

Something flashed across Ragnon's memory. "Can I use your phone?"

"Pay phone—around the corner there, by the johns."

He looked back at Antone, who was following him to the phone. "While I was gassing up and you were in the store—what was it, forty-five minutes ago? I *heard* a damn bike go by—and then a car. I saw the car—a green Plymouth, woman with a red cap driving, and I remember the license. I'll call it in and have it checked."

"Which way were they headed?" Antone asked while Ragnon dialed.

"East."

Outside the bar Ragnon spread a map on the hood of the Bug. The Plymouth's plate belonged to a rental, but they were having trouble running it down. "It was Crown," Ragnon insisted. "It had to be. She's met him, and gone off with him, the damn fool. I asked Poole for a flyover, but it'll take a while to get a plane."

"It didn't sound like Lucinda's description, Sergeant," Antone said cautiously, helping smooth the map and holding down the corners. "Maybe it was Carmen Jones."

"It was Crown, dammit, disguised—it had to be! And Billy Ray was in front of her, going east, maybe an hour ahead of us by now."

"Then even on dirt roads they could be thirty or forty miles away," the Indian persisted. "And there's a hell of a lot of east out there."

"There's also old mining camps. Oro Blanco here." He

pointed on the map, his thoughts racing. "And Ruby, and the Pena Blanca campground at the lake farther on."

"And then the freeway and Nogales and more mining camps east of that," Antone pointed out unkindly. "And side roads that aren't even on this map. A good hundred miles of border just between here and Douglas, and most of it in another county, out of our jurisdiction, and all of Mexico just to the south."

"Are you trying to discourage me, John?" Ragnon asked, tucking a pinch of Red Man in his cheek. He was tired, and the sleepless night wasn't helping his thought process. The damn bike had gone right past him. And worse, he knew John Antone was right. They could still be almost anywhere.

"I'm just considering alternatives," Antone said quietly. "They could even have doubled back through town and headed west. There's the whole Altar Valley then, and Sasabe on the border, and miles of Indian reservation beyond that. Timewise we're right on top of them again, but they could make a right or left turn anywhere and be out of sight over the next hill."

Tom Ragnon shook his head in frustration. "A bike and a green Plymouth, John." He clung stubbornly to that, spat, and began folding the map. "And they're not an hour ahead of us—let's go."

A hundred yards in front of her, Billy Ray suddenly turned off, pulled in next to a roadside ramada, and stopped. When she drove up behind him, he motioned her toward the shaded picnic table beneath it, before stepping over to a greasewood bush. He stood there with his legs spread, his back to her, urinating. "Piss stop," he called over his shoulder. "Want to join me?"

"No thanks. I can wait a while." Getting out of the car,

her handbag in her hand, she stretched. Then she looked around at the cacti-studded hills and a distant mountain she thought must be in Mexico. The wind and the stillness and wide expanse of sky seemed endless.

Turning, he zipped his pants, then walked over to her car and checked it out, opening the glove compartment and looking under and behind the seats. "Your car?" he asked.

"No, a rental."

He stared back down the empty road the way they had come, but no one was following. Then he walked back to the picnic table and sat down on the cement bench in the shade. "Let's talk," he said.

"How far is it to where we're going?" she asked, troubled now as she sat down on the bench opposite him, her bag still clutched in front of her on the table.

"Not far." He fixed her with his hooded, empty eyes. "Let's see your money again."

She tried to anticipate what was coming. Were they really anywhere near the kids, or had he been conning her, bringing her here to—she reached in her bag and took out the little automatic, but his face never changed expression. He just waited.

Placing the gun beside her bag, she took out the roll of bills and held it up. "You want to count it?"

"Later. Right now I trust you—I think." The smile slid across his face again as he looked at the gun. "Such a little piece. You really think that's going to help you if you need one?"

"It has before," Crown responded firmly, meeting his stare.

"You know there's more than me in this," he said. "We've got guns too—big guns. We could just rip you off."

"If that's the way you do business. But you wouldn't get the rest then, would you? This is only the down payment—to be with the child. You don't look stupid to me."

"You really are kinky, lady." The smile again, the stone-dull eyes. "We're both kinks. Maybe we can get along."

"I doubt it. Why don't we cut the bullshit and get going?" She put both the gun and the roll of bills back into her bag.

As they got up, Billy Ray said, "How'd you like to watch the snuff being made?"

The words—the suddenness of the question and its meaning—almost shocked her speechless. "Sure." She hesitated. "Why not?"

"It'll cost you more, of course. We'll probably slip across the border—shoot it down in beaner land."

"How much more?" she asked, not quite sure how far to take this.

"We'll have to discuss that with my partners, but not too much more." He straddled his bike and put on his helmet, his features disappearing behind the dark visor. "Let's go, Norma," he said, and kicked the starter.

She followed him in her car. No one had passed them on the road the whole time they had been there, from either direction, and only a quarter of a mile from the rest stop Billy Ray turned off on a narrow side road that led away into the desolate hills. And Lucinda Crown, taking a deep breath and tightening her jaws, turned with him, eating his dust.

TWENTY-THREE

It was mid-afternoon, with cloud shadows stretching across the land, as she followed Billy Ray around a curve and they drove into a little valley between two hills, winding among the trees of a mesquite thicket.

Lucinda Crown glanced anxiously at the gas gauge on the Plymouth. Still half a tank. But she hadn't picked up her tire at the garage in Arivaca, and she thought they must be at least ten miles from any main road now. She was wondering how much farther it could be when she saw the first adobe ruin through the trees and heard the distant sound of music.

The slanting sunlight burned yellow on the mud walls of a roofless ruin as she passed, a ruin so old that a mature tree was growing out of its middle. Another ancient building sprang up on the left, and then two more on each side in quick succession as the music grew louder. And then she had to slow down because Billy Ray was slowing ahead of her.

The music was really loud now—strong—thunderous— evidently coming from amplifiers and booming through the mesquite grove as Billy Ray braked in a clearing in front of her and she pulled up alongside, rolling down her window.

Raising the visor of his helmet, he looked at her, grinning like a hungry wolf as the music reverberated around them in thunderous waves. And she recognized it now: Wagner's "Ride of the Valkyries" from *Die Walküre*, but most recently from the movie *Apocalypse Now*. It was so real, so vivid and terrifying, she half expected to see helicopter gunships come beating in across the tops of the mesquites, dropping napalm.

Billy Ray had his helmet in his hand as he walked over to her car. "It's my partners!" he shouted above the sound. "They're shooting a session—it's that German opera shit—thinks it gets everybody in the mood!" He waved his helmet at the air around them as the music suddenly stopped and the whole grove turned eerily quiet.

Crown threw open her door and was half out of the car. "Not the snuff film!"

"Naw." Billy Ray laughed. "Just a regular session. Pudge likes to work with the funky afternoon light sometimes." He lit a cigarette and drew deeply, leaning back against his bike. "They'll be here in a minute."

Crown lit her own cigarillo and tried to keep her hands from trembling. And now that the music had stopped, she cold hear the rumble of a portable generator. Looking toward the sound, she spotted the big RV parked across the clearing in heavy shadows under a huge tree. Moments later she picked out the rear end of the Chrysler sticking out of one of the adobe ruins, and then the green van pulled suddenly into the clearing and stopped.

She watched Peter Judge get out on the driver's side, and Carmen Jones step out on the other. So here they were, she thought tensely, all three of them. She wondered if the kids were in the van, and she clutched her bag a little more tightly, waiting.

"This here's the buyer!" Billy Ray called. "She's got five big ones to meet the star of our special cassette, and more when it's shot!"

Pudge was staring at her, his face almost expressionless, but Carmen had a look of curious suspicion about her—or him.

"You brought her back here?" Pudge exclaimed.

"Why not? She's got the bucks and she's alone. Nobody followed us. I made sure."

"You damn fool, Billy Ray." Pudge was obviously angry now, and afraid. "I thought you'd take the kid to her someplace, not bring her here!"

"Relax, man. We ain't gonna shoot the thing here anyway, remember? We're goin' over the border. And she's harmless, 'cept for the little piece she's packin' in that bag, and I told her ours are bigger."

Crown wondered if she should take them now, but she had to find the kids, she had to be sure they were safe. "I want to see the kids," she said.

"Kids?" Carmen asked, suspicion still her dominant feature. "What makes you think there are kids? You're paying for one kid."

"You're making movies, aren't you? They're usually made with several kids. But you're right, it's the one boy I'm interested in. Where is he?" She thought they were probably together anyway.

"Don't worry, he's here," Pudge said, studying her closely. "Come over to the motor home. Have some coffee. Maybe you'll stay for supper long as you're here." He looked over at Billy Ray, who was pushing his bike around toward the back of the RV to rack it. "You see the money?"

He nodded. "She's got a roll would choke a horse—cash."

Pudge opened the door of the RV for Crown as Carmen called, "I'll bring the kid over," and headed back toward the van.

The motor home was surprisingly luxurious and clean, a living room and kitchen combined, and to the right of the door a videogame table with a small chair on either side. "A special treat," Pudge explained, nodding at the table, "for when they perform especially well. Kids love those electric games."

He reached past a TV and VCR and turned on a wall stereo, filling the room with an aria from *Tosca* as he offered her a seat on the long, thick-cushioned divan. His earlier anger and fear seemed to have subsided. She wondered if he was really accepting her, or if it was a sham.

"You've got quite a setup," she observed softly as he poured her a cup of coffee from the pot on the stove.

"Oh, yes—all the comforts. Sugar? Cream?" She shook her head and he handed it to her. "Bedroom, shower, and toilet." He motioned with his hand. "Even a darkroom and storage space for the video equipment." He pulled out a drawer in a small stand and rummaged through some cassettes and still photos, finally handing her a color print. It was a little boy, naked. "That's him. That's Freddie—your boy."

She stared a moment at the picture. The child's expression seemed uncertain, confused. She looked up at Pudge. "Can I keep this?"

"If you've got the money handy." He watched her put the picture in her bag and take out the roll of bills. All the serial numbers had been recorded at the bank.

Behind them, the door to the RV opened and Carmen came in, leading the little boy, the same one as in the picture, except now he was dressed in shorts and a T-shirt. He stared at her blankly and she wondered if he was drugged.

"This is Freddie," Pudge introduced him, "and you are—" He looked at her questioningly.

"I'm Norma Hughes, Freddie," she said softly.

Pudge finished counting the bills and looked at Crown. "You want your session with him now or after supper?"

"Now," Crown answered tightly. His greed had evidently overcome his doubts. Even Carmen seemed pacified by the roll of new bills.

"Okay. Freddie, you be nice to Norma." He looked again at Crown. "The shower's back there. We'll give you an hour. Then we can maybe eat something and talk about the full price of the cassette you want made."

"She might want to watch it shot," Billy Ray said from the open doorway where he had appeared behind Carmen.

"That might be arranged too," Pudge said. "We'll have to talk about it." And he and Carmen stepped out of the RV, closing the door behind them and walking toward the van with Billy Ray.

"I'm not so sure that's a good idea," Carmen said, "letting her watch the shoot."

"It'll be in Mexico," Billy Ray reminded her. "It's a foreign country, and I told you, anything goes in Mexico. The cops can't touch us."

"Except for the Mexican cops," Pudge remarked.

"Which we can buy off for a bent peso," Billy Ray scoffed.

"We'll see," Pudge said. "We'll see how high she wants to go. If it's high enough, maybe we'll take the extra risk."

"You got no balls if you don't, Pudge," Billy Ray said, kicking aside a rock as they walked over to the makings of a fire Pudge had laid beneath a metal grill. Kneeling, Billy Ray put a match to it.

With the sun lower in the sky and more clouds moving in, the slight breeze stirring the mesquites had a nip to it, and holding out his hands to the growing flames, Billy Ray looked back at the RV, where the curtains were drawn and the rumble of the generator was the only sound above the crackling of the fire. "I'll take my bike across the border tomorrow," he said, hunkering down beside the blaze. "Scout out a location for the shoot."

"Not so fast, goddammit," Pudge swore. "I said maybe. I'm still not dead certain about your buyer. We'd better get that weapon out of her bag."

"Shit, Pudge, it's a peashooter—and she's a woman!"

"We've still got to be careful. You'd better get your guns out of the car, just in case." He glanced at Carmen as if uncertain whether to mention something. "We had some other visitors today."

Billy Ray stood up. "What visitors?"

"Just before we started shooting, so they didn't see anything. A couple of Mexicans—wetbacks. They came through camp heading north. Peons, tire-tread *huaraches* and all, but one of them spoke some English. They wanted food and water. I told them we barely had enough for ourselves and sent them on their way."

"Shit," Billy Ray said. "You should have killed the greasy bastards."

Inside the RV Crown sat at one end of the long couch with the little boy at the other. He seemed well nourished, so these maggots were at least feeding them, but he was also small for his age, which he told her was seven. He sat with one leg curled under him, and his body seemed tiny and frail against the big-flowered cushions. "What do

KINDERKILL

you want me to do?" he asked. His large brown eyes were gentle, but somehow lacking the innocence of childhood. "You're not going to hurt me, are you?"

Lucinda Crown swallowed. "No, I'm not going to hurt you. I just want you to listen to me closely—Freddie—is that your real name?"

"No, it's what they call me. My real name is Larry Thompson."

"All right, Larry Thompson. My real name's not Norma either. It's Lucy, Lucy Crown, and I'm here to help you."

"Help me?" His eyes brightened. "How?"

"Help you get away from these people—you and the other kids. Help you get back home."

"Home?" The word seemed almost alien to him; he looked away. "I don't have a home," he whispered so low she barely heard him.

"At least get you away from here—somewhere you'll be safe, where people will treat you—differently."

He studied her closely. "Like you?"

"Yes—like me, Larry. How many other children are here?"

"Two girls."

"In the van?"

He nodded.

"Okay, I'm going to take you all away from here, away from these people."

"Oh, yes!" He moved toward her on the couch. "Please!"

She took both his hands. "But not right now, Larry. I can't do it right away. I've got to get help first, but I'll come back—do you understand? I'll come back with help."

"I—think so—" He shrank away again, as if she had

just let the air out of his favorite balloon, as if he didn't quite believe her now.

Reaching out, she brushed at his hair, wondering again if she dared try to make the arrest now, alone, but deciding against it. They seemed settled in here, at least temporarily. And all she had to do was get to a phone. She could even stall them about the price, or about going into Mexico to shoot it.

Keeping his hand in hers, she led him out of the RV and walked with him over to the campfire.

"Finished so soon?" Pudge asked.

"I'd like to see the other two," Crown told him. "Freddie says they're girls. A friend might want a cassette of one of them too. Then we can talk price."

Peter Judge shrugged. "C'mon, they're in the van." He took Freddie by the arm.

Carmen was adding more mesquite to the fire, building up the blaze against the deepening chill as the sun sank below the hills. But Billy Ray was nowhere in sight. Crown was wondering where he'd gone, when she saw him coming back from the shadows by the Chrysler. He was carrying a bolt-action rifle across his arm like some character out of a B-grade western, and hanging at the end of his other arm was some kind of military carbine with a long, thin magazine. God, she thought with a start, an automatic? And she knew now any chance of taking them alone was gone.

"See?" Billy Ray was waving the carbine as he came up to the fire. "I told you we got bigger guns."

"She wants to see the girls," Pudge called, unlocking the back of the van. "Maybe buy a cassette of them too."

An interior light in the van came on, and as the little boy climbed inside, Crown could see the two girls in the back. They were playing jacks on a board, using a flashlight for illumination, and one of them was clutching a Cabbage Patch Kid doll. But they glanced up only momentarily as Larry Thompson joined them, then resumed the game. "Put that flashlight out," Pudge told them, "you'll burn out the batteries. And all of you, put your sweaters on now before you catch a chill."

"How old are the girls?" Crown asked, her heart pounding.

"Bigger one's seven, same as Freddie; little one's five, almost six."

"My friend really likes them a little younger," Crown said softly, improvising now, stalling. There still might be a chance—

"We can get you one any age you like, Norma," Billy Ray said behind her. He handed the rifle to Pudge and held the carbine across his chest, one finger curled in the trigger guard. "Any sex too. You come down to May-heco with us and I'll even let you pick 'em out. We'll take a little stroll through one of the small villages; how about that?"

"I'll have to think about it. When are you going across?"

"Soon, Norma." He smiled. "Very soon."

"Shall we go over to the RV now and talk price?" Pudge asked. "Carmen can throw some steaks on that fire when the flames die down. Then maybe we can even snort a little coke and I'll show you my special collection of childish delights." He was starting to close the van door when the little boy suddenly cried out, "Lucy! Can't you take us now? Please, don't leave—take us with you now! You promised, Lucy, you promised!"

Lucy Crown's heart almost stopped. Peter Judge slammed the van door and raised the rifle. And Billy Ray was suddenly beside her, his carbine barrel jammed painfully into her side. His stone-gray eyes were no longer dull but full of a quick, malevolent hate. "Lucy?" he whispered hoarsely. "Lucy? Who the fuck are you, lady? What's going on?"

The thought of the Beretta in her bag had barely touched her mind when Billy Ray hooked the barrel of the carbine through the bag's handle and ripped it away, tossing it aside. Then he rammed the carbine into her stomach, hard. The wind left her and she went to her knees, fighting for breath and barely aware of Billy Ray's voice somewhere in the haze around her. "Whoever you are—Lucy," he whispered viciously, "you're dead meat!"

TWENTY-FOUR

"Chief? Rags. We're in Nogie."

"Nice of you to check in. That license we traced on the rental? Name used was Norma Hughes, and she rented it for a week, destination southern Arizona. Description doesn't match Crown, but the credit card she used was good, and the feds confirm it's a cover she's used before, disguised. They want to know where she is, Rags."

"Still my question too, Chief. Put out a new APB."

"I already have. So you had her there in Arivaca. What happened?"

"She met with Billy Ray and disappeared, probably headed east, or maybe into Mexico."

"That's wonderful, Ragnon. *Now* what are you two geniuses gonna do?"

Ragnon ignored the sarcasm. "I don't think she'd go into Mexico—not on her own. But we alerted the border stations, and the sheriff's departments in Santa Cruz and Cochise counties. We can call them for backup when we find our perps, but they think they're in Mexico too. And we checked out the old mining camps at Oro Blanco and

Ruby, and the public campground at Pena Blanca Lake, with negative results."

"Sounds like you're pissing up a rope, Rags. Are you telling me this whole thing has gone sour?"

"No, but we could sure use some help. A little pressure from higher up might move some butts."

"Nobody's got the manpower for a big manhunt, Rags. Especially when they're probably already across the line."

"We don't *know* that, Chief."

"But what you're telling me is they could still be anywhere."

"Somewhere, Chief. They're somewhere."

"Just find Crown, Rags." It was almost a plea now. "And I don't want it broadcast all over hell and back that it's her we lost. The APB is for Norma Hughes. McKittrick's covering temporarily with the Hannigan thing, but the feds want her back now, so you've got twenty-four hours or it blows wide open. And, Rags, if it blows, my balls are gonna be in the crusher, but you can bet your bony ass yours and the Indian's will be right in there with 'em."

Tom Ragnon took a deep breath. "We spent the night here in Nogie, Chief. We're heading out again now."

"Fine, that's good, Rags. Our two flyovers didn't report a thing. We'll try one more. You just keep heading east if that's your thing. A low-flying customs plane did report sighting a big RV and a van apparently traveling together on a back road south of Patagonia at dusk night before last, but no convertible and no green Plymouth, so probably just a coincidence. And no sightings since."

"Thanks," Ragnon said, and hung up. There was no doubt now that it had been Crown and not Carmen with Billy Ray. Damn her eyes. Was she really that dedicated, or just plain nuts? He came out of the phone booth and told Antone about a van and RV being sighted the night before last.

The Indian had spread out the map again on the hood of the Volkswagen. It was 7:40 A.M., and they'd brought coffee and a bag of doughnuts out to the car after six hours of restless sleep in a fleabag motel. "Sounds like this area, if it was them," Antone was saying, drawing a circle with a felt pen. "Harshaw and Duquesne and Washington camp, and half a dozen other old camps and ghost towns, and more farther east."

"Yeah—if it was them. But what else do we have? We'll just have to work our way through the back country, John, then check in again in a few hours with Poole, or Montoya at Pontatoc. They've closed the border station at Lochiel, so the nearest phone will probably be at Parker Canyon Lake." He shook his head, feeling a familiar and uncomfortable tightness that sat like a rock in his guts, and he looked up at the sky, where a vast cloud shadow moved slowly over them like some evil omen. *Where are you, Crown*, he wondered in silent anguish, *where in hell are you?*

Because he was certain that wherever she was, the perps and the kids would be there too. And he'd lost a Mexican partner in a firefight along this border just the year before. He didn't want to lose another.

Lucinda Crown awoke in stifling, cramped darkness and pain, and she was incredibly thirsty, so she knew she wasn't dead. Her lower lip was puffed and crusted with dried blood. Her whole face felt swollen, one eye almost shut. Her ribs hurt when she breathed, and she wondered if any were broken. But at least she *could* breathe, and she was grateful for that.

Her hands and feet were bound tightly behind her and

getting numb, and she was lying on her side. She could smell dirt and grease and gasoline, and when she tried to raise her head she bumped it against metal. Consciousness had come and gone and come again, and she tried to keep the awareness with her this time, trying, too, to push away the urge to panic in the dark closeness, to remain calm and think instead.

As near as she could determine, she was in the trunk of a car, so it had to be the Chrysler or her rented Plymouth, and it wasn't moving. Then she remembered the beating at the hands of Billy Ray, and his sharply repeated words, like metal barbs punctuated by the blows. "Who are you? Who the fuck are you, cunt! Are you a goddamned cop? Are you—huh? Are you a cop?"

It had taken both Pudge and Carmen to pull him off before he killed her, and she had rolled helpless on the ground, desperately going for the steel needle in her disheveled hair, but it was gone. And when they pulled her roughly to her feet, she had fainted.

Now everything hurt, especially when she moved, so she lay still and listened. She could hear the rumble of the generator still going—or was it going again? How much time had passed? Was it still night, or morning? She was achingly aware of her thirst. And then the generator stopped. There was utter silence. And then a bird started singing, clear, distinct. She sobbed, thinking of its freedom. But it must be morning. Birds didn't sing at night—did they?

In the Winnebago, Pudge, Carmen, and Billy Ray were gathered around the kitchen table, drinking coffee. Pudge had the rifle beside him, and the carbine leaned against the refrigerator nearby. "I still say she's a cop," Pudge was saying, dunking a slice of cinnamon toast in his coffee.

"No way," Billy Ray insisted, noting the slight tremble in Carmen's hand as she, too, raised a piece of toast to her garishly red lips. "Some kind of fucking social worker maybe, that's what she is, but not a cop. Cops always have backups, and she's alone."

"Admit it," Carmen whined. "Your contact blew it, or he set us up."

"He was either totally wrong," Pudge agreed, "or he finked on you. She's a cop. If you hadn't beat her unconscious, we could have got it out of her last night."

Billy Ray shrugged. "So we'll ask her this morning. Only this time I'll break some bones, use a lighted cigarette on her. She'll talk."

Pudge pushed the little Beretta automatic across the table toward Billy Ray. "That's a lady cop's gun—the kind they'd use. It's the only thing that explains it—what she asked the kid."

Billy Ray had taken a belt to Larry Thompson until he had told everything that had gone on—or not gone on—with "Norma" who was now "Lucy." She hadn't used him, and she had promised to take him away. She had promised to take all three kids, but she hadn't said she was a cop. "If you're so sure she's a cop," Billy Ray told Pudge, "why didn't you just let me kill her? Just ditch the car and dump her body down one of the mine shafts. We can still do it."

"For God's sake, don't you understand, Billy Ray?" Pudge pleaded. "No cop-killing. They never stop looking for cop-killers."

"Then what the fuck do we do?" They all looked at one another.

"We've no choice now but to run," Pudge said finally.

"It's only a couple of miles to the border from here. There's not much in the way of roads, but it's passable, even for the car. And nothing but a wire cattle fence to cut through along here. And they can't chase us into Mexico."

"What about the snuff?" Billy Ray wanted to know, lighting a cigarette.

"Christ, Billy Ray, forget the goddamned snuff!" Pudge knocked out the ash from his pipe in his empty coffee cup. "At least for now. We've got other problems."

"But we can still make it in Mexico, like we said. Maybe we can even include *her* in it—if it turns out she's not a cop—take her with us and snuff them both!" He looked to Carmen for support, but the he-bitch avoided his gaze, puffing rapidly on her own cigarette and waving away the smoke that got in her eyes. It was making them water and her goddamned mascara was streaking her cheeks. Billy Ray looked back at Peter Judge. "Why the fuck not, man?"

"Because she's probably a cop, that's why." Pudge was losing his patience, yet could feel his resistance ebbing too. Maybe they should at least take her. They certainly couldn't turn her loose here, now. Everything was suddenly too complicated, too dangerous. At least they wouldn't look for her in Mexico.

"We've got no visas to go to Mexico," Carmen suddenly pointed out, "not for us or the vehicles."

"She's right," Pudge said. God, he thought, more complications.

"We don't need no fuckin' visas, man," Billy Ray insisted. "Just to step across the line—that's for trips deep into Mexico. And we're just gonna cut the fence along here and slip across. It's all the same—all a goddamned wilderness on both sides. There'll be a village or two where we can buy gas and food, but they don't ask questions of touring gringos in the back country."

"What about *her* car?" Pudge asked.

"Simple, we siphon the gas and dump it. They find it, and there's a hundred old mine shafts to search for her body—it'll take 'em six months."

Peter Judge looked at Carmen. "You're in this too, dammit. What do you say?"

"Christamighty, don't ask me, Pudge," she fluttered. "I don't know what to do. You two decide."

Pudge was in a hole he couldn't see his way out of. It was Billy Ray they should have dumped, and now he had the aching feeling they had waited too long. Of course there was always the chance the woman wasn't a cop, but then who *was* she? He finally nodded, knowing Billy Ray would have his way in the end anyway. And it was probably the only way now. The woman had seen their faces, the vehicles, the kids—she knew it all. Maybe if they killed her in Mexico and then just lay low for a few months before starting over—but when they did start again, he swore to himself that this time it would be without Billy Ray.

TWENTY-FIVE

Noon. Dark, bruised-looking clouds hovered threateningly low overhead, ready to drench the earth in torrents, and casting a vast gloom across the land. Beneath them, the unmoving air was cool and damp as the desert waited.

The heat from the fire Antone had kindled felt good as Ragnon hunkered down and refilled his mug from the coffeepot resting on the grill. Across from him, the Indian cleaned the last dab of beans from his paper plate and tossed the plate on the flames, watching it blacken and curl. "What now, Sergeant?" he asked.

What now indeed, thought Tom Ragnon. They had hunted all morning, questioned occasional campers, caretakers, a hunter or two, even a U.S. Customs patrol Jeep. Not a trace, not a track, not a clue. "We'd better head for the Parker Canyon campground, John, and call the chief. He's got to give us more help on this. Maybe if—"

Antone suddenly held up his hand for silence. "Listen. Someone's coming. More than one."

At first Ragnon heard nothing, then the faint crunch of footsteps and a rustle of movement in the brush-lined arroyo a few feet away. He saw Antone reach inside his

KINDERKILL

jacket, and his own hand went to the Cobra mounted at the small of his back as he slowly set the coffee mug down and waited.

A ragtag Mexican youth scrambled up out of the arroyo and stepped from the brush, followed by a second, older one. They stopped and stared—illegals by the look of them, and not long across the line. They looked hesitantly from the two men to the car, and then at the fire with its pots of coffee and beans. *"Tenemos hambre,"* the older one said cautiously.

"We smelled your fire and the food," the younger Mexican said in English. "We have not eaten in two days." He looked about eighteen.

"Bien venidos a los Estados Unidos, amigos," Ragnon said, relaxing. "Help yourselves to the coffee and beans." Fortunately Antone had made more than enough, as usual, and he walked over to the open trunk of the Volkswagen and got two more paper plates and an extra mug. Ragnon rinsed his own mug and added fresh water to the coffeepot from their canteen.

Soon the two Mexicans were squatting with them side by side around the fire, eating hungrily and sipping their coffee gratefully. Antone had opened a new loaf of bread and was passing it around as Ragnon asked the younger one, "Where did you learn English? You speak it well."

"From the gringo tourists around Guaymas." He grinned, wiping his plate clean with the bread. "I drove a taxi."

"So what are you going to do around here?" Antone asked. "Not much taxi business." He nodded at the empty desert hills around them.

"We are going to Tucson." He motioned toward his companion. "Jaime's cousin is a foreman in a brick yard. He has promised us work at twenty dollars a day."

"Not much," Ragnon said, "but a lot more than you can make in Mexico, *verdad*?"

"The life is very hard in Mexico, *señor*."

"The life can be hard here, too, *hombre*—for some people." He reached over and refilled both youths' cups with coffee, draining the pot.

The younger of them was looking around now, at their camp, and he saw Antone's rifle in its leather boot leaning against the car. "You are hunters?" he asked.

"Sort of," Ragnon said. "We're policemen." He saw the youngster's sudden look of dismay, and he glanced at the other one, who seemed to have understood the word *policemen*, too, and was suddenly standing.

"La Migra?"

"No, not Immigration. We're regular policemen—detectives. We're looking for three killers—molesters of children—*gente muy malo*."

The younger Mexican translated this, and the older one relaxed a little, saying something Ragnon didn't catch. "He says we are grateful for your kindness," the younger one translated again. "You're not like the police in Mexico. Not like the gringos we saw yesterday either—*ricos* with a big house on wheels and a van and car, but who would not give us so much as a drink of water."

"What?" Ragnon glanced at Antone. "You saw these people yesterday?"

"*Sí*. About this time yesterday."

"Where?"

The young Mexican shrugged. "Miles from here. South and east, almost to the border. We had just crossed."

"Describe them," Ragnon said. "Men? Women? Adults? Children?"

"One man, one woman—sort of. Not young, more than your age I think."

"No children?"

The Mexican shook his head. "We saw none."

"And only two people," Ragnon said, "but three vehicles. What color was the van?"

"Green—I think."

"And the car—describe it."

The younger Mexican glanced at his companion. *"Azul? El automóvil?"*

"Sí, azul," the older one answered, and added something else.

"Blue, and it had a white canvas top—what you call a convertible."

"Jesus—and they were camped, like us here?"

The young Mexican nodded. "Only in an old town—old broken buildings among the trees."

"A ghost town," Antone said.

"Sí, in a shallow valley between two hills."

"With a big rocky wash running down one side?" Antone asked him.

"Sí, an arroyo *grande."*

Antone looked at Ragnon. "Perlyville," he said. "I know the place—the ruins of one of the earliest Anglo mining towns in southern Arizona, and only two miles from the border. It's not even on the map."

Half an hour later the Volkswagen Bug was moving slowly into the little valley between the two hills, barely able to follow the faint trace of a road that ran close beside the big wash. The afternoon had darkened with more clouds, and at the first adobe ruin, brown and stark and silent among the mesquite trees, Ragnon stopped the car and they got out.

Standing motionless, they listened. Only a cactus wren protested their presence, and then a covey of quail scattered from their path as they separated left and right, Antone with the old Winchester leveled as they moved like shadows through the mesquite grove and passed more ruins to the edge of a clearing, where they stopped.

A fire-ring of rocks waited. Nothing else. Then it began to rain, gently at first, then fat, splattering drops as Antone ran to the campfire and probed carefully for any remaining coals among the ashes. He shook his head. "Not even warm." And as thunder shook the sky above them, the rain descended in a sudden deluge, and they both sheltered in the one adobe building that still had a piece of galvanized roofing.

It had evidently rained earlier, obliterating any tracks, and from inside they watched the rain roar down again, soaking the clearing. "Maybe the Mexicans lied," Tom Ragnon said, but he didn't believe it.

"They had no reason to, Sergeant. And they described the van, and the convertible too."

"Yeah, they were here, dammit—I can feel it!"

"We can do more than feel it; we can see it now," Antone said, pointing at the ground beneath their feet where, sheltered from the rain, a set of tire tracks showed plainly. "Not more than a few hours old, Sergeant. They must have parked the car in here. The roof's not high enough for the van."

And as the rain slowed to a drizzle, they searched some more and found the clincher beneath a huge mesquite: dual tire tracks, the same pattern they'd seen beside the dry creek bed on the Malaguena Ranch the week before.

The rain ended as suddenly as it began, and they circled the perimeter of the town in opposite directions. The air smelled sweet, the surrounding desert clean and fresh, renewed. Ragnon felt renewed, too, at least temporarily. Once again they were close, he could taste it. But once again their quarry was gone, and the same freshening rain had also wiped out any further spoor.

They found no new sign of the killers, and no sign of Crown either. His momentary euphoria gone, anger and frustration welled up strong in Ragnon as they met back at the car. "Let's drive around, John. Even with the rain and the wash running, they must have left some evidence—garbage or something. Then we'll head for the border."

They found the green Plymouth on the second trip around the town, nose down behind a big boulder in the wash. Antone stepped into the knee-deep water and felt the engine—cold. And the car was empty. But the trunk lid was sprung wide open and Ragnon had a quick stirring of dread as he looked inside.

But the trunk was empty too—almost. He touched the reddish-brown stains smeared on the tire well and filthy carpeting and smelled them. Blood. And the knowledge momentarily sickened him. Human blood? Crown's blood? Not much blood, thank God, Ragnon thought hopefully.

"If she's dead, she's dead, Sergeant," Antone said softly behind him, resting a hand gently on his partner's shoulder. "But if she's alive—"

TWENTY-SIX

Lucinda Crown was alive. And full of fear and loathing and helpless rage.

Bound naked and kneeling, facing a heavy, half-fallen roof beam with her hands tied around the wood and her ankles roped behind her, she sobbed and gasped, out of breath and aching all over. Again and again she had tried with all her strength to lift the angled beam enough to slide her bound hands off the end, but it was too heavy, or she was too weak. And leaning her forehead against the rough wood, she rested.

She was alone in the nearly roofless adobe ruin of an ancient church. Hours before, Billy Ray had been standing behind her, taunting her as he nudged her bare right buttock with the cold steel of the carbine barrel. "So you're one of them pussy cops, Loo-cee." He had purposely slurred the name. "Not a real cop. Cops are supposed to be tough, but you're soft, weak—I could mash you like a worm—I still might, but maybe we'll save it for the movie, how's that?" He had prodded her again with the cold, hard barrel. "You and the kid'll both be stars, and then you'll both die. Maybe with plastic bags tied over your heads—

that's one of my favorites. Your face gets all screwed up and funny-colored. Only I never killed an adult. You'll be the first, Loo-cee, or whatever your name is. And I bet you'll die just like a kid, crying and begging and scared. Or I might just shove this barrel up your twat and blow you away. . . ."

She had shut her eyes, set her teeth, and said nothing. Her head throbbing, her hands growing numb, she had tried to shut out the sound of his voice, the vicious words, shut out his cruel presence altogether and conserve her strength. Until suddenly he was really gone and it was silent in the old church. She wondered what would happen next.

Oddly enough, none of them had abused her sexually, yet. Not even Billy Ray, who had been brutal in his physical abuse—but no rape, no sodomy. He evidently reserved his sexual aberrations for children, at least up to now.

Early this morning, when they had let her out of the trunk of the Plymouth and fed her, and let her go to the toilet in the wash with Billy Ray watching her every move, she had told them she was a cop before he could get any rougher. She wasn't sure they even believed her, but maybe it had saved her life, or at least delayed her death. She had even tried to convince them they'd be better off submitting to arrest now. Billy Ray had laughed loudly at that, and forced her into the trunk of the Chrysler. And in minutes the roughest ride of her life had begun.

Later, hauled out of the Chrysler, she had been dumped on the ground in front of this old Spanish mission. Once boasting twin bell towers, it wasn't even much of a building now, only a tumbledown ruin. She knew it must be over two hundred years old, its adobe walls blackened by countless fires, and probably burned originally by

Apaches. Now it was nearly roofless, the great wooden beams fallen in on the dirt floor and lying at odd angles against the walls, the niches carved in the adobe long emptied of icons, and the altar crumbling. An empty, desecrated, lonely place, a place of stark sunlight and deep shadows and gloomy silence as they had led her inside, stripped her, forced her to her knees on the packed earth floor, and made her clasp one of the fallen beams while they bound her hands tightly around it.

Only Billy Ray had remained to taunt her. "See you later, Loo-cee," he had finally said, stepping out through the broken, sagging wooden doors. "We're gonna snort a little coke and make some plans, but I'll be back—count on it!"

She had waited, listening, making sure that he had really gone. Then she had tried to free herself from the beam. She had tried again and again as the hours passed, but it was useless. Now her breathing had quieted once more, but she was exhausted. She could hear some tiny animal rustling against the wall behind her, and wondered if it was a captive too. The lowering sun seemed to stand still as she rested. And then she resumed what she knew was a tedious, frighteningly fragile chance at best: the slow, methodical sawing motion of the thick rope against the ragged edge of the beam.

She wasn't sure just how soon she heard the new sound—a scuffling of feet—and she froze, motionless, then turned her head, twisting painfully to see over her shoulder. If Billy Ray was returning . . .

The scuffling sound moved closer. Then a small voice whispered behind her, "I'm sorry, lady. I'm sorry I gave you away."

"Larry?" She twisted hard to see him, the pain shooting through her shoulders. But he was there, in a corner in the shadows. "Larry—where are the other children?"

"Still in the van. I came to find you, to tell you I didn't mean to—"

"Never mind. Come here, will you please?"

When he stood beside her she nodded. "That's it. Now, I've got to get free. Can you reach under the beam and unfasten the knots?"

Kneeling, the boy worked at the thick rope with his small fingers, but finally shook his head. "I can't—they're too tight."

"Then see if you can help me lift the beam. Just a little so I can slip the rope off the end."

Still on his knees, the boy crawled under the slanted end and put his back against it. "On three," Lucy Crown whispered, "one, two—three!" She lifted with him, straining against the nausea and fatigue.

On the third try, with the end of the beam poised briefly a couple of inches clear of the dirt floor, she slipped her bound hands off the end and the wood thudded down again. She was free of the beam but not of the ropes, and she began gnawing at the knots and talking between breaths. "Where are the adults?"

"In the motor house." He stood there, watching her as if fascinated.

"All three of them?"

The boy nodded. "Are you going to take us away this time?"

"Yes. Now go back to the van, Larry. Get the girls, but warn them to be very quiet. Just bring them here while I get out of these ropes."

With the boy gone and her heart beating with anticipation and dread, she continued her attack on the knots with her teeth. Several minutes passed in silence before they finally loosened and her hands came free. Massaging her wrists to restore the circulation, she went to work on her roped ankles, finally getting the knots loose enough to slip one foot out and then the other. Getting stiffly to her feet, she stretched her aching muscles and staggered over to the open mission doorway and peered outside.

Where there had once been a high-walled courtyard around the church, now there were only fragments, the low adobe barrier broken completely through in a dozen places and melted down to a height of only three or four feet. Beyond was a grassy clearing and a mesquite grove, with the big RV and the Chrysler pulled in side by side under the trees. Around them the sunlight was fading to a pale yellow. There was music, not amplified now, but coming from the motor home—some vaguely familiar operatic aria she couldn't quite place. She thought the van must be elsewhere in the grove, out of her line of sight, but where were the kids? And how much time would she have when they got here?

She looked around inside the church again, resting against the wall and still not in full control of her nerves and muscles, which were cramped from the long confinement on the beam. She saw her clothes strewn against the opposite wall where Billy Ray had thrown them, and made her way to them, dressing clumsily while she tried to orient herself.

Bounced around in the darkened, stifling trunk of the Chrysler, her hands bound and her mouth taped shut, she had tried to keep track of the time and direction of movement after leaving the campground. She had to assume they had started directly south toward the border, and it was relatively smooth at first. Then they must have left the road and headed across country, stopping once probably just to get across the border itself, because not much later they were on a fairly smooth road again.

Minutes after that they had slowed, going through a village. She had heard the sounds of children calling to each other in Spanish, a mule braying, a passing truck badly out of tune, and more Spanish voices when they stopped for gas. And then a rougher road for just a little while, and they had stopped—here.

So the border had to be north, and not far. She estimated maybe a half mile back to the village, and then not more than a mile from there back into the United States. After that . . .

At the quick sound of footsteps she whirled around, fighting the rising panic, but it was only the three kids, Larry leading the two girls hand in hand. They weren't dressed for a cool desert night and neither was she, but it would have to do. One of them still clutched the Cabbage Patch Kid protectively. Crown could still hear the music coming faintly from the RV, and she had the feeling that when it stopped . . . "What are they doing now, Larry?" she asked the boy.

He shrugged. "Just doing dope and playing music." The two girls stood close beside him, silent, staring at her as if she were from another planet. She considered trying to steal the van or the Chrysler, but knew it was too risky. They were too well armed. They even had her Beretta now.

The sun slipped below the horizon, and a chilling breeze stirred the dust in the clearing as she made her decision. If they could at least reach the village . . . There was no telling how long they had until Billy Ray decided to shoot a session, or simply take the kids some supper, but it couldn't be long. Hopefully she wouldn't need long. Even on foot they could be back across the border in an hour.

Less if they could get a ride in the village or maybe find the police—yet she wasn't sure she could trust the Mexican police. "Let's go," she said, taking Larry's hand. "And don't make a sound, any of you." Then the four of them slipped out of the church through a hole in the back wall, and as the day died in torment beneath a blood-red sky, they found a narrow, winding road leading north.

TWENTY-SEVEN

The crimson sky had faded. Dark clouds laced with distant lightning crushed down upon the whole western horizon, leaving only a narrow band of brightness exposed beneath them as Ragnon and Antone pulled up a dozen yards from the tall cement column and barbed-wire cattle fence that marked the Mexican border.

They had left the dirt road ten minutes before and driven cross-country, cutting for sign, and found it here where the fence had been broken through and several vehicles had crossed, one with dual wheels.

While the Volkswagen engine idled noisily, Antone got out and knelt to examine the sign. He looked up at Ragnon. "The same dual-wheel pattern, Sergeant, and three vehicles—but the tracks are hours old."

Tom Ragnon wasn't surprised. Spitting, he got out and looked south across empty rolling hills that were softening from brown to gray in the fading daylight banking off the low clouds in the west. He spat again. "You ready for an armed invasion of Mexico, John?"

"Wherever the trail leads, Sergeant. Nothing else is going right with this case."

They got back in the car, but as Ragnon shifted into low, Antone put a hand on his arm. "Wait—look."

At first he didn't see anything, then movement low against the dark side of a hill—a figure stumbling on foot, with several more tiny figures running beside it. "Jesus, John—it's Crown! And she's got the kids with her!"

They came out of the dusk, holding hands as they worked their way along the side of the low hill, across a shallow arroyo, and then up beside the tall concrete border marker, where they stepped through the opening in the fence and slumped down, safe.

Antone held open the door of the Volkswagen while Ragnon ran over to Crown. "We missed you, Lucy" was all he could say, trying to ignore her tattered, bedraggled appearance and the purplish bruises that were obvious even in the fading light. He suppressed his outrage and anger and incredible relief—and the myriad questions he wanted to ask. Until she reached out and took his hand and then drew herself hard against him.

"You're not gonna cry, are you, Crown?" he asked gruffly, a lump in his own throat.

She looked up, the tears welling. "No, dammit, Rags, I'm not going to cry!" And then she did. "Oh, Rags," she sobbed, "it was awful—they're awful!" Turning, she held out her hands to the kids as she squatted down.

"They had these three in the van. We're okay now," she told them. "We're safe."

Ragnon glanced around at Antone. "John, better get the kids in the car." He looked back at Crown. "Are they really all right?"

"I think so—they will be. Kids are amazingly resilient, but they'll need a lot of therapy."

"How about you?"

While the Indian led the children over to the Volkswagen, Lucinda Crown put her arms around Ragnon again. "I'm all right too—really. Just hold me a minute, till I stop shaking." And he held her, stroking her tangled hair. "They're over there, Rags," she whispered against his chest, "the three of them, with the big RV and the green van and the convertible. God, but he's vicious, cruel, that Billy Ray—" She couldn't seem to stop talking now, until he hushed her.

"Easy, easy, Lucy. Hey, c'mon, you made it, partner. You're a ball-buster, remember?"

She wiped her eyes. "There's a Mexican village about a mile to the south," she told him more calmly, "and then an old abandoned Spanish church, a ruin, a quarter mile or so southeast of the village. They held me there. And Billy Ray's got some kind of military carbine—I think it's an automatic—and there's a bolt-action rifle, and they've got my Beretta. I couldn't find a phone in the village, not even a police station, so we just kept on toward the border." Her breathing was getting rapid again, her emotions barely controlled.

"It's okay now, Lucy," Ragnon said, still holding her. "It was crazy, but you did good. You're safe, the kids are safe. That's what matters most."

"But they'll steal a Mexican child now, find a real buyer, and still make the damn snuff!" She looked back south, staring into the gathering dusk, then looked at him again. "We haven't lost the bastards, have we, Ragnon? They're not really going to get away?"

Tom Ragnon was staring south, too, and he knew what she meant: They were in Mexico. "No, Crown," he said softly, "we haven't lost them, I promise you that." He looked around and watched Antone getting the kids settled in the backseat of the Volkswagen. "You take the car—get them into Pontatoc."

"I want to go with you, Rags."

"Use your head, Crown—look at you. Get yourself and the kids back to Pontatoc, now, and all of you see a doctor. John and I will finish this business."

"My God—how? On foot?"

Ragnon was watching Antone, who was already pulling his Winchester and their flak vests from behind the seat. "You say it's only a mile or so," he said. "With the advantage of darkness we'll find 'em and hit 'em just before dawn, while they're sleeping. We'll have them out of Mexico before anybody knows we were there. You call Poole—he'll be at home. Just tell him we're still hunting and we're close."

"He'll guess what you're doing, Rags. Poole will know."

"I want him to know. He won't admit he knows. Now go." He watched Antone help her into the car, and waved as the noisy little beast's lights came on and it disappeared to the north around the bend of a hill. Then he looked at the Indian, who came walking toward him carrying their flak vests over his shoulder with the old Winchester hanging easily at the end of his arm. "You look like you're ready, John," he said as he checked the loads in his own Cobra.

John Antone merely nodded. And with a few stars already showing in the blackness to the east, and only a faint gray streak of daylight slashing the line of dark clouds in the west, they stepped through the opening in the fence and headed into Mexico on foot.

The same dusk had settled over the old Spanish ruin a mile and a quarter to the south. Billy Ray Lee, with his carbine in one hand and a flashlight in the other, stood tensely by the sagging door, playing the light over the dirt

KINDERKILL

floor and tumbled roof beams inside. Her pile of clothes was gone. *She* was gone. Only the tangle of rope remained at the foot of the beam.

Carmen and Pudge stared over his shoulder as he muttered fiercely, "How the fuck?" But it didn't matter how. They were gone—the woman *and* the kids.

Billy Ray had finally brought the kids' supper out to the van and found the back door open and the vehicle empty. He hadn't even thought of locking it down here. Where could they go in Mexico, for Christ's sake?

"They've freed the woman and taken off," Pudge spoke up anxiously behind him. "Now what the hell do we do?"

"They won't get away with this," Billy Ray said tightly as he tucked the flashlight under his arm and clutched the carbine against his chest, clicking the safety on and off and working his way through the tangle of debris to the back of the church. Carmen and Pudge had flashlights, too, and it was quickly evident that their quarries were nowhere inside. They knew for sure when Carmen said, "There," and pointed her light at the large hole in the bottom of the back wall and the dust around it full of obviously fresh, small footprints.

Stooping and shining his light through the hole, Billy Ray tracked their path on out to the road that led to the village.

"And the border's only a mile or so away," Pudge said behind him. "Even on foot they could be there by now."

"Unless she stopped in the village," Carmen added.

"Damn!" Billy Ray swore. "Either way, we've got to find her, and fast." He turned to the others. "Go get the other guns, and the van and car. I'll get the bike and we'll spread out, converge on the village. She'll probably be there, trying to get help. I doubt if there *is* any help—there probably isn't even a phone—but we've got to get the bitch back before she makes trouble."

Dusk had settled over the village too, and Sergeant Luis Jaramillo of the Sonoran judicial police sat on a bench in the paint-chipped gazebo that dominated the center of the little plaza. He was smoking a long black cheroot and watching the lights come on in various places around the town. Some shone with the bright incandescence of bare electric bulbs, and some with the softer, dimmer glow of kerosene lamps. Behind him, his black, unmarked Bronco sat at the curb on the street in front of the darkened church, and he had been sitting there alone for nearly ten minutes, pondering the situation.

Dressed in hand-tooled leather boots and sharply creased Levis, with his Colt .45 holstered beneath a brown corduroy jacket, he smoked and watched the lights come on at his particular point of interest—the town's combined Pemex gas station and grocery that was on the southwest corner across from the plaza, where it had all started.

Here on the far edge of his jurisdiction there was seldom much to profit from, so Sergeant Jaramillo didn't even come this far too often, and never stayed long when he did. But this trip was different. He had passed through the village a few hours earlier and stopped for gas. The station's owner was Angel de Fuentes, his informant in the area, and he had a curious story.

Since de Fuentes pretended to speak little English with occasional *turistas*—so it was easier to make "mistakes" when changing pesos to dollars and liters to gallons—they usually talked freely in his presence. But this particular trio of gringos, two men and a curiously mannish-looking woman, had said practically nothing. They had come through just this morning in dust-covered vehicles: a big

Winnebago, a green van, and a Chrysler convertible. They were obviously wealthy. But the village was off the regular tourist route, miles from the nearest legal port of entry. There wasn't even a nearby paved road except for the concrete drive around the plaza itself, and it was full of potholes, while the village's rutted dirt streets angled off at the four corners of the plaza like spokes off the hub of a wheel.

They had bought gas and groceries, and managed to ask simple directions where they might camp somewhere out of the way. The grocer had suggested the old mission church ruin southeast of the town—there was even a well. But it was when he had gone into the back room and peered through the peephole into the women's toilet that he had gotten the real surprise: The "woman" had stood facing the bowl, and held her dress up to pee.

"Un tranvestidor," Sergeant Jaramillo had muttered when the grocer had finished his story. But it had set him to thinking, wondering, for the next couple of hours. Nothing impressive had happened in this village in the three years since he had made sergeant. But the three dust-covered vehicles bothered him. What were they doing here, miles from the nearest port of entry, yet so near the border? Had they entered the country illegally? And if so, what were they doing—running contraband?

And then something else had happened. The grocer had called him away from his evening meal and *cerveza* at the Olvidos Bar, where he was even then thinking of paying the gringos a visit at the old church. Just before dark, the grocer had said, another gringo woman with three gringo children had passed through the village on foot, coming from the south. This was what had finally made Jaramillo decide that an investigation was definitely called for.

He had checked first to the north in his Bronco, but the light was already getting so bad he couldn't pick up any tracks of people on foot. What he had found were the fresh tire prints of several vehicles suspiciously close to the border. He had then returned to the village, where the whole episode continued to mystify him. What was going on?

He had decided to wait in the gazebo on the plaza until full dark, and then visit the gringos down at the old mission. But now it looked like they were going to save him a trip. A late-model green van was slowly entering the village from the southeast, and he watched it pull up on the paved apron on one side of the Pemex station. Moments later a small Chrysler convertible coming from the southwest pulled up on the other side of the station's concrete apron, and he could hear what sounded like a motorbike approaching, also from the south.

Crushing his cheroot under his boot, Jaramillo stood up, adjusting his shoulder holster and then waiting motionless in the darkness of the gazebo as the sound grew louder, until the biker, too, came in on the dirt road southeast of the station and circled the concrete drive around the plaza once before parking in front of the station.

De Fuentes hadn't mentioned a bike, but it could have been carried inside the van, and all three drivers had now gone into the Pemex station together. So where was the Winnebago, Jaramillo wondered. Left at the old mission? Moving silently to the front of the gazebo, he slowly descended the steps. It was time to find out about these *chingasos* gringos.

As he walked across the street and onto the cement apron fronting the station, he noted the New Mexico license plates on the bike and van. The convertible was on the other side of the pumps, but he thought its plates would probably be the same.

Stepping inside, he greeted Angel de Fuentes, who appeared now to have been convinced by these gringos that he knew more than a little English. "No, *señores*, no woman here, no kids—I speak the truth," he was telling the young muscled gringo with stringy blond hair.

"Are these the ones?" Jaramillo asked the grocer in Spanish.

"*Sí, por seguro, Sargento,*" he answered, and looked relieved.

"*Buenas noches, señores, señora,*" Jaramillo greeted them pleasantly enough, and introduced himself in English. "I am Sergeant Luis Jaramillo of the state judicial police, at your service. Your identification, *por favor*."

There was a moment of stunned silence. The young muscled gringo, standing to his left with the grocer, looked over at the older gringo, who was standing in front of him with the "woman."

"Look, officer," the older gringo said. "We know we shouldn't be here. We—heard about the old mission south of here and just came over to see it. We didn't want to drive all the way to an entry port, and there was an opening in the fence. We're going back in the morning—or right now if you wish." He was reaching for his wallet. "We'll even make it—"

"Shut up, Pudge," the young gringo snapped. "You don't need to make a fuckin' speech, and we don't need identification."

Sargeant Jaramillo realized too late the young gringo had moved farther to his left and behind him. Close up he could see they were not the simple gringo tourists he could prey on, and he started to step back, reaching for the .45 holstered under his arm, then stopped as he felt the cold, hard metal of a gun barrel jammed painfully into the hollow under his left ear.

"Here's our identification, *Capitano*, you bean-eatin' bastard," Billy Ray whispered viciously behind him, and the click of the hammer being thumbed back on Crown's little automatic was loud in the sudden stillness of the Pemex station.

TWENTY-EIGHT

Deputy Ruben Montoya had the duty when Lucinda Crown and the three kids entered the sheriff's substation in Pontatoc at exactly 7:04 P.M. by the old pendulum clock on the station wall. But even with her description lying on the desk in front of him, he didn't recognize her. "Can I help you, miss?" he asked, glancing from her to the equally bedraggled-looking children.

"I'm Crown, Ragnon's partner—Rags and Antone. I don't have my ID, I've been undercover but—"

"*Híjola*, of course! They've been looking all over for you!"

"They found me. Rags and Antone—found us." She placed a hand on Larry's head to indicate the children.

"Oh, Christ, sure." He came around the counter. "What the hell happened? Where's Ragnon?"

"Answers later. Just see if you can arrange a night's shelter for these kids while I call Lieutenant Poole."

She put the call through on one of the two phones at the front desk, trying his house first and surprised at how relieved she was to hear that gruff voice growling irritably, "Yeah, Poole here."

"This is Crown, Lieutenant. I'm in Pontatoc—just shut up a minute and listen. I've got three kids the pedophiles had with them. We lost the perps themselves, but we're closing in."

"Where the hell are Rags and the Indian?"

"Still on the border. I just brought the kids in safe. I'm going back."

"The hell you are! You're off the case, Crown. Your people want you back—now."

"No way, Lieutenant. Tell them to put me on sick leave—I'm hurting—tell them, Lieutenant. Now I've got to go."

"Wait! That bitchin' Ragnon is in Mexico, ain't he? He's putting on one of his fuckin' dog and pony shows!"

"He's getting the job done, Lieutenant. Now I've got to go, it's my bust too."

"Okay, Crown, I can't stop you from here without having you arrested. But you can tell Rags if his ass gets burned over there, I'm not gonna kiss it and make it well."

"You're all heart, Lieutenant."

"And you can give him another message—a real one. His father died a few hours ago, just slipped away in his sleep. Tell him I'm sorry."

Lucinda Crown hung up the phone slowly, turning as Montoya came back in the front door. "I put the kids up with old lady Oates over at the Palace. What's the matter now?"

"Ragnon's father died. Poole just told me."

"Madre Santísima!" Montoya crossed himself. "And he doesn't know?"

She shook her head. "I'll have to tell him. Look, can I borrow a gun? I have to go back."

"A gun? Hey, shouldn't you take it easy—see a doctor? You really don't look all that great yourself."

"I've got to find Rags and John. They're close to a bust."

"When—tonight?"

"Now."

"Then let's get help. A SWAT team."

"I don't know where they are exactly, so a team won't help until I find them. A gun—please?"

"Okay, you can check one out. But you'd better take a walkie-talkie too. If you're not out of range, you can let us know when you find them. Meanwhile, I'll try to get a chopper to stand by." He unlocked the gun cabinet first and she picked out a .357 Magnum revolver and a box of shells. She hoped Montoya didn't notice how her hand was trembling.

In the darkness Tom Ragnon and John Antone approached the Mexican town plaza on opposite sides of the dirt street, both wearing their flak vests, and Ragnon carrying his Cobra at his side while Antone held the Winchester barrel down along his leg.

Both of them kept to the shadows as much as possible, eyeing the scattered bright glimmer of electric bulbs and the dimmer glow of lamps in various houses as they passed. But mainly they watched the plaza ahead, with the darkened gazebo in its center and the well-lighted Pemex station on one corner, where a suspicious-looking van was parked on one side and a small convertible on the other.

With a hand signal from Ragnon, they crossed the street simultaneously and converged on the dark gazebo, which was empty. "Looks like the van and the Chrysler," Ragnon whispered, peering through the lattice, "but no Winnebago."

"There's a bike," Antone said. "See it on the apron over by the sign?"

Ragnon grunted. The sign said GASOLINA—ABARROTES. To the left, an old tow truck was parked in the open gateway of what looked like a junkyard behind the station. The concrete in front of the station and the street surrounding the grassy plaza were the only paved areas in the town. From the plaza the dirt streets led off diagonally in four directions.

"The RV could still be at the old mission," Antone said. "Looks like several people inside the station."

Ragnon was looking around them in the darkness. The gazebo commanded the whole plaza, which had a shaggy eucalyptus tree standing at each of its corners. To the right, across the street, were single-storied Sonoran row houses. To the left, and also across the street, was a darkened church with twin bell towers. A black Bronco was parked in front of it, the only other vehicle in sight.

"I think they're on the move, John," Ragnon said. "I'm going in closer. Cover me from here with your rifle."

"Okay, Sergeant, but you'd better take this too." He handed him his Redhawk revolver, then glanced skyward as an early-rising moon lifted blood red above the clouds on the horizon while Ragnon sprinted for a corner tree and crouched in the shadow of its trunk, directly across from the Pemex station.

Suddenly the lights went out in the station. Ragnon glanced back at the gazebo but couldn't spot Antone. Flattened on the ground beside the tree, the Redhawk braced in front of him, he wondered if he'd been seen because of the damned moon. It seemed to pop up even higher now, drained of its redness and shrinking even as its brightness flooded the plaza and the town.

Maybe they were simply closing the station, but no one had come out. And Ragnon waited, staring across the street, trying to see into the darkened windows but unable to make out anything but shadows.

Inside the darkened Pemex station Billy Ray Lee whispered tightly, "I tell you, someone's out there around that plaza—I saw 'em move!" He stood away from the door, pressed against one wall, his carbine covering both Sergeant Jaramillo and the Mexican grocer, de Fuentes. He had them both on their knees, hands clasped behind their heads and leaning forward with their foreheads resting against the high wooden counter. And he had the Mexican lawman's .45 tucked in his belt.

"I don't see anyone, Billy Ray," Carmen whispered hoarsely. She held the .25-caliber automatic now, reluctantly, and was cowering in one corner and peering anxiously out the wide front window. Pudge had brought the bolt-action rifle from the van, and he stood in heavy shadow beside a darkened display case, the weapon held tightly in sweating hands. "Are you sure you—" he started to ask.

But another voice boomed suddenly from the darkness outside, "Billy Ray Lee! Or Billy Lee Ray! My name's Ragnon—Sergeant Ragnon, Mimbres County Sheriff's Department! I've got a warrant for your arrest—you and the other two, Peter Judge and Herman Henry Spears, alias Carmen Jones! It's over—throw your guns out on the street!"

Billy Ray glanced at the two Mexicans still kneeling against the counter as Carmen whimpered bitterly, "Oh, sweet Jesus, what're we going to do?"

"Shut up!" Billy Ray stared out the open door at the dark plaza beyond, then shouted, "Go fuck yourself, cowboy! You're outta your jurisdiction—where the fuck you think you are? This is Mexico!" He turned and jabbed the

Mexican cop in the back with the barrel of the carbine, then grabbed him by the collar with his free hand and lifted him to his feet. "Tell him, goddammit, greaseball," he snarled, moving the carbine barrel up to the man's neck and marching him to the door. "Keep those hands on your fuckin' head and tell him who you are!"

"Sergeant Ragnon?" Jaramillo called out to the darkness. His voice had a slight tremor. "I am Sergeant Luis Jaramillo of the Sonoran judicial police! With me is Angel de Fuentes, the station operator! These people are armed and we are hostages—go back where you came from!"

"Shit," Tom Ragnon muttered under his breath. He looked around the mostly darkened village and saw two more lights go out. No place to go for help. Nobody wanted this kind of trouble. He hadn't even seen a police station, but now the significance of the unmarked black Bronco parked nearby was clear.

As a drifting cloud dimmed the face of the moon, he darted back to the gazebo, keeping the tree between himself and the station. But even so, a burst of automatic fire from the doorway sparked off the pavement behind him.

Antone was flat on the floor of the gazebo. "With an automatic weapon and hostages," the Indian said, "maybe we better withdraw."

Ragnon sat down on the gazebo steps and peered under the rail. "I had a football coach once, John, who said the game's not over till it's over."

"But the hostages—"

"Are dead meat anyway if we leave. You think he's gonna let 'em go?"

"So what do we do?"

Ragnon looked around in the darkness again. He knew he should simply find a phone somewhere, call in the

Mexican police, and get the hell back across the border. But then the hassle of formal deportation for these scum might take weeks—if they didn't just buy their way out of it and disappear. No, he had them, dammit, here and now, all three, and he wasn't about to let them go.

"Cowboy?" Billy Ray shouted suddenly from the station. "Cowboy!"

"John," Ragnon whispered, "move with the next cloud that shadows the moon—across the street to that church. Get up in one of the bell towers with your rifle and wait for a clear shot. If we can get Billy Ray, the other two might give it up."

Antone nodded silently, and disappeared over the back side of the gazebo, running even as another burst from the carbine momentarily lit up the doorway of the station with its muzzle flash, and ripped up the grass on the plaza.

"Cowboy! You son of a bitch, you still out there?" Billy Ray called. "I'll *kill* 'em, goddammit!"

"You'll kill 'em anyway, Billy Ray!" Ragnon called back. "Won't you?"

Pudge, still standing as if frozen in a shadowed corner, whispered in near panic. "Let's get outta here, Billy Ray! Let's just run for the van or car and go!"

"Shut up, you gutless wonder, and keep your gun on these two!" He motioned to the two Mexicans, who were sitting now, their backs to the counter and their hands still clasped behind their heads. "We're in control, cowboy!" he shouted at the open door. "*We're* in control!"

Not for long, Tom Ragnon said quietly to himself, and slipping under the stair rail of the gazebo, he dropped to the ground and stepped between the slats into the blackness under the platform.

He knew Antone must be in the church tower by now, and feeling around among the abandoned trash and litter under the gazebo, he found what he wanted: a fat, unbroken bottle. Moments later he was back at the tree on the corner of the plaza, peering across at the station, where nothing moved.

As the clouds thinned, more stars appeared. The moon wore a halo, and there wasn't a single light left on in the village now, though it wasn't even eight o'clock. Glancing once behind him at the darkened church beyond the gazebo, he stepped out from the tree and lofted the bottle in a high overhead arc, like a hand grenade. Then he drew the Redhawk from his belt, and as the bottle shattered on the concrete apron right in front of the station door with an explosive crash, he dashed diagonally across the street to his right and into the deep-set shadowed doorway of one of the Sonoran row houses.

Inside the Pemex station, the sudden explosion of the bottle had unnerved them all. Peter Judge jerked the trigger on the .30–.06, and the shot shattered the drinking-water bottle mounted on the cooler beside Jaramillo and de Fuentes as Carmen screamed and dropped her pistol. And Billy Ray sent a long, angry burst of automatic fire out into the darkness of the plaza.

Sergeant Jaramillo, his hands still clasped obediently behind his head with his arms aching and his rage at the bursting point, was now covered with water and broken glass. He didn't know who all these *pinche* gringos were or what they were doing here, but he had no fantasies about the chances of himself or the trembling grocer living much longer if he didn't act. Hurling himself at Billy Ray, he tried to wrench the carbine from his hands.

But he was off balance and Billy Ray easily jerked the weapon away, and then stunned the Mexican cop with the butt end of it. But as he raised the carbine again to finish the Mexican off, he saw a quick movement in the street outside and instead whirled and fired another burst out the door.

A figure in the street staggered and fell, but someone returned fire, and three booming shots brought the plate-glass window of the station crashing down and slammed into the shelves of canned goods over Billy Ray's head as he turned, dove over the counter, and then disappeared through a curtained doorway at the rear.

TWENTY-NINE

Tom Ragnon, stuffing the smoking Redhawk back in his belt, rushed over to Antone, who had pulled himself to the curb of the plaza. "I caught one, Sergeant," he said through clenched teeth, "a ricochet." His rifle still beside him, he was holding his left thigh. "Nothing broken—I think—but it hurts like hell. Can I borrow your shirttail?"

Ragnon pulled out his shirt and began ripping it. "What were you doing out of the church tower, John?" There was blood, sticky and dark in the moonlight, but fortunately not pulsing from an artery. As he helped the Indian bind up his thigh, Ragnon thanked whatever gods there were, including his own, that the damage seemed superficial, almost a through-and-through. He could feel the hole where the slug entered, and the lump near the surface of the skin where it had lodged.

"I had no clear shot from the church tower, boss," Antone explained. "Moonlight was reflecting off the windows, couldn't tell one shadow from another in there, so I came back just as everything hit the fan."

When they were finished, Antone clung to his rifle while Ragnon helped him over to the tree at one corner of the plaza and propped him sitting against the trunk in shadow. "Now, stay put, partner, while I see what's happened in the station. It's too damn quiet over there."

"Maybe one of your shots got Billy Ray," the Indian said, "but don't count on it. He could come out smokin', so watch yourself. I'll try to cover you from here."

Pulling the Redhawk and running in a crouch, Ragnon darted across the street and into the shelter of the old tow truck parked in the entryway to the junkyard, where he paused and replaced the three rounds he'd fired. The yard itself was all stark moonlight and deep shadow, and there was still no sound or movement from the station. Jesus, he thought, had they all gone out the back somewhere?

Rushing from the shadow of the tow truck across the apron, he crouched beside the station doorway, then cautiously peered inside over his gunsight. A Mexican he assumed was Jaramillo stood against the wooden counter, and he had Carmen and Pudge spread-eagle on the floor at his feet, covering them with a small automatic. Another Mexican was cringing fearfully in a corner, but there was no sign of Billy Ray. "Where's the other one, Sergeant?" Ragnon whispered, lowering the Hawk and stepping inside.

"Through there." Jaramillo nodded toward the curtained doorway behind the counter. "I heard a door slam; the grocer here tells me it leads to the junkyard out back." The Mexican cop was holding the little pistol in one hand and had his other hand against his head. Ragnon could see a dark stain leaking from beneath his fingers down the side of his jaw. "How bad are you hurt?" he asked.

"The *pinche cabrón* hit me with his carbine. I'm all right—just dizzy. The grocer says there's no back exit from the yard, Sergeant, just a high corrugated-iron fence topped with coils of razor wire."

"Then he'll have to pile some junk against it to get over," Ragnon said, "or scramble up a pile already there, but I haven't heard any noise. My partner's hit, too, but he's covering the front gate. I'll go around that way if you can watch this doorway."

"If he shows, I'll kill the *hijo de la chingada*."

"You've sure as hell got my permission," Tom Ragnon said. Turning back outside, he signalled Antone, then slipped past the tow truck, and sticking to the deepest shadows, he entered the silent moonlit yard.

Nothing moved, and there were no sounds, not against the back fence or anywhere else. Only the slight noise he made himself as he moved cautiously forward, stepping as lightly as he could. Still, the crunch of his boots on the cindered yard seemed loud as he started down between the rows of tumbled refuse: old appliances, rusted car bodies, stacks of pumps, motors, generators, all piled high on either side. As his eyes tried to separate the different shadows from the stark moonlight, raw fear began to climb like prickly cactus along his spine.

It wasn't until he was working his way along a second row that he paused in the shadow of a tilted refrigerator, listening, and suddenly sensed the presence of extreme danger. His adrenaline soared—too late. He heard the quick, screeching movement of the refrigerator coming down. Stretching, he threw himself forward in desperation, but not quite far enough. The full weight of the appliance caught the back of his knees, pinning his legs. Only the partially open door had kept it from crushing them, but he was stuck, held fast as a figure lunged from behind it and a fiery burst from the carbine ripped up the ground beside his head.

The noise temporarily deafened him, and he found his gun hand had caught under his side as he fell. By the time he pulled it free, Billy Ray was off and running, a shadowy figure heading for the front gate as Ragnon lined up his sights and squeezed off three shots while shouting, "John! He's coming! The bastard's coming!"

One shot must have nicked Billy Ray, because Ragnon saw him stagger—saw the muzzle flash of another frenzied burst from his carbine as he lurched from the tow truck to the van still parked beside the station door, where he disappeared. And Ragnon heard something else now—a familiar sound at the back of his consciousness even as he saw Antone, still braced with his rifle against the tree trunk across the street—the noisy roar of an engine coming from north of the plaza, a Volkswagen engine! His Volkswagen? he thought wildly. Crown, in his Volkswagen?

Billy Ray had made it into the van and was cranking the engine. Ragnon strained to free himself, but it was useless. He emptied the Hawk at the van's tires even as it fired up and lunged forward into the street, and someone, probably Jaramillo, began firing a pistol at it from the station doorway. But the van was already rolling across the street, headed straight at Antone when the little yellow Volkswagen, traveling without lights, squealed its tires coming around the corner of the plaza and swerved into the path of the van, where it braked to a stop.

The van crunched heavily into the car, and Billy Ray shifted quickly into reverse, but the engine died on him and Lucinda Crown was aiming a revolver out her side window with both hands. Before she could fire, Billy Ray had grabbed up his carbine. But it was Antone, still braced against the tree with his Winchester, and Jaramillo, standing in the station doorway, who got off the killing shots, firing almost simultaneously, the roar of the rifle and crack of the pistol echoing and blending even as Billy Ray was slammed back against the seat, drilled cleanly through the chest and head.

It took the combined efforts of both the Mexican cop and the grocer to lift the refrigerator enough to free Ragnon's legs. Limping between them, he made it to the tow truck. The station lights were on again, and there was Lucinda Crown standing in the reflected glow. "You got some kind of death wish, Crown?" he asked, but he was smiling and shaking his head, not quite able to chastise her as he leaned against the truck's fender.

"I had to come back, Rags. We're partners, aren't we? Sorry to bang up your car."

Tom Ragnon shrugged. "Like me, it'll recover."

"Which reminds me, I've brought bad news—about your father."

Ragnon frowned. "How bad?"

She hung her head. "Poole says he died in his sleep—just this afternoon."

Ragnon looked away. "Goddammit," he murmured. With the danger past, he felt a little nauseated and surprisingly weak anyway, and the news of his father's passing wasn't exactly the high point of the day. Finally his eyes focused again on the van, where Billy Ray's body was still slumped over the wheel. "And John got him?"

She nodded. "John and this man here." She indicated Jaramillo. "Are you sure you're okay?"

"Yeah, I'll be fine. But John took a hit in the thigh earlier. Slug's still in there. How's he doing?" Ragnon could see the Indian's shadowy form still propped against the tree across the street.

"No complaints, but I'm sure he's felt better. I used the military first aid kit in your Volks for a temporary dressing and gave him a shot of morphine. Your shirttail just wasn't cutting it. That'll hold him till a doctor can take the bullet out."

"You should have seen a doctor yourself, Crown, instead of coming back, but thanks."

"Maybe we can go together—the three of us." She smiled her sharky little smile, and in spite of her battered appearance he knew she was going to be okay too.

"Where's the other two?" he asked the Mexican cop, who was watching in silence as Ragnon tucked a pinch of Red Man in his cheek and promised himself it would be his last.

"Handcuffed together inside, Sergeant. What did these *cabrones* do that brings you with guns into Mexico—breaking our laws."

"They are killers, defilers of children. We were in pursuit." It was a lame excuse, he knew, but what did the guy want, for Christ's sake? And how was he going to get them out of Mexico now?

Jaramillo grunted unenthusiastically. "Then why not kill them too?" he suddenly offered. "I can do it if you wish." He shrugged expressively. "Killed while attempting to escape."

Tom Ragnon looked at him. The guy was serious, and Ragnon—angry, hurting, and exhausted—was sorely tempted. But he wouldn't go quite that far, even though he knew they might get off under the American legal system. He'd have to take that chance. What he didn't want was the hassle of getting them returned through official channels. The paperwork alone could take weeks—never mind the legal technicalities he'd violated. Though some time in a Mexican jail might be a kind of justice too. But they were only a mile inside the country. "No, Sergeant," he said, "no more killing. But I *will* make you a deal. We caught them before they crossed the border, okay? It'll save a lot of paperwork for both of us."

Luis Jaramillo's eyebrows rose. "I suppose such a thing could be arranged, Sergeant," he said cautiously, curious but not quite convinced.

"In their RV, right? We need it for evidence—and the bike and the van."

"Perhaps—it could be worked out." He was getting the idea but was still hesitant.

"Of course, any cash you find on them is yours—minus a roll of marked bills that belongs to Crown here. And the convertible we don't know anything about, okay? You won't have any problem with the registration and plates?"

A wide grin slowly creased the face of Jaramillo beneath his thick black mustache as he looked across the gas pumps at the dusty late-model Chrysler LeBaron that was now his. "*Por seguro, Sargento,* no problem."

"*Mil gracias* for your help," Tom Ragnon said, shaking Jaramillo's hand firmly.

"*Por nada, Sargento,*" the Mexican cop answered, his expression somber again. "Law enforcement on the border is always a cooperative effort."

Jesus, Ragnon thought, spitting. He actually said it with a straight face.

EPILOGUE

It was after 11:00 P.M. by the big clock on the squad bay wall above the map of Mimbres County. And Crown and Ragnon sat at his desk, where a small lamp offered the only illumination in the room. They were alone. They'd spent the previous night and much of the day with Antone at the hospital, where they'd been checked over themselves and released. They'd even gotten a few hours sleep before going to work on their reports, which they'd turned in by five o'clock, and gone out for steaks and a movie.

But the message on Crown's phone recorder when they got back to her apartment said the chief of homicide wanted to see them both—privately and immediately—no matter what the hour, and here they were.

"I really didn't think they'd swallow all of this, Rags," Crown was saying, nervously grinding out her second cigarillo in the ashtray. "It's too incredible."

"Relax. The first hurdle is Old Iron Balls, and he'll swallow what he has to. He'll gag a little maybe, but he'll back us."

Because it had been quite a parade, with Antone on the couch in the RV watching Pudge handcuffed to the wheel in the driver's seat, followed by Carmen in the van with Crown and Billy Ray's body, and Ragnon bringing up the rear in his crumpled yellow Bug. They had reentered the U.S. near the concrete marker and stopped. Then, while Ragnon stood in a pouring rain and shot up a small area of brush and rocks, leaving spent shell casings from the different weapons and fresh bullet scars on several big boulders to create the "scene," Crown had called in help on the walkie-talkie.

Then they'd set fire to a gasoline-soaked mesquite to light up the site for a helicopter pickup, and left the vehicles to be impounded for evidence by the deputies.

"You think the case itself is tight enough to stand up?" Crown asked, lighting another of her slim black cancersticks in spite of Ragnon's scowl.

"Should be." Ragnon had thus far resisted his pouch of Red Man, but he had almost finished a pack of gum. "Forensic evidence in the RV and van should be enough to clinch it, but you never know. Why? You think we should have let Jaramillo shoot 'em?"

She gave him her sharky little grin. "It probably would have been a lot easier than this—"

They both heard the elevator doors whoosh open, and then the heavy footfalls coming down the hall, where before there had been only the soft hum of the janitor's buffer. The chief came in, puffing a cigar and motioning them into his office without a word of greeting. It was a bad sign. Following him, Ragnon limped over to the long black Naugahyde couch, while Crown took the straight-back chair and Poole lowered himself behind his desk and turned on the lamp. "Well?" Poole glanced from one to the other as if daring either to speak first.

"Well what, Chief?" Ragnon ventured. "John is fine. He'll be back on duty in a couple of weeks."

"That's dandy. Now what the fuck happened?"

"You read what happened, Chief. It's in the report."

"I want to hear it with my own ears from you two, because I don't believe what I read in that so-called report—nobody'll believe it."

"I don't know why," Ragnon said easily. "It was simple enough. We caught 'em in darkness just this side of the border. There was a firefight. John was wounded and one perp was killed. It was all in the shooting statement."

"Fuck the shooting statement." Poole's cigar had gone out, and he relighted it with his big bronze horse lighter, putting on his angry-walrus act again as the blue clouds rose around him. "I mean, what *really* happened, Rags? Just between you and me and my wastebasket you're so fond of spitting in. And how come you're not messing it up now? You're not nervous enough?"

"I quit that bad habit, Chief. But if you persist in this line of questioning, I just might have to start up again. Everything's in the report, and we all three signed it."

"Bullshit is what's in the report, Rags, and you damn well know it." But he put on his half glasses and looked at it again anyway. "Let me see if I even got it straight. Antone caught a slug in his thigh from Billy Ray's carbine. Later, propped against a tree, he puts one from his Winchester through the van windshield and into Billy Ray's chest, and Crown here pops him in the head with her .25-caliber, almost simultaneously."

"That's the way it went down, Chief."

"But Crown checked out a .357 in Pontatoc." He turned on her as if catching her in the act, and his leer was awesome. "Why would you shoot him with that peashooter of yours?"

Crown kept her cool. "What can I say, Lieutenant?

When the chips were down, I relied on the gun I was most familiar with."

"There should be matching shell casings and fresh bullet scars on the rocks, Chief," Ragnon added innocently enough, "if we can find the exact scene again."

"Oh, I'm sure you can, Rags." His voice was oozing sarcasm. "I hear there's a hole cut in the fence big enough to drive a motor home through—plus a van and a car. How the fuck do you explain that?"

"Someone's always cutting holes in the border fence, Chief. The border patrol is repairing them all the time."

"And your injured leg—give me that again."

"Fell into an arroyo—bank gave way. Cross my heart. I got off several shots with John's Hawk, and one nicked Billy Ray, but he made it to his van."

"Where Antone and Crown took him out, right? And the other two surrendered in panic."

"You got it, Chief." Ragnon glanced at Crown and smiled confidently.

Sidney Clayton Poole leaned back, shaking his head futilely. "So this is gonna be your report—your *official* report?"

"Something wrong with it, Chief?"

"Well, for openers, Rags, you know those two surviving perps are claiming something a little different, don't you?"

"I suppose they would." He was still smiling. "I know *I* would."

"Like all of this took place illegally, in another country—totally out of your jurisdiction."

"Pure fantasy on their part, Chief. Perps will dream up anything for an out."

"So will wild-assed detectives."

"So it's our word against theirs, right?"

"Not quite." Chief Poole ground out the stub of his cigar in his big onyx ashtray as Ragnon felt a bead of sweat trickle down his side under his arm. "I had that village on the other side checked out this evening, Rags." Poole glanced at Crown, who looked uncertainly back at Ragnon. "And this state judicial cop who works the area—" He glanced at his notes. "One Sergeant Luis Jaramillo—you know him?"

"Never heard of him," Ragnon answered with a straight face.

"Of course not. Well, I just got the report back an hour ago, and he says there *was* something going down on the night in question. He even admits the perps were all three in the village, but he found them 'acting under suspicious circumstances'—his words, Rags—and he generously escorted them back to the U.S. border and saw them across, all unofficially, through the hole they'd cut in the fence."

"Well—there you are, Chief." Ragnon glanced triumphantly at Crown as Poole continued.

"This Jaramillo says all the reported noise—the yelling and shooting and cars crashing—that occurred later in the village was just a local drunken celebration that got out of hand. And of course he doesn't know anything about any Chrysler convertible, and he never heard of you two or Antone either. He swears to it all in an affidavit, and no one swears otherwise except the perps." He leaned back and began peeling the cellophane from a fresh cigar. "So who knows, Ragnon, could be it's enough to get you off the hook—this time."

He fired up and blew some smoke while he stared at his homicide specialist over his half glasses, then shook his head hopelessly. "Rags, you're more trouble than a sackful of wet cats." Then he turned to Crown. "And I'm glad as hell I don't have to put up with *your* shit anymore, lady. God knows I don't need two of you. Now, get outta my sight while I dream up something for my own goddamned report."

In the hall outside, they waited for the elevator and Crown glanced at Ragnon. "I'm really sorry about your dad."

Ragnon sighed. "It was time—" And he felt the guilt of a burden lifted. "I've got to arrange for the burial tomorrow. How about you? Back to the old grind—more kiddie porn?"

She shook her head. "Not for a while. I've got some days coming and I'm going to get lost somewhere."

"Oh? Want some company? I've got a few days coming myself. After I get my dad put away—"

"No thanks, Rags." But she smiled to soften the blow. "You're a little too much of a good thing—for me anyway. I think I better try someone new."

Tom Ragnon frowned. "Just so it's not McKittrick."

"No, definitely not McKittrick, not anymore."

The elevator doors whooshed open and he held them for her. "You go ahead. I'll catch the next one. I forgot something in my desk."

"Be good to yourself, Tom Ragnon," she said as the elevator doors were closing. "You deserve it."

"You too, Lucy."

Ragnon walked slowly back to his desk and sat a while in the dark. He really hadn't forgotten anything. He had just wanted to send her on her way, out of his life. Maybe she'd been too much of a good thing for him too.

He saw the diffused light from the chief's office coming through the frosted glass door, and thought about him working on his "goddamned report." He wasn't sure how it would all turn out for Peter Judge and Carmen Jones. He'd taken a chance, going into Mexico after them. He might even have handed their defense attorney a free ride on technicalities. But at least no kid would have to worry about Billy Ray anymore.

And with an anguished tenderness he thought fondly of his own kids, safe at home on Old Father Road. And then he thought fondly, too, of Angie. He glanced at the luminous dial of his watch. She was working swing shift this week, so she was off at midnight. Maybe he'd just drop by, have a cup of coffee or something, and see which way her stick floats.

Of course he knew he'd better call first. And he did.